HAWKRISE

Hawkrise is the final volume of Aileen Armitage's enthralling saga set in the Yorkshire mill-town of Hawksmoor. It is 1911. The small community of Hawksmoor mirrors the hypocrisy and upheaval of the wider world. Vincent Gregg, first Socialist MP for the valley, incurs bankruptcy to support his luxurious lifestyle. In contrast there are the Pearson boys: Hal, the true idealist, and his younger brother, Eddie, who puts duty before self when he follows his father to become an engineer. Into their lives the First World War brings horror and change...

HAWKRISE

HAWKRISE

by
Aileen Armitage

Magna Large Print Books
Long Preston, North Yorkshire,
England.

British Library Cataloguing in Publication Data.

Armitage, Aileen
 Hawkrise.

A catalogue record for this book is
available from the British Library

ISBN 0-7505-0942-2

First published in Great Britain by Arrow Books Ltd., 1988

Published in Large Print November, 1996 by arrangement
with the copyright holder.

Magna Large Print is an imprint of
Library Magna Books Ltd.
Printed and bound in Great Britain by
T.J. Press (Padstow) Ltd., Cornwall, PL28 8RW.

ONE: 1909

'Things'll never be the same again, you just mark my words, Annie lass. They'll never be quite the same.'

James Stott Pearson spoke the words with quiet pride as he took his wife's elbow and steered her carefully through the still jubilant crowd of party workers towards the door. She looked tired, pale and lined after the weeks of campaigning, but there was a flush on her cheeks which owed as much to the party's success as to the heat of the town hall. At the tram stop she leaned against his shoulder with a sigh.

Instantly he felt concern. Never one to complain, Annie would not tell him if the day's activities had been too much for her. 'Are you all right, love? We could have left earlier if you didn't feel up to it.'

'Nay, I'm all right, truly I am. And we couldn't leave till the results were read. Nay, I were just wondering if Hal had managed to get tea ready on his own—I left the makings, but you know what lads are.'

James snorted. 'For heaven's sake, lass,

he's close on eighteen years old! He's quite capable of seeing to himself and Eddie. They'll not starve just because we're out all day.'

'No, I suppose not, but it just doesn't seem right to leave them alone so long, no one there to greet young Eddie when he comes in from school and all. I've never been one to do that, even with all the Band of Hope lectures and Co-op meetings.'

James sighed, tearing his gaze away from her forlorn face to look up the road. 'Never fret, love—you've been the best mother anyone in their right minds could wish for. Any road, seeing as our Harold is off to college very shortly he'll have to learn to fend for himself sooner or later—good practice to get his own tea ready just for once. What's more, he'll say himself it was all in a good cause once he hears the news. Ah, here comes the tram.'

Once aboard and seated, Annie snuggled up close to her husband. He sensed that, had it been seemly, she would have leaned her head on his shoulder. Under the yellow glow of the street lamp she had seemed to have more colour than she did now, and his conscience twinged. All those weeks of campaigning on Vincent Gregg's behalf had taken their toll, but she would never admit it. To be by her husband's side, toiling and supporting in all his efforts, was

Annie Pearson's ambition; nothing would ever deter her from it, and he loved her the more for her loyalty.

Loyalty: that had always been Annie's strong point, right from the day he met her, all those years ago. It had been their common interest in the evils of drink that first brought them together. A devoted church worker at St Thomas's who suffered from the unpredictability of a drunken father, she had been all too eager to join him in working for the temperance movement. Under his guidance she had developed into a skilful lecturer, and the Band of Hope had taken her all over the area. No stay-at-home housewife, Annie had been a wonderful wife and mother to their two sons none the less. But she was ageing fast; at forty-two it was only reasonable that she should slow down.

Her mind seemed to have been travelling along the same direction for she turned her face up to him with a faint smile. 'I've been thinking, James. It would be rather nice to spend a weekend over at our Fanny's. I'd be glad of a bit of a rest. Shall I write and ask? The change'd do you good and all. We've had that busy a time of late.'

He looked down at her and hesitated. 'Aye, if you like. But happen not just yet a bit—I know the election's safely over, but I've still got a lot of union business in hand. There's that matter of young Fairbank's dismissal, for instance. I've got to help him sort out his appeal—I can't just leave him in the lurch, for he relies on me.'

'Aye, love. Everyone does.'

He recognised the tone of resignation in her voice and felt again the twinge of his conscience. The tram clattered to a halt and bodies began heaving past them towards the door, bodies smelling of sweat and factory grease and ale. The night-shift workers were making their way to Hopkinson's, and he heard the crash of clogs on cobbles as they dismounted. Annie fanned her face, but whether from heat or to waft away the stench of ale he could not tell.

'Not far now, love, and then we'll soon be on the tram to Lindley.'

She smiled wearily. 'I'll be that glad to be home, put me feet up and have a cup of tea. But it's been a grand day, James, it has that. First Labour MP we've ever had—I'm that proud. All those years we've had a Liberal, and at last we've made it. A socialist MP for the valley, and we helped to put him there.'

He squeezed her arm. 'Aye, we did that, love. We've summat to be proud of. Like I said, things'll never be quite the same again. The workers have begun their fight back against the capitalists. Just wait till we tell Harold.'

At last the tram clanked into St George's Square and James helped his wife to climb down. The evening air was blowing chill, and he felt her arm shiver in his as they walked up Station Street, past the imposing offices of the Hardcastle estate buildings, towards the tram stop. Annie stood in silence for the five minutes it took for their tram to arrive, but he noticed that she pulled up her fur collar closely about her neck.

The tram rumbled away uphill out of the town towards home and comfort. As it clanged its way past the Bay Horse, James felt his wife stiffen momentarily as she caught sight of the drinkers tumbling out of the inn, laughing and joking noisily. At last the clock tower came in sight which old Sykes had had built for his workers' benefit. Ever since its sonorous chimes began to ring out the quarters there had been no excuse for anyone to turn up late for work at Sykes' mill. James helped Annie out of her seat.

'Here we are, lass. Won't be long now to that cup of tea.'

Letting go of his arm she walked the twenty yards from the tram stop to the little row of three cottages set at right angles to the road. As they turned into the

11

cobbled approach James read with pride the inscription carved in the gatepost. Hollin Row. The name had filled Annie with delight, he remembered, the day they moved as newly-weds into the centre cottage nestling between the smaller two. He could see a light burning in the living room window as Annie took out her latchkey.

Hal was sitting hunched in the chair beside the range. He looked up sharply as his parents entered the room, blue eyes eager and brows raised in question.

'Well? You made the last tram then—had the results been declared?'

James pulled himself erect. Annie sank into the other chair and smiled. The youth's gaze travelled from one to the other.

'It's a proud day for the West Riding, lad,' James said slowly, conscious of the historic import of the occasion. 'For the first time we have a socialist MP in the area—Vincent Gregg won the seat they said none but a Liberal would ever hold.'

Harold took a deep, slow breath. 'He did it!' he breathed. 'My God! He's done it!'

'Don't blaspheme, Hal,' murmured Annie, her eyes closed.

'I'm sorry. What was the poll, Father?'

'Eighty-eight per cent. Best poll ever.

12

Narrow margin, though. Gregg only won by a hundred and fifty votes.'

His son smiled broadly. 'Who cares? He won, didn't he? I'll bet they sang "The Red Flag" like they've never sung it before, once the results were out.'

'They did that,' murmured his mother. Then, opening her eyes, she added, 'Has our Eddie gone to bed?'

There was only a tiny pause before Hal answered.

'Yes.'

Annie noticed the hesitation. She craned her neck to see his expression. 'What's up, Hal? Has he done his homework? Did he ask you to help him again, is that it?'

James saw her look of concern and intervened. 'Now come on, lass, what about that cup of tea you promised us, eh?'

'Just a minute, James, there's something Hal's not told me, I can sense it. What is it, Hal?'

'Nothing really, Mother. He's done his homework all right, and with no help from me. It's just that...well....'

Annie sat bolt upright. 'Just that what? Tell me, Hal.'

The youth hung his head. 'He were out late, that's all. But he got his work done all the same.'

James frowned. It was not like young

13

Edward to disobey and, what was more, it was important that James Stott Pearson's family was seen to set a good example, pillars of the Church and respectable society as they were. Annie, her face pale with exhaustion, beat him to the question.

'Where was he, Hal? Did he tell you?

'Yes. He was at chapel.'

James started. 'Chapel? But we're Church. What chapel?'

'Queen Street.'

'The mission? But that's Methodist! What on earth was he doing there?' Annie looked aghast.

Hal shrugged. 'Idle curiosity, so far as I can tell. There's no harm in that, Mother. He went with his chum Denton.'

His mother sat forward, seizing the poker and jabbing at the fire through the bars of the grate. James could see she was disturbed but could not quite identify the cause of her unease. He joined in the attempt to soothe her.

'Nay, like Harold says, there's no harm done, love, even if we are Church. But he shouldn't be out late alone and without telling us. I'll speak to him about it in the morning.'

Annie sprang to her feet, all sign of fatigue vanished. 'I'll speak to him about it right now, asleep or not, that I will.

14

I'll have no child of mine, only eleven years old and all, going to chapel. They could warp his young mind for life, they could.'

James moved towards her. 'Nay, don't take on so, Annie lass. What about that tea now, eh? Harold, pull the kettle over the fire.'

She brushed past him. 'No, I've got to talk to him now, otherwise he'll be going to sleep with his little head full of the Lord knows not what. Let me be, James.'

He stood aside, knowing better than to argue further once her mind was made up. Harold cast his father a significant look and reached into the cupboard for the big brown earthenware teapot and the caddy. His father seated himself in the chair Annie had just vacated.

'It were a right grand day, sun shining and all. I reckon many folk couldn't have gone to work today, there were that many folk there.'

'Was the Countess there?' Hal enquired.

'Nay. I didn't see her. She's supported him at most of his campaign speeches though. Couldn't expect her to come up from London again, I reckon. Pity. She'd have loved seeing the crowds going crazy with joy. Just fancy, Harold—we've a man after our own heart to represent us in Parliament at last.'

'Well, not us, but it gives us hope that we'll get our man in for Hawksmoor next. And Gregg's not really one of us, is he? I mean, I've never seen such a dandy in my life. Fine clothes, whisky, cigars....'

'Don't let appearances fool you, Harold. He comes from the slums of Liverpool, remember, and a man doesn't easily forget his origins. He's worked hard, college and all, to get where he is. That's what college can do for you.'

'Well, he does talk sound socialism, that's for sure,' murmured Hal as he poured hot water from the kettle into the teapot, swished it round and tipped it into a dish.

'Talk?' echoed his father. 'He doesn't just talk—he's the most eloquent speaker I've ever heard, and that includes Tom Mann. He's a natural-born orator, is Gregg—knows how to move his listeners to action, and by thump, that's just what they're going to do. We could do with more like him in the party.'

'Aye,' said Hal, busying himself ladling spoonfuls of tea into the pot. 'I'll do my best, Father.'

James smiled. One could always rely on Harold to recognise where his duty lay.

In the small bedroom Annie Pearson surveyed her son by the light of the

16

candle on the bedside table. He looked so vulnerable, far younger than his ten years with his wide green eyes fixed penitently on her.

'I'll not scold you any more, Eddie, so long as you don't go near chapel again—promise me, for it distresses your father, and you wouldn't have that, would you?'

'No, Mother.'

'You want to please me, don't you?'

'More than anything, Mother. I do try.'

She sighed. 'I know you do, love.' It wasn't really his fault if his judgement was sometimes a little erratic—James really should make some allowance for the boy's age. He couldn't be expected to match up to Hal just yet a while.

Eddie half sat up. She patted his hand. 'No more chapel then, remember. And your father doesn't really care for those Dentons, you know, so it might be wiser to choose another playmate.'

The boy's face furrowed into a frown. 'But he's fun, Mother—he showed me where there are graves in the cellar at the mission. It was creepy down there.'

'Graves? Now Eddie, how can you call that fun? Anyway, it's no longer allowed—chapel folk have to bury their dead in graveyards same as the rest of us now. Come on, put that book away and

I'll nip out the candle. You should have been asleep long ago.'

She bent and kissed his cheek swiftly, longing to hug him close but mindful of James's warning. Eleven-year-old boys were on the verge of manhood and must not be encouraged to behave effeminately. As she pinched out the candle and went to the door, she paused, aware of the heavy scent of candle wax and conscious that her son needed another word.

'Goodnight, son, and may God bless you and love you as I do.'

There was the sound of a deep sigh as she closed the door behind her.

Outside the town hall the cheering crowd showed no sign of thinning. The Countess smiled happily.

'They're not going to let you go yet, Vincent,' she remarked to the handsome young man at her side. 'You're the hero of the hour—the first socialist member of the House for this part of the country. They're not going to let you sleep tonight. Go on, you'll have to speak to them again.'

With pride she watched him go out once more, and heard the cheers swell to a roar on his appearance. From here she could just make out his words as he held them spellbound by his eloquent tongue, as he had done so often over the last few weeks.

'And this victory has rung the death knell of the capitalist system,' she heard him conclude, and at once the crowd broke into a roar again, a cry that was at once jubilation and adoration of this man. Tired but triumphant he came back inside.

'For God's sake, somebody pour me a drink,' he muttered hoarsely. 'My damn throat's giving up on me again.'

The Countess nodded to the election agent. Vincent pulled out a silver cigarette case, put a cigarette between his lips and struck a match. Then he took the glass and drank deeply.

'This has been a wonderful day, Vincent, both for the cause and for you personally.' The Countess sank into an easy chair. 'What do you plan to do next?'

He stretched his arms above his head, revealing an expanse of silk shirtcuff and expensive gold cufflinks. 'Tonight? Go back to the inn, have a couple more drinks to ease this damn dry throat, and then sleep.'

She smiled indulgently. 'I meant to-morrow, Vincent. And after that. Do you want to keep my car, make any more speeches before you take up your seat?'

He shook his head slowly. She marvelled at the way his oil-smooth hair never seemed to get out of place, whatever the excitement and jostling he had to endure. Ever the

19

epitome of suave, urbane gentleman; no wonder all the millgirls adored him.

'No thanks, Countess. I've done with speechmaking for a week or two. I think I'll go back to Liverpool tomorrow.'

'To see your parents?'

'My mother—my father is dead, remember. I know she'll be delighted with the news.'

The Countess was enchanted. It was typical of the man to want to please his mother, the woman who, despite her own poverty, had striven to give her son the best education she could. Not many working-class mothers could boast a son of Vincent's attainments.

The agent cleared his throat and stepped forward. 'Shall I get you out the back and escort you to the inn, sir? The people will never let you pass if they see you.'

'No, it's all right,' cut in the Countess. 'I'll take Mr Gregg in my car.'

'No need, Countess,' Vincent smiled amiably. 'I'm sure you're ready for bed after all the excitement—you go on, and I'll follow when I'm ready. Another whisky please, Arthur.'

The Countess rose reluctantly. 'If you're sure....'

He took her hand. 'I am most grateful to you for all you've done, Countess. You and Mrs Pankhurst and Mrs Glazier. Never was a man so blessed with friends.' Bowing over her hand, he kissed her fingertips. The Countess smiled and withdrew her hand.

'Ever the charmer, Vincent. You'll go a long way.'

He watched her leave, then sank into a chair. 'I'm worn out, Arthur. Another whisky, and then tell Mrs Longden she can join me, and you can go.'

'But getting back to the inn, sir....'

'I'll make it, never fear. Do as I say, there's a good fellow. Is Mrs Longden still here?'

'Aye, sir. She's been waiting.'

'Then show her in, Arthur. And then you can go and have a well-deserved night's sleep. You've earned it, and here, take this—have a drink to celebrate.'

The agent nodded, pocketed the sovereign and left the room. What Mr Gregg, MP, did in his own time was his own affair, and he wasn't a man to meddle.

TWO

Jubilation over Vincent Gregg's triumph continued for days. Annie Pearson's neighbour, Mrs Charnock, was no less excited than anyone else in the valley.

'Who'd have thought it, Annie? A stranger to these parts and yet he topples them Liberals after all these years! Eh, but he's a grand fellow—why, Rosie Sykes told me he talked to the lasses as they came out of the mill—he flicked his hair back and asked them if they liked it. They fair laughed, she told me, he were that nice and friendly.'

'Ah yes,' agreed Annie. 'He has the gift of making folk feel at home with him. He's no snob, for all he's a gentleman.'

Mrs Charnock gave a shiver of delight. 'A body can't help feeling that things'll look up now, with him. Don't tha think so, Mr Pearson?'

James lowered his newspaper and regarded her solemnly. 'Indeed, Mrs Charnock, we sincerely hope so, but don't forget that Mr Gregg has made no great promises, you know.'

'Aye well, happen not, but he's a Labour

man, isn't he, and that's summat.'

'To be sure it is, but not supported by the ILP or the official Labour Party. He's the valley's choice, a true socialist, but he knows what he's up against when he gets to the House of Commons—that's why he makes no promises. Remember what he told us—we won't see socialism in our time, he said, and perhaps not even in our children's time. He's a realist, Mrs Charnock. Don't expect miracles overnight.'

'Nay, nay, I don't, Mr Pearson. But it does give a body hope when we get a Labour man in at last. Our Jack says the weaving shed were all done up with bright red ribbons yesterday, the men were that happy. And I heard tell as folks stayed up all night singing and dancing when they heard the news.'

'And well they might,' said James with a smile, turning back to his newspaper. 'As you say, Mrs Charnock, it gives a body hope, that it does. It says in my paper here, "Mr Gregg is in deadly earnest and is absolutely sincere. He has made social reform his religion and has found in it his inspiration." I think we can agree with that.'

'Then let's hope he can do summat about improving our way of life,' remarked Mrs Charnock, 'for the Lord knows we

23

could do with it. I'd best be off now to get our Jack's tea ready, or he'll be back afore I've peeled the spuds. Goodnight to thee, Annie lass.'

Annie came back into the living room after seeing her neighbour out and sank into the chair opposite her husband. 'Read me some more from the paper, love,' she said softly. 'I'm that tired I'd be glad of a chance to close me eyes and listen a bit.'

James adjusted his half-framed spectacles and cleared his throat. 'It says that Mr Gregg deliberately makes his appeal to those people who are better off—that's us, you see, folk who have work and a reasonable standard of living, not the poor and starving. It says he makes his appeal to the imagination of the people, preaching the fuller life, for that is what the people are yearning for. Valley folk are not discontented, but they are unsatisfied.'

'That's what you've always said, James.'

'And that's why we've worked at setting up the Co-op education classes, love. People do need a fuller life, something to satisfy the mind as well as the body.'

'I'm glad Mr Gregg thinks as you do, love.'

'As we all do, Annie, and every artisan and skilled man in the West Riding. He knows it's more than quick, small gains we're in need of—more to hope for than higher wages or shorter hours. It's hope we want, hope of a better and fuller life for our children. Mrs Charnock was right—Gregg gives us that hope.'

Annie sighed. 'It's a big responsibility for a young man of twenty-five.'

'He's old enough to recognise what he's taking on—why, our Harold knows the meaning of socialism well enough, and he's much younger. It's the way a man's brought up that counts.'

Annie fell silent. She knew how he had set his heart on his sons following in his own dedicated footsteps, and indeed Hal did seem to have imbibed all the socialist ideals James stood for. Eddie, now, was a different kettle of fish. James seemed a little apprehensive about the way his younger son was turning out.

With some reason, perhaps, she was forced to admit to herself. The lad had played truant from school yet again today. She still had in her pocket the note from Mr Ward, the headmaster; a very crisp note which she had not yet shown to James.

'*If this occurs again I shall have no alternative but to inform the School Board officer,*' he wrote, and her heart sank at the prospect. James, sitting on the bench as he did, would never tolerate such disgrace

25

from his own son. She had to speak to Eddie about it.

'Where were you then, if not at school?'

'Up in the woods. Watching squirrels.'

'But why? Why didn't you go back to school?'

He shrugged. 'Wanted time to think. Everyone does.'

He refused to be drawn on what he was thinking about, but then that was Eddie, ever quiet and keeping his own counsel. She refused to contemplate the word secretive in relation to her cherished son. But she felt sick with guilt at the thought of keeping the matter secret from James.

A guilty secret, or a blazing row? The former seemed by far the lesser evil in the circumstances. James's anger was a cold and terrifying thing; he never raged and shouted, believing that to be a sign of lack of self-control. But his tight-lipped face and austere and icy manner were all the more frightening for that, both for Eddie and for her. She dreaded James's displeasure, and for that reason she would not tell him about the letter.

'Nay,' said James, 'it's about a great deal more than wages and hours, is this struggle, and Gregg's the man to lead it.'

Sir Marcus Hardcastle fumed as he

sat drinking port with his guests, the wealthy stockbroker Lawson and millowner Tunnycliffe, both highly-respected and influential men in Hawksmoor. Both were magistrates and town councillors.

'Damned insufferable, if you ask me,' Sir Marcus rumbled. 'What is the world coming to? Bloody upstart from Liverpool slums, to represent the valley? What impertinence! What can he know of land and property-owners' problems? Bolshevik! All he'll want is shorter working hours and as much as ten pounds a week wage, I'll be bound. You'll have to watch out for yourselves, you millowners.'

Tunnycliffe nodded. 'Aye, but he'll not be that outrageous, surely—I mean, not ten pound a week. That's very likely more nor I get meself.'

'We all have money problems,' murmured Lawson. Sir Marcus rumbled agreement. 'But so far as I can gather, this Gregg is no anarchist.'

'He's an agitator, isn't he? Why, he stood as a Revolutionary Socialist,' Tunnycliffe reminded him.

'Only because he had to have a name—the official socialists wouldn't have him. But he's not a typical product of the slums—intelligent, educated, charming, eloquent—and he has tastes better suited to gentlemen like ourselves.'

Sir Marcus eyed him shrewdly. 'So perhaps he's not that much of a rebel then—is that what you're saying? A moderate man even?'

Lawson rubbed his chin. 'Well, I wouldn't go so far as to say that, but it seems to me we may be panicking rather too soon. After all, an educated man, trained for the ministry too, is more likely to take a moderate line than a hot-headed fanatic from the lower orders.'

'That's true,' agreed Sir Marcus, 'and he is being backed by Philip Snowden, so if that's anything to go by—'

'Ugly little cripple,' cut in Tunnycliffe.

'But with a brilliant mind,' added Lawson. 'He's one of the socialists' main assets.'

'But lacking this Gregg's charisma, is that what you're saying?' enquired Sir Marcus.

'Exactly. Gregg is a folk hero already, and therefore a man to be watched.'

For a moment the men were silent, mulling over Lawson's words. Then Sir Marcus reached for the port bottle.

'Well, all that remains now is to see how he conducts himself in the Commons. It'll be interesting to see what he has to say for himself. I'll keep an eye on Hansard, that I will. Fill up your glass, Lawson?'

'And all I say is, thank the Lord we've

such a big Liberal majority in the House,' added Tunnycliffe. 'That'll put a stop to him doing too much harm—Bannerman and the rest of them will see to that.'

Next morning in his hotel in the centre of Hawksmoor, Vincent Gregg stretched lazily, savouring the crisp, cool feel of the sheets against his skin. It was going to be another steaming July day.

He reached across and pulled the bell which would fetch the waiter with his shaving water, then lay back against the pillows. God, what a day it had been yesterday, the culmination of all his hopes and dreams—well, perhaps not the culmination, for his real work and the realisation of his dreams still lay ahead. He could recollect that there had been a great deal of cheering and back-slapping at the town hall, wine flowing and repeated singing of 'The Red Flag', but what occurred after the Countess left was now only a hazy memory.

Ah yes, Louise. There had been warm lips and limbs, heat growing to a stifling climax, and then peace. She must have got up and left during the night or very early this morning, anxious to avoid gossip. Like others of his fervent female party workers, Mrs Longden was willing to offer more than just canvassing on his behalf. He had a dim recollection that Mrs Saxby had been very pressing last night too, her husband being away in the south somewhere. Still, Louise had been very responsive and satisfying....

There was a light tap at the door.

'Come in.'

Vincent watched indolently as a fair-haired young man entered, a jug of hot water in one hand and fresh towels in the other. He looked fresh and clean in his neatly fitting uniform, and he moved with easy, catlike grace to the washstand where he placed the jug next to the flower-patterned bowl. He draped the towels neatly over the towel rail and turned to Gregg.

'Will there be anything else, sir?'

'Not at the moment. I'll ring for breakfast later, when I'm ready. Pass me my robe, will you.'

There was plenty of time to have a leisurely bath and digest a hearty breakfast before he had to catch the train to Liverpool. He watched the waiter move around the bed. There was something pleasurable in the way he moved, gracefully and with no undue haste. As he bent to pick up the robe from where it had slithered off the bed, Vincent experienced a leap of pleasure.

'Thank you. I'll ring for you later.'

The youth bent slightly. 'At your service, sir.'

Tuesday nights were always Band of Hope nights and a source of pleasure to young Eddie. There was usually quite a crowd up at the Lindley Brass Band's rooms, where the meetings were held, many of them his own schoolmates who, freed from the restrictions of school and Mr Ward's strictness, could be relied upon to join in a game afterwards. Knocking at doors and running away was becoming a bit boring, though; they'd have to think up something more exciting.

Denton was hanging about outside the bandroom door. 'Where've you been? I've been hanging about here for ages for thee. Slide show tonight, I heard tell.'

'Great.' Lantern shows were fun, even if the story was always basically the same.

'Then a lecture,' Denton informed him. 'Not your dad again, is it?'

'Can't be. He's at a union meeting.'

Eddie wished he didn't have to feel so apologetic about his father. Trouble was, he was a cleverer man than most, so he was always giving lectures or chairing meetings or sending criminals to jail. He never seemed to have the time to do the things other dads did, like going fishing in the reservoir or breeding pigeons. He could hardly imagine Father with animals—it was as much as he could do to tolerate the kitten in the house and even that, he said, made him sneeze because of the cat hairs on the furniture.

'Hey,' said Denton, tugging his arm, 'look at that big trombone in the corner—wish I could play that.'

'It's a euphonium,' said Eddie.

Denton sneered. 'Don't show off to me, Pearson. Just because tha can always spot what note it is Miss Fairley plays on the piano and they let thee sing solo in the Board concerts, that doesn't mean tha knows everything.'

'I wasn't saying that,' Eddie protested.

'No, and tha'd better not, neither. Hey up, here comes the chap with the slides.'

But first there was the usual opening hymn, and while he sang, Eddie's gaze was still on that gleaming euphonium. Like Denton, he would dearly have loved to try to play it. Ever since he was little he had wanted to make music. Hal sometimes let him play his violin for a few minutes, but only if Father was out, and sometimes Mother too would let him play on her beloved piano. But Father had stated emphatically that there was no money for another violin or tuition for him, because it cost so much to set Hal up ready for his college career.

Not that Eddie envied his brother anything, for Hal was a kind and thoughtful brother, not like Denton's, who was always punching him. He always smelt of beer too—a pity he didn't come to the Band of Hope.

As the hymn ended, Mr Guest rose to his feet to introduce tonight's speaker, a wiry little man with a moustache. As Mr Guest sat down Eddie felt a sharp sting on his neck and saw the paper pellet that fell at his feet. Some more of his schoolmates must be sitting behind him, but he did not turn round. The little man rose and cleared his throat nervously. Most of the lights went out.

'Once I was a prosperous tailor, with my own business in Leeds,' he announced, 'but demon drink got hold of me and destroyed my life. Let me tell you how it happened, and how I struggled to overcome it, as in the end I did, with the help of friends such as Mr Guest here.'

He gestured towards the chairman and then signalled to the man at the back of the hall who was dealing with the slides. On the blank wall behind him appeared a picture of a shop.

'It was a thriving business,' the little man said, and Eddie wondered why the name over the shop front was not the same as the little man's. 'I worked very hard, leaving my wife and children alone at home while I worked until late at night. Then one day I thought I would stop and have a drink before going home—and that was a bad mistake, for gradually I went more often, stayed longer, and drank more and more. Meanwhile, my wife and children saw less of me than ever.'

He signalled again, and the picture changed to that of a woman and her weeping children seated at a table.

'I became sour-tempered and impatient of my wife's pleas. I let my work suffer, and when she wept, I hit her.'

There were moans and cries of 'Shame' from the audience. The little man flung up his hands.

'You may well cry shame on me, my friends, for I lost the respect of my family and my friends, and finally my self-respect. I lost my home because the landlord threw me out for not paying the rent. My business was in ruins and I was up to my ears in debt. I had to sell the shop to clear the debts. My wife took the children away, and I was left penniless, destitute and alone. No one wanted to know me.'

The picture on the screen changed to that of a slumped man on a street corner in the rain, his hair unkempt and his clothes ragged and awry. His eyes stared unseeingly into the gutter, but again Eddie wondered why no one in the room questioned the fact that the face on the screen was not that of the speaker. Voices could be heard muttering disapproval. The little man held up his hand.

'This, my friends, this is the picture of a man who has reached the depths of degradation. This is what demon drink can do; this is why we should shun it like the plague. But for the intervention of my good friends here....'

Eddie felt his attention beginning to drift. The story was always the same every week; only the narrator was different. At one time the stories used to make him shudder and filled his nights with horrific dreams, but nowadays the stories had lost their terror. The Band of Hope meant to him not so much the desire to prevent heavy drinking as the promise of treats, of processions on Whit Sunday followed by bunfights in the hall, of outings on the charabanc in the summertime to country delights like Cope Bank, with its stalls and sideshows and candy floss and rides on the boat.

Denton's heavy clog gave him a sharp flick on the ankle. Eddie looked at him. Denton nodded to the girl in the row in front. Peering in the dim light, Eddie saw what was delighting him. With a touch surprisingly delicate for a lout, Denton had tied Sally Parkinson's pigtails together with one of the innumerable rubber bands he always carried amongst all the other paraphernalia in his pockets, and then lacquered the ends of her hair with sticky gobstopper.

'She'll never notice till she gets home,' Denton hissed in pleasure.

Eddie pulled a face. 'Ah, that's rotten,' he murmured. 'You wouldn't like it.'

Denton sneered, his pudgy face looking even coarser in the gloom. 'Afraid, art tha? Scared we'll be thrown out? Tha'rt a right namby-pamby, thee.'

'I'm not.'

Applause broke out as the speaker sat down and the chairman rose again. Further argument had to be delayed until after the final hymn was sung and the audience began to emerge from the hall into the warm summer evening. By this time Denton had gathered his cohorts.

'Pearson's a scaredy-cat,' he jeered. 'Scaredy-cat! Scared Sally Parkinson'll scratch his pretty face, aren't tha, Pearson? Pearson's scared of a lass!'

The other lads were laughing, and Eddie felt his face grow hot. 'I'm not, I'm not,' he protested, but his small voice only provoked more raucous laughter. Sally Parkinson, passing the group with her girl friend, cast a disdainful look at the

36

noisy group and passed on by.

'Yes, tha art! Tha'rt a cissy!' shouted Denton, and the others all took up the chorus.

'Cissie! Mother's boy! Pearson's a cissie!'

It was more than flesh and blood could bear. Eddie felt the anger burning in his throat rise into his head, and reason fled. Without thinking, he found his right arm swinging back and then flying forward, aimed straight at Denton's sneering face. But the bigger boy was too quick; he ducked and the blow swung clear over his head.

Eddie staggered, thrown off balance, and stumbled. Denton stood immobile, startled by the attack. Suddenly Eddie's reason returned. After that, flight was advisable rather than staying to try and bluff it out. Numbers were against him. Before Denton could recover either wits or voice, Eddie turned and ran, as swiftly as his legs would carry him, back to the safety of home.

Vincent Gregg put down the cup and saucer and looked around his mother's little parlour in a small house in the back streets of Liverpool. It showed evidence of its owner's pride in her possessions; her china ornaments on the sideboard were carefully dusted and the brass fire irons gleaming. Kindling lay ready in the hearth against the day when the weather turned cool.

'Aye, I read it all in the papers,' Mrs Gregg was saying dreamily. 'It made me that proud when folks asked about you and said how pleased they were. I always knew as you'd do well, Vincent.'

He smiled at her. It was true; she'd never lost that devout belief that one day the world would come to know of Vincent Gregg, and he felt a twinge of remorse that ever since he'd left home to go to college he'd given little thought to her. She was part of the past, the struggle and the poverty, and had no place in the glittering future.

'More tea, love?'

Vincent waved a hand and started to rise. 'I'll have to be getting a move on, Mother. I've to be in London the day after next, and I've a lot to do.'

She nodded at the cigarette packet on the arm of his chair. 'You'd best not forget them, else where will you be?'

As he pocketed them she watched him with half-closed eyes. 'You look well, anyhow, love. Just don't smoke too many of them things—or drink too much, either.'

He laughed at her concern. 'I'm a grown man now, Mother. I'll be all right.'

She frowned. 'I'm not so sure, folks in London being what they are. Don't let them lead you astray.'

'I won't, I promise. Now I must be off.'

She levered herself out of the chair to accompany him to the door. Vincent looked down at her, thinking how diminutive and vulnerable she seemed in her faded apron, with her thinning hair crimped tightly after just being released from metal curlers. Her lined face looked grey as she looked up at him and smiled.

'I'm glad you found time to come, Vincent. It were very good of you when you're so busy. I'm grateful.' He started to protest, but she interrupted him. 'Like I said, love, I always knew you were cut out for something special; you're way ahead above the rest.'

He laughed uncomfortably. 'Well, they always say a seventh son has special powers....'

'And you be sure you make the most of yours. But that's not what I meant. You're different from the rest of the family. Go on, you'd best be off or you'll miss that train.'

In the tiny vestibule Vincent bent and kissed her cheek, briefly and without emphasis, for she hated fuss. 'I'll always be grateful to you,' he said huskily. 'You've done more for me than most mothers would.'

'Go on, get off.'

From the parlour window she watched through the lace curtains as his tall figure strode away down the street, head bent against the drizzle that was beginning to thicken into rain.

'Ah, Vincent Gregg,' she murmured in a voice so low it was almost inaudible against the ticking of the clock on the mantelshelf, 'but there was a rare star shining the moment you were born. The time had to come when the world took notice of you, and it's only just begun.'

THREE

In the heat of a late July afternoon Vincent Gregg walked slowly and purposefully down the gangway of the House of Commons towards the Speaker's chair. He was flanked on either side by two of the Labour Party's most eminent members, Snowden and Clynes. If their progress was slow, due largely to Snowden's disability, it only served to heighten the stately solemnity of the occasion.

Near enough four hundred Liberal MPs were watching as Gregg approached to take the oath, as well as a hundred and fifty Tories and a mere thirty of his own persuasion. One of these was unable to resist crying out triumphantly 'Good Old Red Flag', and Gregg's lips curved into a smile.

A Tory back-bencher leaned to murmur to his neighbour, 'So this is the young firebrand they've all been talking about, is it? It will be interesting to hear what he has to say in his maiden speech.'

The elderly gentlemen next to him shrugged. 'Not a great deal, I expect. Maiden speeches are always a bit of a bore because they have to be non-controversial.'

After the session had ended, Gregg made for the outer lobby. A tall, shambling figure was coming towards him, and he recognised Hobson, who he knew was connected with the *New Age*, the newspaper well-known for being the voice of intellectual discontent. Hobson was one of the most respected rebels of the ILP. Gregg held out his hands warmly.

'Hobson, how wonderful to see a friendly face,' he said with genuine enthusiasm. The other man's face lit up.

'Gregg, my old friend! Congratulations! You really showed 'em in the valley—wonderful!'

Gregg grinned with schoolboyish charm. 'That we did—but the real work is yet to come. I'm looking forward to that.'

Hobson's smile faded into a frown. 'Look here, Gregg, I don't want to intrude on your affairs, but I know it's not easy to get settled in London if you're not exactly flush with money....'

Gregg laughed with easy grace. 'I see my reputation for profligacy still pursues me. Well yes, it's a fact I am hard up, but I'll get by.'

Hobson glanced over his shoulder and lowered his voice. 'Do you have any money? Have you a place to sleep tonight?'

Gregg shook his head, but the smile did not leave his handsome face. 'I've a shilling or two only, but I never thought of finding a place to stay. But don't let it concern you, my friend—I'll be all right.'

The older man took his arm. 'Tell you what, you stay at my place until you find some suitable digs. How's that, eh? Give you chance to look around and learn the lie of the land, so to speak. Come on, it won't take long to get there. You'll be quite comfortable with me.'

'That's very good of you. I would appreciate the opportunity until I sort myself out....'

'Say no more. It's settled,' said Hobson. 'Come on, we've time for a cup of tea before we set off.'

Eddie leaned against the doorway of his brother's bedroom, hands thrust in pockets.

'What you doing, Hal?'

His brother straightened and brushed back his hair. 'Having a sort-out, getting ready for when I go away.'

Eddie felt a stab of disappointment. He wasn't ready to let Hal go out of his life yet. 'Will it be soon, Hal?'

Hal crossed towards him and ruffled his hair. 'No, you goose. I don't go till the end of September. That's when the college terms starts.'

43

Eddie felt his spirits rise. The end of September—that was autumn, a long way off. 'Can I help you do your sorting, Hal? If you're clearing out those soldiers....' He nodded with what he hoped appeared to be indifference towards the collection of lead soldiers on Hal's bookcase. His brother smiled. 'They'll be yours, I promise you, but not yet. I want to finish painting them if I have chance before I go away.'

'I could help you—I'm quite good at that.'

Hal threw back his head and laughed aloud. 'You're a cunning little blighter, Edward Pearson, but I'm not taken in by you. You and your wide-eyed innocence. It conceals a shrewd little brain, I know.'

Eddie preened, flattered even if he was not quite certain whether it was meant to be a compliment or not. Hal was busying himself sorting out sheaves of papers, murmuring as he did so. 'You'll do well, young Eddie. You know what's important to you.'

Encouraged, Eddie came further into the room. As a rule his parents did not like him to disturb Hal. He leaned confidentially against the edge of Hal's desk.

'What's important to you, Hal, the most important thing?'

His brother looked up, an expression

44

of surprise on his face. Eddie noticed with envy the hint of whiskers on his chin as Hal fingered it. 'Let me see,' he said thoughtfully, 'my conscience, I think. Doing what I know is right, and not necessarily what I'd like to do. Acting according to conscience even if the rest of the world doesn't agree with me, if need be.'

He smiled ruefully, as if suddenly conscious of the pompous sound of his words. 'Come on, you can help if you like. Tell you what, see which of my books you might like to have, instead of reading those Deadwood Dicks all the time.'

The sound of Father's footsteps plodding heavily up the stairs made Eddie pause. Maybe he should leave. Father appeared in the open doorway, newspaper in hand. He was evidently on his way to the toilet, where he could read undisturbed.

'I take it there is serious discussion going on here,' he remarked. 'My sons are debating the evils of drink or of capitalism, or possibly they are outlining the attributes of the newest socialist MP, Mr Gregg.'

A flush spread over Eddie's face but Hal came to the rescue. 'Indeed, Father, we did mention that Mr Gregg's strong belief in pacifism was to be admired, since so many of his colleagues do not share his views.'

Father's expression darkened. 'That is

so. Many of us recognise that fighting for one's beliefs is at times inevitable. Don't you believe that too, Hal?'

Eddie watched his brother's reaction, saw his face set and his shoulders stiffen. 'My views are the same as Mr Gregg's on that score, Father. Fighting is wrong; the taking of life is unforgivable, a sin as the Bible teaches us.'

Fearful though he was, Eddie felt proud of his brother's courage. His father's voice remained calm but his pale blue eyes held an icy look.

'In some circumstances fighting for a way of life may be unavoidable, son, but I will respect your opinion even if I can't share it.' He paused, and Eddie thought how reasonable he was being. Hal plunged on.

'In my opinion, all differences, national or even international, ought to be able to be resolved by reason and discussion. I could never bring myself to take up weapons against another human being—nor, I think, would you. You fight for men, not against them.'

Eddie breathed a sigh of relief. Clever Hal, flattering Father. It was true, too, for Father spent hours on behalf of his union workers. Though he was employed at Syke's mill, he would never let the millowner dismiss a man willy-nilly without good cause. Many a union man in the area had cause to be grateful to James Pearson for his fearless campaigning in the interests of justice.

Father sighed and turned to go. 'Aye well, as I said, I'll respect your opinion though I can't share it. Eddie, be off and leave your brother in peace.'

Down in the kitchen Mother was baking bread. Eddie sat on a stool to watch as she kneaded the dough, looking forward to the last little piece which she always kept for him to fashion into a little man or a rabbit or whatever his fancy dictated.

'Did Hal say if he's going up to the Clarion?' she asked, in that absent-minded way she always spoke when she was busy.

'He didn't say. Will he take his bicycle to college with him?' If not, Eddie realised with hopeful anticipation, he could go to the cycling club in Hal's place.

'I expect so, dear. He'll need it there to save on tram fares.'

Hope faded. 'Can I have my own bicycle then?'

'Afraid not. We can't afford it.'

Hope vanished. Eddie picked up a discarded crumb of dough and chewed it. It tasted horrible, and he spat it out.

'But I think you're old enough now to sign the pledge—then you'll get a little gift,' she said softly as she greased the loaf tins.

That sounded more promising. 'A gift?' he repeated.

'Only a small one, not as big as a bicycle, but it's better than nothing.'

Hal's voice echoed down the stairs. 'What time is it, Mother?'

Eddie answered for her. 'Quarter past ten.'

'He is going up to the cycling club then,' said Mother. 'Better put the kettle on for his drink before he goes.'

Hal appeared in the kitchen doorway. 'I'm off,' he said. 'Arthur will be waiting for me at the clock tower.'

Mother wiped the flour from her hands, a slight frown rutting her tired face. 'Are you sure you ought to go out with that Arthur, love? He's a bit of a hothead, they tell me.'

Hal patted her shoulder fondly. 'Don't fret so much, Mother. Arthur's all right. He's a bit of a firebrand, I agree, but that doesn't mean anything. He's very ardent in his beliefs, and I find him stimulating company. I'll have to go now, or he'll have given me up.'

Mother nodded. 'Will you be back for tea, love? Remember we have Mr and Mrs Iredale coming.'

Oh please, thought Eddie, be back for

then, Hal. That woman always pats my head and says how big I've grown if I'm here on my own!

'Probably not,' Hal called back over his shoulder. 'Don't worry about me—I'll have tea out. Give my respects to the Iredales, won't you?'

As the front door banged behind him Father came downstairs. 'Hal gone out?'

'Yes, dear. Shall I make us a pot of tea?'

'That would be nice. And Eddie, what are you doing in the kitchen, bothering your mother? Go on up to your own room and amuse yourself.'

Mother put her arm around the boy's shoulder; then, catching sight of her husband's disapproving expression, she withdrew it quickly. 'I was just saying, James, I think maybe it's about time our Eddie signed the pledge. Don't you agree?'

'Aye, why not? Do you know, Annie, it says in the paper that Lord Cromer is to be pensioned off with fifty thousand pounds—just think of that!'

Eddie wandered disconsolately out of the kitchen. He could just hear his mother saying, 'And who is this Lord Cromer when he's at home?'

In the crowded House of Commons,

Labour's newest recruit was making his maiden speech. For a time there was hushed attention as his husky voice filled the chamber.

'He's never going to talk about that grant to the ex-governor of Egypt, is he?' one back-bencher whispered to another.

'That's what I heard,' his neighbour replied. 'Listen.'

Gregg's voice was waxing eloquent. 'One hears questions of a very similar character from both sides of the House.... One begins to wonder what question is being discussed.... Has someone finally found a solution to the poor problem? Or are they introducing a measure of pensions for incapacitated workmen? Or has the rumour slipped out that the new member is about to speak? I find it surprising that such enthusiasm can be evoked from these crowded benches with the full support of the Opposition on the question of giving a grant of fifty thousand pounds—to an Egyptian official.'

Ignoring the cries of 'Shame', Gregg continued: 'Outside these walls people are starving. Men and women who have given good and substantial service to the state are tottering towards paupers' graves. The attitude of this government could not be better devised if the object were to help the most revolutionary schemes; the most

50

energetic propaganda is being carried on for socialism, not by socialist propaganda but by the impotent statesmen of this impotent government who have deserted the pledges they gave to the people at their election.'

There was uproar in the chamber. Gregg waited patiently until it had died down and then went on: 'If this policy is persisted in, there will not be only one electoral change, but we can look forward to the day when all the front benches are occupied by socialists.'

There was loud laughter from the Liberal benches as Gregg sat down, but his handsome face maintained its expression of contempt. It was still there as he sat at tea with Hobson that evening.

'It was a challenging speech for a first-timer,' Hobson remarked gruffly. 'Not what the House is used to.'

'Why should I concern myself with outmoded traditions?' Gregg replied carelessly. 'It's high time those smug blighters were shaken out of their complacency. Much has got to be achieved, and it won't be done playing around with antiquated procedures.'

'You'll have to take care not to upset the others, those of our own party, I mean. Keir Hardie himself has agreed to accept parliamentary procedure.'

51

'As part of a bid for political respectability, I know,' said Gregg, 'but I'm afraid I remain unconvinced.'

Hobson grunted, and evidently decided to change the subject. 'Are you staying in tonight?'

'No. Why?'

Hobson shrugged. 'It's just that you've been out just about every night since you came here. I thought you might be staying in for once, that's all.'

Gregg shrugged. 'So many invitations, Sam, people are so pressing....'

'You don't have to accept them all. I know they're curious to see the new phenomenon, to hear you speak, but you don't owe it to them to accept them all.'

'Ah well, they're not all speaking invitations, Sam. I'm being asked to a literary lunch tomorrow and another party in Mayfair—it's useful to get to know people.'

'I see.' Hobson could indeed see. Gregg was enjoying the lionising, and why shouldn't he? He was the socialists' newest and rising star. Just so long as he didn't let it go to his head and forget why he came here....

Sir Marcus Hardcastle's always temperamental digestion was not being helped by what he read in his newspaper.

'Young popinjay!' he exploded as his son pulled up a chair to join him at the breakfast table. 'Who the devil does this Gregg think he is, to insult the likes of Lord Cromer, I'd like to know? Quibbling over the man's pension, and after he's given so much service to his country too!'

Robert Hardcastle shook out his napkin and spread it carefully across his thighs. 'Oh, he's not such a bad chap, Father, quite bright for a socialist, in fact. Speaks well, dresses well—you could almost take him for one us.'

'Balderdash! He's an upstart. Came up out of nowhere and now he thinks he can tell the elected government what they should do! Downright criminal, if you ask me, to let a man of his type represent the masses. He'll stir the mob to violent action if we don't watch him.'

Robert helped himself to a liberal portion of kedgeree. 'Oh, I don't think so. He's really quite amiable when you talk to him. Very cultured, actually, and terribly knowledgeable. I liked him.'

Sir Marcus's jaw dropped. 'Talk to him? Are you telling me you've actually talked to this fellow?'

His son smiled, in that gentle, rather effeminate way which always irritated Sir Marcus. 'Now don't act so outraged,

Father. You encouraged me to cultivate intelligent and useful people, didn't you? You won't find many more intelligent than Vincent. He's really rather intriguing.'

'But are you telling me you've actually met him?'

'Of course. I couldn't have talked with him otherwise, could I?'

Sir Marcus swallowed hard, trying to control his anger. His voice sounded strangled. 'Where, and when?'

'Last night. At the club, with Bottomley. He was terribly witty. Really, Father, he would be an asset at anyone's dinner table. You might think of asking him to come here—or to Byram Hall when he's in Yorkshire.'

His father splutterd into his second cup of tea. 'Invite him here? You must be out of your mind! I'll not have any socialist here, preaching his Karl Marx claptrap. What would my friends think?'

Robert smiled and spread butter thickly on his toast. 'I think they'd be captivated, just as everyone at the club was last night. He's a natural raconteur.'

'That's as may be,' retorted his father in heavy tones, 'but he opposes everything we stand for, everything our family has fought for, for generations. He hates capitalism and enterprise, and I'll remind you that the Hardcastles have struggled for four hundred years to get where they are today.'

'Oh, don't be so pompous, Father.'

Sir Marcus got up from the table abruptly. 'No, you listen to me. The Hardcastles would be nothing still, if we'd listened to the likes of that fellow Gregg. You wouldn't be enjoying the standard of life you do. No, he's not setting foot in my house—any of my houses—so don't you think of bringing him, not while I'm alive and master of the Hardcastle estate. Do you hear?'

Young Robert sighed. It must be frightfully tedious to be fifty, but that was thirty years ahead of him yet, thank goodness. 'Very well, Father. Talking of Byram, why don't we spend a few days there? I've got that new fishing rod I want to try out, and it would be such fun—that is, if it isn't still raining cats and dogs up there like it was last time.'

FOUR

Sir Marcus and Lady Hardcastle were late for the Hon Mrs Beauchamp's soirée; not late enough to overstep the bounds of politeness, but late enough to attract sufficient attention. It would be a great pity if Lady Hardcastle's new emerald necklace were not commented upon as a clear sign of her husband's generosity, and that would have ruined Sir Marcus' evening. That the emeralds were also an investment and were already heavily insured was beside the point.

Robert Hardcastle followed his parents up the steps of the elegant Belgravia mansion, stifling a yawn. He hoped sincerely that there was going to be someone interesting present at the gathering tonight, for these society functions could be ineffably boring on occasions. It was a bit much, really, when a chap's mother insisted on always taking one along to these do's, as if twenty wasn't old enough to be allowed to choose one's own evening entertainment.

'Sir Marcus—and Alicia, my dear. How nice to see you both—and young Robert too!' Mrs Beauchamp enthused. 'I'm so glad you could come.'

As if anything would have kept Father away, thought Robert morosely. He'd go anywhere he thought there were contacts to be made or influential people to curry. As he handed his cloak to the maid he caught sight of Adeline Hamilton and groaned. Simpering daughter of a fabulously rich stockbroker, she was in Mother's eyes a highly suitable catch for any ambitious young man, but if she started her ludicrously obvious matchmaking games again tonight.... He headed with determination towards the billiards room.

The Hon Mrs Beauchamp endeared herself instantly to Sir Marcus. 'Alicia, my dear! What a magnificent necklace you're wearing! My, but you'll be the envy of every woman here!'

Lady Hardcastle preened. 'A gift for my birthday,' she murmured.

'Really?' The honourable lady's eyes widened.

'From me,' added Sir Marcus.

'Who else?' laughed the hostess. 'Never a breath of scandal attaches itself to dear Alicia's name. Come now, I'd like you to meet some of the new people I've got here—a rather intriguing little pianist chappie from Hungary, I think, or it could be Armenia, I can't remember. Anyway, he's got the most amusing accent and such a charming, old-fashioned courtesy about him; he quite puts our English men to shame, and the girls are all enchanted by him.'

'If you'll excuse me,' cut in Sir Marcus, 'I'd like to have a word with someone I can see over there—business, you know—but you go on, Alicia. I'll join you later.'

'By all means,' assented the hostess. 'By the way, Alicia, did you know we'd just returned from a spell at our place in Nice? Such fun, such interesting people—why don't you go abroad more often? You never seem to go further than that Yorkshire place of yours. A spot of sunlight would do your complexion a world of good.'

'Ah well, it would mean missing Henley and Ascot, and that would never do,' rejoined Lady Hardcastle. One in the eye for the Hon Mrs Beauchamp.

The hostess shrugged sequin-covered shoulders. 'Oh, I always think the season is far more important, the hunt balls and the Court presentation—oh, but I was forgetting, the presentation would not concern you, would it, not having any daughters.'

There was no time to think up a witty retort as the lady's daughter joined them at the wine table. Her mother beamed broadly. 'Don't you think Sophie grows prettier every day, Alicia? I'm quite looking forward to presenting her. And as Frederick is making over a handsome allowance to her on her eighteenth birthday, I fear we may be hard-pressed with suitors at the door before very long. Which reminds me—where has young Robert got to? He and Sophie used to be such good friends when they were small.'

Lady Hardcastle bit her lip, trying hard to control her vexation as she took the glass of wine she was offered. She would hate this woman to arrange a match between her daughter, however pretty, and Robert, but it would be best to hold her tongue. Marcus could very well think it an excellent match....

'I think I saw him in the billiards room, Mother, with Mr Gregg,' Sophie remarked.

Lady Hardcastle could foresee the next move and spoke quickly to avert it. 'This Hungarian pianist you spoke of—I'm terribly keen on music—do find him for me and introduce us, there's a dear.'

'To be sure. Ah, Sophie, will you take Lady Hardcastle to meet Stefan—I see the Fordyce-Joneses have just arrived. Do excuse me.'

'With pleasure,' said Lady Hardcastle.

59

'I must confess, Mr Gregg, I didn't expect to come across you here this evening,' Robert remarked as Gregg signalled the maid to refill his glass. 'It's such a pleasure to come across some intelligent company and not just the usual boring crowd.'

'Please call me Vincent,' his companion murmured as he held out his glass to be replenished. 'But I can't say I find the company boring—quite the contrary, in fact. Still, it's a whole new way of life to me, but I expect you've always lived with it. Well, you've asked me all about my job—now tell me about you. What do you do?'

'Do? Work, you mean?' Robert's expression was one of surprise. 'Well, I dare say I'll manage Father's business one day. I'll have to learn all about the investments in manufacturing and industry and manage all his estates. He keeps suggesting I go up north and spend some time with his estate manager there to learn the ropes, but I keep telling him I'm not likely to take over from him for centuries yet, so what's the hurry?'

'None, it would seem. Life is for living, for enjoying while we can. What are your pleasures, Robert—I may call you Robert, mayn't I?'

'I'd be glad—after all, we must be much of an age, you and I. And to answer your question, I like opera, the odd visit to a variety show, a game of cards....'

'And a glass of whisky now and again,' added Vincent with a smile, laying aside his wine glass and heading towards the side buffet, where waiters stood ready to serve. Robert followed and, when he saw Gregg order a double, followed suit. They were standing by the arched doorway when Sir Marcus entered.

'Ah, Robert,' he said cheerfully, 'I believe Sophie wants a word with you.' Catching sight of the elegant man with his son, he raised his eyebrows interrogatively.

Clearly he did not notice his son's hesitation before he spoke. 'Father, allow me to introduce to you'—Sir Marcus' hand was already beginning to rise—'the new Member of Parliament, Mr Vincent Gregg.'

The light died in Sir Marcus' eyes. His hand did not fall but his manner became at once cool. Gregg's hand touched his only briefly.

'My father, Sir Marcus Hardcastle,' continued Robert.

Gregg nodded. 'A pleasure to meet you,' he murmured.

Sir Marcus stiffened. 'Wish I could say the same,' he grunted. 'You're the fellow who rants all that bolshie stuff I keep reading about, aren't you?'

Gregg smiled an amused little smile. Robert flinched. 'Well, I would hardly expect a landowner like yourself to share my views,' Gregg admitted, 'but I think I speak for the majority of the population.'

'The devil you do!' exploded Sir Marcus. 'Well, I don't want to waste my time listening to the meddlesome, trouble-making claptrap you talk—nor, for that matter, does my son here! Robert, your mother wants you.'

He turned abruptly and marched away. Robert watched the receding fat little figure in alarm, and then the alarm began to subside. Vincent Gregg had dealt with him coolly enough; he could do the same.

Gregg was watching him, spinning the remains of the whisky around in the bowl of his glass and that slight smile of amusement still curving his lips. Robert was filled with admiration of his cool, suave manner.

'Well?' said Gregg. 'Hadn't you better go?'

'When I'm ready,' Robert replied. 'I want to talk to you.'

'Some other time, perhaps.'

Robert's heart leapt. 'We could meet again? I'd like that. Where, and when?' His handsome young face fell. 'I can't invite you to our place, I'm afraid.'

Gregg laughed as he returned to the buffet. 'I think I can see why. Never mind. Tell you what, how about meeting me at my club one night and we can perhaps go to the opera together?'

'Oh yes, I'd like that very much! It really is a nuisance, you know, living with my parents. Can't have a life of my own. I really must see about getting a bachelor flat for myself soon.'

Gregg patted his arm as he made to go. 'Don't worry, I won't embarrass you with your father. He and I are not exactly anxious to meet again, holding such diametrically opposed views as we do. Now you'd better go and join your mother—and this Sophie.'

Robert grimaced. 'Women! She's always trying to push me at some girl or other. I'd much rather go to the opera with you—I'll really look forward to that.'

'And so will I, Robert.'

'Let's fix a date,' the boy urged, following Gregg. 'What about Friday?'

Gregg turned, his easy smile fading. 'Ah well, I think I'd better leave that for the moment. In a week or two, perhaps. Fact is, I'm not exactly flush at the moment, but....'

Robert's anxious look vanished. 'Oh, is that all? Then there's no problem—it will be my treat.'

For a moment Gregg looked uncomfortable. 'I really don't think I can accept.'

Robert waved an impatient hand. 'Of course you can. I have a very good allowance, so we'll say no more about it. Your turn next time. Friday night then, agreed?'

Gregg spread his graceful hands expressively, and then reached into his pocket for his silver cigarette case. 'How can I possibly refuse?' he said huskily as he extracted a cigarette. 'I am delighted to accept.'

The Hon Mrs Beauchamp was chatting to another of her guests in the drawing room. Mrs Patricia Anstruther was listening inattentively, her deep green eyes never leaving the open doorway.

'So I suggested to Sophie that perhaps she and young Caroline—'

Mrs Anstruther seized her hostess's arm. 'Forgive me, Charlotte, but who is that devastating young man over there—the one smoking a cigarette?'

The Hon Mrs Beauchamp half-turned on the sofa to glance over her shoulder. 'Oh, that's Vincent Gregg—you know, that new socialist MP. He's the latest darling of London society—everybody who is anybody is inviting him these days. I just had to ask him to my little soirée.'

Mrs Anstruther's eyes gleamed, and she smoothed down the folds of her pale green watered silk skirt. 'You must introduce us, Charlotte,' she murmured softly. 'You really can't hog such a gorgeous creature to yourself.'

'Really, Patricia!' her hostess reproved. 'Wasn't Hugo able to come with you tonight?'

Mrs Anstruther smiled. 'Afraid not, my dear. He's abroad on business yet again. In Rome or Paris, I forget which. Now do introduce me, there's a dear, before that wretched Bella Sinclair beats me to it—he'll never have a chance of escaping her clutches once she gets her talons in.'

Her hostess sighed. 'Very well, come along. But take care, Patricia, for he's a protégé of the Countess, and she won't like it if you tarnish his reputation.'

Mrs Anstruther chuckled. 'I—tarnish his reputation? From what I hear he's managing very nicely by himself. Come on, lead the way.'

An hour passed and Gregg was still deep in conversation with Mrs Anstruther, and he was in no hurry to get away. The lady was not only very pretty but witty and vivacious too. She had an intriguing way of skirting dangerously near to ribaldry at times, but always managing to stay on the right side of the fine dividing line between propriety and downright naughtiness.

'No, please,' she was saying, 'call me Patricia, and perhaps when we know each other well enough you may call me Trixie, as my friends do—but not yet.'

He made a slight bow. 'I am honoured—and I look forward to the further honour.'

'Then that's agreed. I think we shall find we have a lot in common, you and I. Rather different from the rest, a little apart and not afraid. Who was it said, *"Qui s'élève, s'isole"*? Whoever it was, I'm sure it referred to us—shall we drink to it?' She gave him a wry little smile.

He smiled too, his generous mouth widening and an impish expression in his eyes. 'Why not? An excellent idea.'

He turned and beckoned, and glasses were placed in their hands. She raised hers, casting him a challenging look over the rim.

'To our better acquaintance then,' she murmured.

'I'll drink to that.'

'Friday? I'm having a few friends to dinner.'

He frowned and lowered his glass. 'Ah, Friday I can't manage, I'm afraid....'

She shrugged. 'No matter. I know you're a very busy man. Monday, perhaps?'

'Monday is fine. Your husband will be home then?'

She shook her head, and inwardly he could not help admiring the way her red-gold hair caught the light from the chandelier. 'He won't be home until the end of the week. You won't be bored if we dine à deux?'

He laughed softly. 'As we say in the House, a rhetorical question, dear lady. I look forward to Monday.'

Annie Pearson sank into the chair by the fireside with a sigh. James had gone to his Co-op Education Committee meeting, but for once she had no commitments and could spend the evening at home with Eddie. She looked fondly at him, his fair head bent in concentration over the album as he sat at the chenille-covered table.

'Turn the light up, love, or you'll strain your eyes. Another postcard from Hal?'

The boy straightened, pushing back the wayward front flick of his hair. 'No, Mother. I'm just mounting the ones I already had of Kirkstall Priory and Robin Hood's grave—the ones Mrs Iredale sent me this summer.'

'Let me see.'

She could sense his pleasure in the eager way he passed the album over then sat back, eyes aglow, to watch her reaction.

She felt a pang of guilt, mingled with nostalgia. So little time she had with her son these days—he was growing into a man before she had shared his childhood.

Inside the front cover of the leather-bound album was pasted the pledge, Eddie's declaration, and she screwed up her eyes to read the words:

'I hereby agree, with God's help, to abstain from all Intoxicating Drinks as beverages so long as I retain this card of membership.'

Signed by the officials, Sidney Aspinall and Frederick Fowler, there then followed the prayer: *'Oh God, give me, Thy young servant, grace to withstand the temptations of the world, the flesh and the devil, and with a pure heart and mind to follow Thee.'*

Lowering the book she looked over the top of it at his eager young face. 'Aren't they pretty,' he said, 'especially the coloured ones.'

'They're lovely, indeed they are.'

He flushed with pleasure. 'And I've put in some of your Christmas cards as well, and the card we had from Mrs Booth with Blackpool Tower on it. The ones from Hal with all the views of York are further on—shall I show you?'

She could not resist smiling at his evident enthusiasm. 'Not just now, love. My eyes are tired. Will you read to me a bit from the paper?'

The invitation clearly pleased him for it was usually James's function to read to her. As Eddie fetched the newspaper from the sideboard, still smooth and folded since James had had no time to open it, she watched him sit in his father's chair and, back erect and solemn-faced, clear his throat just as James would do.

'What shall I read to you, Mother? About this murder in Whitechapel? Or Mr Gregg's speech about the Irish trade unionists?'

Annie lay back, eyes closed. 'I don't know,' she murmured. 'Not murders, I think. Too depressing. And the papers never have a good word to say about Vincent Gregg these days. Ever since he made that speech about the people having broken bottles instead of shrapnel, and then those Belfast strikers used bottles against the military, he can't do anything right, it seems. Your father says he's sometimes too extreme in what he says and he ought to be more moderate, like Mr Macdonald.'

The boy remained silent. It was pointless to expect a reply from him; he was too young to understand and, unlike Hal, he seemed unaware of the world around him. Except for birds and bees and butterflies, that was—they were the real world to Eddie.

She opened her eyes. Eddie was reading silently. He caught her look and hastened to explain.

'It says here that the Amalgamated Society of Railway Workers are angry at not being recognised as a union, and they've had a poll. They're ready to serve strike notices.'

'Goodness,' said Annie. 'More and more people are beginning to air their grievances against the Government. If it goes on like this, heaven knows where it might end....'

'Mr Gregg is grumbling about the rich too,' Eddie remarked without looking up from the paper. 'The aristocracy especially. Does that mean people like those Hardcastles you talk about?'

'Possibly. What does he say?'

Eddie cleared his throat again. ' "The upper classes, driven to—to ennui..."—what does that mean, Mother?'

'I'm not sure. Boredom, I think.'

' "Driven to ennui by the daily round of insincerities, markedly yearn for new games and excitement. Their brains are becoming atrophied, and their soul is so much salt to keep the body from putrefaction. The working classes, harried and hustled by the problem of living, gaze with bleared eyes upon the perplexing medley, and down again at their chains with the dawning glint of a new hope." I don't think I understand all that, but it sounds strong.'

'A new hope,' repeated Annie softly. 'That's what we all need.' She was about to doze off to sleep when she suddenly sat upright. 'Oh, Eddie, I've left some old blankets at the top of the stairs—will you get them and tie them up in a bundle for me? I must take them down to the centre tomorrow when I do my turn at the soup kitchen.'

Obediently Eddie rose to go and do as she asked. As he did so he heard her murmuring to herself again. 'Aye, there's plenty as could do with a bit of hope these days, that there is.'

The House had heard enough about unemployment. Trade was abysmal, strikers were threatening violence and London's streets had been crowded with the army of unemployed who marched from Manchester to plead for action. But the King's speech at the opening of Parliament had foretold legislation only for education, for licensing and for pensions for the aged—only so much was possible within one parliamentary year, so the heated outpourings of this rabid socialist fellow were really more than flesh and blood could bear. But today he was at it again.

'As a socialist I have no hesitation in saying that it is more moral, more manly, infinitely more preferable to steal when you are starving than to die of hunger....'

'No! Shame!'

'I have nothing but the profoundest contempt for the man who allows his wife and children to starve, and accepts this as being according to the supposed will of God.'

A pause until the uproar died, and the husky voice proclaimed again. 'I know I can trust you not to steal from the needy man or woman. If you're going to steal, steal from those who have; they won't miss it. They'll be saved from indigestion.'

And with a smile, the insolent fellow seated himself again.

There was a light still burning in the living room window when Gregg arrived back at the house. Sam Hobson was sitting wrapped in his old woollen dressing gown by the burnt-out embers of the fire.

Gregg threw his coat over a chair. 'Dreadfully sorry to be so late again—Mrs Anstruther offered me a lift in her car but there was some trouble with the carburettor, or something and the chauffeur had quite a job fixing it. Wouldn't have been half so late otherwise.'

He took out a cigarette and lit it. Hobson fanned the air with his evening paper and wished for the thousandth time that

Gregg wouldn't chain-smoke. The curtains, armchairs, carpets—everything reeked of tobacco since Gregg moved in.

'Well, at least you've thought up a new one,' he remarked.

'New what?'

'Excuse. It's a different one every time.'

'Reasons, my dear fellow, not excuses. It really is the reason why I'm so late.'

'Aye, well, it's not for me to tell you what to do. A grown man needs no telling. But I wanted a word with you any road.'

'You would rather I moved on. Well, I think I can oblige you, Sam. I've found a place....'

'Nay, that's not what I were going to say, but I can't say as I'm sorry. Nay, I were just going to caution you to take care, that's all.'

'Caution me? About what?'

'About taking too strong a line in the house—'

'Nothing's too strong for that feeble-minded government we're stuck with.'

'Happen not, but it's strong meat for your own side too. They don't like the way you're going about things.'

'I say no more than they ought to be saying. People are starving, Sam.'

'Aye, but where many socialist members began by agreeing with you, the more militant ones, even they are losing sympathy with you now.'

Gregg exhaled a perfect smoke ring and watched it float to the ceiling. 'Who, exactly? What are you trying to tell me, Sam?'

The older man eyed him solemnly. 'Snowden, that's who. Watch out for him, Vincent lad. He may have walked with you to the Speaker's chair, but he's not with you now—and that's a fact. He'll do you harm, he will, if you don't watch out.'

Gregg considered for a moment, then ground out the cigarette in an ashtray. 'I thought you were going to lecture me about my private life, Sam.'

'That I'll not—there's plenty others finding fault with you about that already. Mind you, I don't think much of you making speeches in Hawksmoor to the ordinary folk wearing your best evening suit....'

'Nonsense. They like it. And more to the point, so do I. But as to Snowden, well, let me tell you, Sam, I've no intention of moderating my words for him or for anyone else. People are without work, without self-esteem, and above all, without food or hope. Someone has to speak for the starving, and in the strongest terms possible. And I'm the man to do it. To hell with Snowden, and his ilk.'

Hobson regarded him thoughtfully for a moment and then eased himself out of his chair. 'Aye well, I felt it were up to me to warn you, and now it's up to you. I've done what I can.'

As he made to pass the younger man he caught the heady smell of whisky. 'And another thing,' he added slowly, 'you're drinking too much. Best cut it down, especially afore you speak in the House.'

Gregg laughed, but there was a bitterness in the sound. 'It's not alcohol in my blood that causes heated speech, Sam, I assure you—it's the fire in my blood.'

'Aye, maybe, but you do drink too much. Now I'm off to my bed, where I should have been hours ago. Goodnight to you, Vincent.'

FIVE

Robert Hardcastle waited impatiently on Leeds railway station, turning up the fur collar of his coat against the cold and wishing the time away until the train for Hawksmoor was due.

How tedious of Father to make the sudden decision to send him up north just now, when travelling was so uncomfortable in the depths of winter and when the fun in London was at its peak. It would also mean having to stay in the house alone—heaven grant that the housekeeper had warmed the place sufficiently to thaw out his frozen bones when he arrived. And the prospect of having to go over all those boring old ledgers with old Whatsisname, the estate agent, was far from exciting. Fancy wrenching a fellow away from the pleasures of a winter season to exile him to the bleakest, dirtiest part of the country! Father could be so unreasonable at times. The only consolation lay in the knowledge that Vincent would be up here soon.

Robert could not resist a wry smile. In his anxiety to remove his son from temptation, Father had overlooked the fact that Vincent's constituency immediately adjoined Hawksmoor and that their dedicated Member returned there often.

'Time for a cup of tea, sir, in the refreshment room if tha wants it afore the train comes.'

For the first time Robert became aware of the broken-veined face of the old porter standing guarding his valise. The old man looked peaked and blue with cold. No wonder, living in this God-forsaken place. A cup of tea...that wasn't a bad idea, but it would probably be ghastly. Still, a hot drink might help to keep this damnable cold at bay.

He was peeling off his gloves to fish in his pocket for coins when a voice hailed him.

'Hardcastle! Well, bless my soul! Fancy meeting you here!'

Robert turned, startled at hearing his name, and stared unrecognisingly for a moment at the tall, fair-haired young man smiling at him.

'Colville! What on earth are you doing here?'

The young man gripped his hand in a strong handshake. 'I was wondering the same thing when I caught sight of you, Robert. I thought you lived in London still.'

Robert drew himself upright. 'I do. Just

up here on business for my father. What about you?'

'Going back to college in York. Decided to pick up on my education again, having misspent my youth so badly.' He tossed back his head and laughed, and Robert felt a frisson he remembered so well from the past.

He gave an embarrassed little laugh. 'Ah yes, but I regret nothing. I have fond memories, James,' he murmured.

Colville looked at him, eyebrows slightly arched. 'Ah, yes, I was not referring specifically to that—you were my fag, you know, and it is not uncommon for a bond of deep, ah, affection in such circumstances. I still think of you fondly, Robert.'

'Do you?' Robert instantly regretted the inadvertently eager tone in his voice, for he saw the light that leapt into James's eyes. 'I'm sorry, I didn't mean—I meant I'm happy you can recall the time with pleasure, that's all.'

'Of course. I understood. Just so long as you would not wish to....' His voice tailed away, a note of enquiry faintly discernible.

'No, no, of course not. It was all a long time ago.' If only he could have masked the alarm in his voice. It was true he had hero-worshipped James once, even been foolish enough to write him passionate letters declaring his worship.

'Yes,' agreed Colville. 'It was a long time. Tell me about yourself. Not married, are you?'

Was it Robert's imagination or was there a hint of a sneer in his voice, as if he considered Hardcastle incapable of loving a woman?

Robert sighed, enacting as casual a manner as he could achieve. 'No, but my mother is trying hard enough to pair me off. How about you?'

'Likewise. Scheming mothers can be the very devil, but I have other plans for my future, and they don't include marriage yet a while.'

'What kind of plans?' This was safer ground to tread.

James made an expressively airy gesture, waving a gloved hand. 'Oh, projects, deals, entrepreneurial games, you know.'

'At college?'

James gave him a pitying smile. 'A front, my dear fellow. And a degree will add prestige, in any event, if I do manage to get one.' A bell clanged over the station-master's office. 'Ah, the York train—are you catching that?'

Robert shook his head. 'No, the Hawks-moor one.'

James's eyes gleamed. 'So you'll no

doubt be seeing the redoubtable Gregg again before long,' he remarked drily. 'Well, nice to see you, Hardcastle. Perhaps we'll meet again in town some time. Cheerio.'

The venerable old porter came shuffling back and touched the peak of his battered cap. 'It's in now, is the Hawksmoor train, sir. I'll see thee and thy bag safely aboard in the first class.'

Seated in the corner of an otherwise empty compartment, Robert watched out of the window as the train steamed out of the station. His unseeing eyes were looking at the grey slate roofs of tenements as the train clattered on out of the city, but inwardly he was seeing again dusty school corridors and candlelit dormitories. Colville's handsome face permeated all his dreams in those days, and he remembered the ache of waiting and hoping to be called to the prefects' study to fag for the school hero. Colville, lithe-limbed and athletic, excelled at everything physical, from cross-country running to cricket and rugby, both of which he captained for the school. He was every schoolboy's fantasy hero, and Robert, steeped in adoration, had been envious of any other boy who earned a word of praise on the cricket field from him. He recalled how jealous he had been of young Faversham when Colville actually touched him, clapping him on the shoulder to express his admiration of a particularly fine catch.

The greyness of the city gave way to green fields intersected by random drystone walls and an occasional squat farmhouse. It was curious, thought Robert, how the sight of James Colville could give him a shiver of excitement still. The old feeling of something powerful, something enigmatic and possibly even ruthless in him made one feel he could still be a force to be reckoned with if one were ever foolish enough to get on the wrong side of him. Curious, too, how the fellow seemed to know about his friendship with Vincent Gregg—had he perhaps seen them together at the theatre in London, or been told by others?

And however he knew, why should he comment upon it in such an odd manner? Not jealousy, surely, after all this time. Robert's letters had left no room for doubt as to how he had once felt, but the fellow was not petty-minded, and in any event Robert did not feel the same way about Gregg.

No, of course he didn't. He enjoyed Gregg's company enormously. They had many interests in common, that was all. Vincent's conversation was a delight, and his taste was impeccable, in dress and reading and theatre. He was such fun, too. And he was affectionate, unashamed to put his arm about a fellow's shoulder as he talked. Father would have hated such behaviour if he had known, but what the eye doesn't see.... No, Robert simply enjoyed Gregg's company, that was all, and preferably alone.

Which was not as often as he would have liked, dammit, because those women were always in hot pursuit of him. Just lately it had been that wretched Bella, anxious to prove that she could be just as enticing a hostess as Trixie Anstruther. And Mrs Anstruther had no business to be asking Vincent to dine so often, with her husband away. It would only harm Vincent's reputation if she went on....

Evening clouds were beginning to roll across the smoky horizon and gaslamps starting to glimmer. That must be Mirfield—not far now to Hawksmoor. He shivered at the prospect and hoped fervently that the housekeeper would have a good log fire burning and hot bricks in his bed, not to mention a nourishing hot meal ready, preferably with some of that delicious Yorkshire pudding with the crispy edges she excelled in making.

'Hawksmoor! Hawksmoor!'

In the ensuing hour Robert forgot his cold, cramped limbs when he reached the house and found that the housekeeper's preparations had excelled even his hopes. Good humour restored, Robert was about to savour a large brandy before bed when the maid entered the dining room.

'By the way, Mr Robert, this letter came by the afternoon post.'

The letter was from Vincent. By the time he had read it his good humour had vanished.

I'm sorry I won't be able to meet you this time as we planned—Trixie has arranged a do specially in my honour on Friday night so there'll just be time for me to give my speech in Halifax and then catch the early train back to town. Sorry, old man. Better luck next time.

Yours, Vincent.

Robert screwed up the letter and threw it irritably in the direction of the fireplace. It ricocheted off the fender and rolled along the rug.

'Bloody women!' he exploded. 'Why can't they leave him alone?'

It had been wonderful having Hal back at home for the Christmas vacation from college, but the house seemed empty and lonely now he had gone, Eddie thought, as he trudged wearily up the cobbled street leading towards the station square, lowering his head against the icy sleet.

Hal's stories of college life had opened up a whole new vista for Eddie. It wasn't all writing long essays and working far into the night; there were also clubs and societies, such as the debating society and the socialist club and the cycling club—and it was about this Hal was most excited.

'Lovely places to visit, like Beverley, where we rode last weekend, and the exhilaration of riding in the countryside whatever the weather—even the rain is exciting when you're well wrapped up. And the conversations we have, far into the night—the people you meet with like minds—oh, it's all so good.'

The sparkle Hal brought into the house seemed to vanish with his departure. Mother and Father were, as always, busy with all their work. School was all right, but with no close friend and a continuing battle with Denton and his cronies, it was not as happy as it might have been.

Still, there would be more postcards from Hal to look forward to, more pretty pictures of York and Beverley to mount carefully in his treasured album. Eddie was deep in thought as he turned the corner into the square.

At this time of day it was usually quiet enough, apart from passing trams, but today a small crowd was gathered about a tall man who was waving his arms as he spoke. Eddie approached, curious about what was going on.

The tall man was no ordinary man, for he was not dressed in everyday clothes but in a long black overcoat which swung loose, and beneath it Eddie could glimpse his stiff white shirt and black bow tie. He was clearly a gentleman, and dressed ready for some special evening occasion even though it was not yet four o'clock in the afternoon.

'And so I urge you all, dear friends, not to give up but to continue the struggle with a manful heart. For the day will surely come when your children will be free to hold up their heads in pride that we, the socialist workers, never lost heart in the campaign to secure their future....'

Political talk again. Eddie lost interest in the words that seemed to pour so effortlessly from the gentleman's lips and watched instead the graceful movements of the slim hands. The hands stopped waving. One moved to a pocket in the overcoat and withdrew a flask. For a moment the gentleman paused in his speech, took a long swig from the flask, and then continued. A plump, middle-aged woman with a shopping basket over her arm nudged Eddie.

'Don't he talk lovely? I'd give my vote

for him any time, I would, if I had one.'

'Vote?' repeated Eddie. 'Who is he then?'

'Why, it's Mr Gregg, Member of Parliament, didn't tha know? Not for Hawksmoor, more's the pity, but he's a grand lad all the same.'

Her enthusiasm was clearly shared by the rest of the crowd, thought Eddie, for despite the sleet they stood there, huddled into their coats, and listening intently. Now and again they cried out their approval, and the gentleman held out his arms as if embracing them. The church clock struck four, and Eddie continued on his way home, turning over in his mind that this was the famous Gregg he had heard so much about. No wonder people thought so well of him.

There was much talk that evening about a bazaar. Mrs Charnock was excited about the prospect and Father could hardly get a word in edgewise.

'Mr Fletcher said as it were to be an international do. I don't know why, but that's what he said it were—'

'Because we are anxious to show that workers all over the world are united in socialist principles,' Father interjected.

'Aye, well, he said I'm to give a hand on the Indian stall, and it's all to be done out like an Indian palace.'

'That's right,' said Mother. 'I'm helping on the Japanese one, a tea-house.'

Mrs Charnock ignored her. 'So I thought I'd have a look in the Co-op for some stuff....'

Eddie heard her voice droning on, but he was already lost in his own day-dream. The Co-op. Of all the large buildings in the centre of town, the Hawksmoor Industrial Society was probably his favourite. Whenever Mother took him there to buy a new winter shirt or socks he was always fascinated by the network of wires criss-crossing the ceiling, and the way the assistant would put Mother's money into a wooden cup, screw it into a container on one of the overhead wires and then pull a cord. The cup would go winging its way across the wires towards the cashier's desk, and moments later reappear overhead bringing Mother's change.

'Eddie—are you listening?'

Startled, he sat upright. 'Yes, Mother.'

'Have you done your homework?'

His gaze slid away from hers. 'Yes, Mother.' The rest of the arithmetic could wait till morning.

'Then you'd better go and practise the songs we've chosen. We don't want to let Mr Glasier and Mr Gregg down.'

Interest sparked into life. Father was

talking about the huge numbers of people expected, and how gratifying that would be for Mr Snowden, and even Mr Hardie if he were able to attend. Words burst from Eddie's lips.

'Mr Gregg—I saw him today—he looked that grand and talked so fine—'

'Eddie! How many times have I told you not to interrupt? Go upstairs at once.'

Father's voice was stern. Mother looked at him and spoke softly. 'Let him tell us, James. I agree he's very rude, but did you know Mr Gregg was in Hawksmoor?'

Father might have relented, as he usually did when Mother intervened, but for Mrs Charnock. The wrinkles around her thin mouth deepened.

'Children these days! I don't know what the world's coming to, I don't really!'

Father's voice lowered an octave. 'You heard me, Edward. Upstairs.'

Eddie shambled out miserably. It might have helped to enliven the banishment if he knew which songs he had to practise. As he closed the living room door behind him he heard his mother spring to his defence.

'He was only showing an interest in politics at last, dear. He could do worse than admire Mr Gregg.'

'He could have chosen a more moderate man like Mr Macdonald, but that's beside the point. Children interrupting their elders

88

cannot be tolerated,' boomed Father.

'Quite right,' agreed Mrs Charnock, 'now what was I saying...?'

Vincent Gregg sprawled at his ease in a deep armchair, a cigarette between his fingers. Mrs Anstruther stood before the mirror, twisting her head to inspect the green chiffon hat nestling on her red-gold hair.

'All in all, it sounds like a rather dreary trip,' she remarked. 'You must be glad to be back in the land of the living.'

'Not at all, my dear lady. Chairing the bazaar thing was rather fun, actually,' he replied in that deep, husky tone which enraptured so many.

'Didn't Keir Hardie turn up there too? That's what I heard, and that you refused to share the platform with him.'

Gregg smiled. 'You never miss a thing, do you? Yes, that's true, and I never will. But the bazaar was a great success, none the less. The Hawksmoor party workers were very proud of themselves—and well they might be. They raised over twelve hundred pounds, and that's a lot of money from the pockets of the working class.'

She turned away from the mirror and, placing the hat on the sideboard, stood playing with the folds of chiffon. 'A sum which would barely keep you in cigarettes and whisky for a year,' she remarked drily, 'but I'm really not terribly interested in these parochial events. I'd much rather know whether you met the Hardcastle boy again while you were in Yorkshire.'

He glanced up at her, curiosity in his dark eyes. 'Why do you ask?'

Slim shoulders shrugged. 'He often seems to crop up wherever you are, and I know he's been in Hawksfield—'

'Hawksmoor.'

'Because Alicia told me. Did you see him?'

'No, actually. There wasn't time.'

'Otherwise you would have?'

'Possibly. What is all this, Trixie? You're just as bad as he is, always asking me about how often I see you. Honestly, I'm beginning to think you could be jealous. You're not really, are you?'

She moved away to the drinks cupboard and took hold of the whisky bottle. 'Don't be silly. Have another drink?'

He watched her pour the amber liquid into his glass and set the bottle down on the wine table, then ease herself on to the arm of his chair, her slim arm along the chairback behind his head.

'Tell me, Vincent,' she said softly, 'wouldn't you like to live a rather more—exciting life?'

He frowned, puzzled. 'Exciting?'

'Well, more fun, shall we say. I know the kind of people—' She stopped in mid-sentence and he smiled, recognising her game. Exciting curiosity was a cunning ploy he sometimes used himself when the occasion called for it. He decided to fall in with it.

'What people? What kind of fun?'

She patted his arm. 'There, I knew you would be interested. Are you by any chance free the weekend after next?'

'I think so.'

'Then keep it free. I'll arrange the rest. Just you leave it to me, and I promise you you'll enjoy it—and don't worry, they aren't the kind of people who can do your reputation any harm either; quite the contrary.'

'Aren't you going to tell me any more?'

She rose and went to pick up her coat from the corner chair, then turned and gave him an impish smile. 'Not yet. You'll have to be patient, but I think you'll find it well worthwhile. Goodnight, Vincent.'

She turned up her face and he bent to kiss her lightly on the cheek. 'Shall we meet tomorrow?' he asked.

She turned away, shaking her head. 'Not until next Wednesday when he's off again to Paris. It wouldn't be wise.'

Gregg made no comment. She spoke as if they were lovers, and he wondered if that too was a ploy to lead him on. If so, he was far too shrewd a campaigner to fall for it.

'Your car is outside?'

'Yes. And Dawson will hate me for keeping him waiting in the cold. Goodnight.'

After she had gone, Gregg took out of his pocket the letter which had arrived by the afternoon post. Laying aside his cigarette and reaching for the bottle, he poured himself another whisky before re-reading its contents.

My dear Vincent, I was heartbroken that you hadn't time to see me. This is such a dismal hole without your smile to brighten my life. I expect you are still in need of a spot of the ready, so please find enclosed something to tide you over. Oh, my dear Vincent, I miss your presence more than words can say! Never was man more loved than you are, by

Your devoted, Robert

Gregg sighed, took a deep draught of the whisky and leaned his head back against the linen antimacassar. The money would come in useful, especially with the style of living he was now becoming accustomed to. All those parties, the new clothes, the cost of cigarettes and drink.... No need to acknowledge the money though—Robert

92

would understand.

Gregg drank deeply from his glass again, the cigarette smouldering in the ashtray forgotten.

In the privacy of the room lately Hal's but now his, Eddie rolled on the bed, his beloved album in his hands. He was about to add the latest card from Hal, the one that came today and which Mother and Father had already savoured. How fortunate that cards could be mounted in the album in slots and did not have to be pasted in, or Hal's messages would be lost to sight forever. He sprawled on his back and held the latest above his head.

Dear Eddie, Hope you are all well as I am. Rode out to village of Cottingham this morning—a very pretty place. I'd really like to show you this part of Yorkshire some day. Met a delightful fellow coming in off the sports field and had tea with him—we're to meet again for a run over the fields on Sunday. Such a charming chap, name of Colville. Kindest regards, Your loving brother Hal

Eddie sighed, but it was with pleasure rather than envy. Hal was really living life, and maybe he too could do the same one day.

SIX

It was a lavish party even by Trixie Anstruther's expensive tastes and she had enjoyed it enormously during the early part of the evening. Now it was beginning to slide downhill, as it invariably did with this set, into the usual round of schoolboy antics. Francis and Rupert had just begun their party piece, duelling now with soda syphons across the littered dining table.

The King was no longer in the room; he'd probably gone to a quieter spot to continue his pursuit of that pretty little actress girl. Vincent lay sprawled on a settee in the alcove, watching events through half-closed eyes and pulling on his cigarette, while that insipid Topping woman knelt alongside, stroking back his tousled hair. He glanced up as Trixie approached.

'You didn't warn me it would this kind of party,' he murmured. 'A small evening, you said.'

The Topping woman gave Trixie a nervous, apologetic smile and moved away. 'That's what Edward likes to call these little unofficial gatherings,' Trixie explained, 'in

94

contrast to all his official banquets and balls at Marlborough House. Just his friends, in a situation where he can relax.'

He watched the flying jets of soda moodily. 'Relax?' he muttered. 'Act the fool, you mean. Never in all my born days before have I seen grown men sliding downstairs on tea trays and throwing rugs aside in their host's home to start capering like lunatics and squawking like Red Indians. Not to mention putting tablets of soap in the cheese board and mixing sennapod juice in the wine. That poor devil with a moustache has been running back and forth all night—haven't seen him at all since midnight.'

A stray jet of soda caught Trixie's bare arm as Rupert swung round. She shook it off, then moved Vincent's feet aside so that she could sit beside him. 'Nor are you likely to see him again before morning,' she remarked drily. 'He has a dressing room next to Cynthia's.'

'Who?'

She nodded towards the taller of the duellists. 'Young Rupert's wife. Oh, you needn't worry, Rupert knows, and anyway he's next to his light-o'-love too, so all's square.'

She couldn't help smiling at the way he stared ahead of him, eyes not focusing on the scene, as he tried to digest this information. It wasn't easy with a drink-fuddled brain. Vincent drank far too much these days, and he had not been his usual scintillating self at the dinner table as she had hoped. Right now, with his bow-tie askew and his elegant shirt spattered, his oiled hair awry and his dark eyes glazing over like the Serpentine in winter, he looked positively disreputable—but then, so did everyone else in the room.

He took a gulp of champagne and took out another cigarette and lit it. The last one still lay smouldering unfinished in the ashtray.

'It's criminal,' he muttered. 'Bloody sinful, that's what it is.'

She patted his hand. 'Yes, I suppose you would call it adultery, like the rest of our boring, conventional society. But we take our lead from His Majesty, and what higher authority....'

He snatched his hand away. 'You know what I meant, Trixie. It's criminal that some can live like this—just look at them, spoiling more food than ordinary men and women see in a week, while others are starving out there. It's enough to make any man lose faith in the existence of a God.'

Trixie sighed. He was in danger of becoming a downright bore if he started on his political hobby-horse, and this was decidedly not the place. She glided a gentle hand along his knee.

'Come now, Vincent. You haven't told me yet how you like my new gown. Don't you think this shade of pink becomes me well?'

He gave her the briefest of glances. 'Very pretty. I bet it cost enough to keep six East End families for the week.'

She leaned closer. 'Why concern yourself about anyone else outside this room, my dear, when Harriet has carefully contrived to place you in the room next to mine? I know for a fact that it's taken her the best part of a week to plan everything strategically so that everyone is satisfied. Now you aren't going to be a bore so that I don't feel inclined to make the best use of it, are you?'

He brushed her hand away. 'How can you say that, not care about others outside? Don't you realise what they're suffering? Don't you care? Dammit, does anyone here care, just so long as they can sup champagne till it comes out of their ears and then lay someone else's wife? God, woman, it makes me sick!'

Her back stiffened and she tossed her head. 'And you make them sick too, ranting on the way you do, and all the time you're supping as much of His Lordship's champagne as you can swallow, and smoking his cigars. You enjoy the good life just as much as anyone else here, and you can ill afford it. Do you truly believe your constituents will vote for you again when they find out what manner of man you really are? What kind of hypocrite are you, Vincent Gregg?'

His dark eyes widened in a startled stare. 'I care! I try to do something about their plight. Why, I spoke forcefully in the House only yesterday—'

'I heard,' her icy voice cut in, 'interrupting a debate on licensing to do it, and succeeding in getting yourself thrown out by the Speaker for being out of order. I heard. You were drunk again, it seems. A fat lot you'll achieve for your precious working-class chums when you're banned from the Commons for disruptive behaviour.'

Vincent's eyes smouldered. 'I'll fight for them in whatever way I think, Trixie. I cannot contain my anger when I see so clearly what is happening and no one else seems to care. Just look at them!'

He swung his arm in a contemptuous gesture at the young men now giggling as they wheelbarrowed one another, neighing and whinnying and laying bets on their respective mounts as they careered drunkenly around the littered floor.

Trixie regarded his glitter of anger and

rose. 'I think I'll go to my room,' she said quietly. 'I'll see you in the morning. Goodnight.'

He was frowning and did not look up as he replied, 'Goodnight, Trixie.'

'Call me Patricia, if you please.' And stepping carefully among the overturned glasses and snoring jockeys, she swept from the room.

Harold Pearson sat on the edge of the bed in James Colville's study-bedroom and watched the lithe figure of Colville, as he bent to place another pile of books on the floor.

'Great game that,' smiled Colville, 'and now I've got the very devil of a thirst. Have some wine with me—or perhaps you'd prefer a beer?'

Hal shook his head. 'No thanks.'

'Oh sorry, I forgot. Ginger beer, then?'

'Really, I'm not thirsty. Got to get back to my room in a minute anyway to finish my history essay. Done yours?'

Colville's blond head swung back as he laughed. 'I'm nowhere near as diligent as you, Hal. More interested in watching the market and racing results.'

'It's got to be given in tomorrow.'

'I'll get up early and do it then. Have you read in the paper what your friend Gregg has been up to lately?'

'I don't know him personally,' Hal demurred.

'But he comes from your God-forsaken part of the country, doesn't he? And young Hardcastle too—do you know him?'

'I know of the Hardcastles, of course—everyone in Hawksmoor does.'

'Young Robert Hardcastle is a devotee of your Gregg, so they say. An adoring spaniel, follows him everywhere.'

'I know nothing of him. I've seen Gregg at local meetings and heard him speak. Fine man. Views I respect.'

'I agree he's charming, or so I'm told, but one can hardly agree with his views surely—a bolshie, a feminist—'

'Not a feminist, James. A suffragist, yes, for he does support Mrs Pankhurst.'

'And a pacifist too, Hal. Now no one can admire a man who would not fight for his country if called upon. Still, even if one finds that unpalatable, he could still be a useful voice for the unwashed masses, I suppose, if only he could learn to control his unruly tongue.'

Hal's voice was gentle, but there was no mistaking the firmness in his tone. 'As it happens, James, I agree with him very strongly over the question of pacifism. My conscience dictates non-violence, whatever the provocation.'

James stared for a moment. 'Ah well, if

it's a matter of conscience then I won't argue with you. I can only state my own case, that I could and would fight to protect my interests, but if you feel otherwise then perhaps we should leave the matter alone.'

Hal looked up at him soberly. 'You would enjoy carrying arms, spilling another man's blood?'

James returned his look squarely. 'I told you—I'll always fight to protect my interests. There is nothing I would like better than to be a soldier. In fact, when all this degree nonsense is over, I think I'll take a commission in the Army. Now, how about a mug of cocoa before you finish that essay?'

Later that evening, Hal chewed the tip of his pen thoughtfully. He pulled out of his desk drawer a postcard with a pretty coloured photograph of Bootham Bar. Eddie would be delighted with this for his collection.

Hope you are all well as this leaves me at present. College work is still hard but rewarding on the whole. Weather awful, having rained since Sunday. Hope you'll like this picture. People sometimes disappoint, but beauty of places like this never fail to please and inspire.

Your loving brother, Harold.

Missing you so dreadfully. Please tell me when we can meet again.

Your devoted, Robert.

Vincent Gregg stuffed the letter irritably into his desk and glanced at the clock. Eleven o'clock—the Countess would be calling at any minute and his head still felt like a hollow cavern after the night's carousing. His mouth tasted awful too, but he lit up another cigarette.

She entered the room with grace despite the thickening waist and over-ample bosom, trailing a wake of expensive French perfume. He kissed her on the cheek and watched her sit in the one comfortable chair his lodgings boasted.

She was surveying him critically as he turned away to light a cigarette. 'You're not looking well, Vincent,' she remarked. 'Too much drink and nicotine, too much campaigning and speechmaking....'

'It has to be done, Countess. I'm needed on the platform.'

'To ensure your return at the General Election, you mean? I wouldn't bank on it, my dear. Public opinion is not so strongly in your favour as it was, and your health is suffering too. It's time you had a rest. Why not take a holiday away from it all for a while?'

He felt the irritation that rose inside him. 'Oh, for heaven's sake, Countess, you know I couldn't afford it, and anyway....'

'Anyway, you never listen to advice, I know. Then let's change the subject. Was Bertie at the party—the King, I mean?'

'Yes. I didn't see much of him.'

The Countess chuckled. 'He hasn't changed much, it seems. I was his favourite once, you know—oh, a long time ago, admittedly, but he was terribly infatuated. I still have his letters in a little box at home.'

'Love-letters? From the King?'

She shrugged. 'He was only the Prince then, and terribly indiscreet. He's learned to be more cautious since then. Ah yes, those letters could have earned me a vast sum of money if I'd been that kind of lady....'

'Blackmail?' Vincent looked at her in amazement, seeing her in a light very different from hitherto.

'An ugly word, my dear, but it was mooted at one time. I couldn't go through with it. I was too fond of Bertie ever to bring him sorrow. Now, what about that cup of coffee you invited me to have with you—my car is outside, so shall we drive to the Ritz?'

As Gregg picked up his coat and followed her outside to the waiting car, he felt in his trouser pocket to see whether he had sufficient money both to pay for the coffee and tip the waiter. Dammit, this money problem was probably the reason for his continual headaches, not to mention the insomnia. Now the wine merchant was refusing to deliver any more Scotch until his bill was settled, and he couldn't get his other dinner jacket back from the tailor's until he too was satisfied.

Perhaps he had better write back to Robert and say he would call and stay at Byram for a few days with him. After all, he'd be going up to Yorkshire to speak at that meeting in Pudsey next week anyway. Every opportunity to speak was vital now if he was to have a chance of being returned in the coming election. God, if only this awful headache would let up!

'Do have another cup of tea, Mrs Iredale—and I wish you would try one of my fairy cakes.'

Emma Iredale gave a shy little smile and accepted. 'I'd be delighted, Mrs Pearson. And don't you think that we've known each other long enough for you to call me Emma?'

Annie felt the flush of pleasure redden her cheeks, and looked across to James for guidance. He smiled, and handed her his cup to refill.

'I'm sure we'd be honoured, Emma,' he said. 'And you must call us James and Annie.' He glanced good-humouredly at Emma's husband, but Edgar Iredale did not appear to be listening.

Emma laughed softly. 'As always, Edgar's mind is far away, on business probably, but I know he agrees—don't you, dear?'

Edgar snapped to attention. 'Oh—sorry —yes, of course. Forgive me, James. Thinking about the shop, that's all.'

Emma's lively little face dimpled, and Annie marvelled that she could look so young when she knew for a fact that they must be of an age, she and Emma. It must be because she had remained childless, whether by design or accident, that she could look so carefree. Edgar had a tidy little drapery business down at Longroyd Bridge and their modest home nearby lacked for nothing.

'Eddie not at home today?' Edgar asked as he reached for more bread and butter.

Annie sensed that the words were spoken more out of a sense of politeness than of genuine interest, but she answered warmly.

'He's gone camping up in Swaledale with the Boys' Club—he's really taken to camping. Loves every minute.'

Emma gave a shiver. 'In this weather? Ooh, rather him than me! How brave of him!'

James spread jam liberally on the thinly cut brown bread. 'Ah, he's a deep one, is our Edward, but afraid of nothing. Now what about this election, Edgar? Will you be campaigning? I've promised to help in Mr Gregg's campaign again—he could have lost a lot of support after walking out of the House like that, calling them murderers, so he'll need all the help he can get. What about you? Are you going to help?'

'Ah, no, I think not.' Annie could hear the complete lack of interest in his voice. Poor man—what with the shop and all the church work he did, it was unreasonable to expect more of him. He hadn't James's stamina and fierce determination.

'I won't, of course,' giggled Emma. 'All this political stuff is way above my head. Don't know how you manage to understand, Annie.'

'Annie is a very devoted worker for the party,' James said with pride, 'and has now become chairman of the Women's Committee too.'

Emma lowered her dark eyes, abashed. Annie felt sorry for her. James was not impressed by silly, helpless women.

'Are you taking a holiday this year?' Annie cut in. 'We thought we might have a few days with relations in Knott End—that's near Fleetwood, you know.'

'Nice,' said Emma. 'We haven't planned anything yet. Depends on Edgar, really, and when he can get time off from the shop. Assistants aren't all very reliable. Isn't that so, dear?'

Edgar, staring down moodily at the slab of seed cake on his plate, made no answer. Emma nudged him in the ribs. 'Dear me,' she reproved, 'aren't we miles away? And to think we've been looking forward all week to having tea at the Pearsons'. High spot of the week, that is.'

Edgar folded the linen napkin and laid it alongside his plate. 'I'm sorry. James, do you think we could have a talk—on our own? I'd appreciate it.'

Annie saw the look of surprise in James's eyes quickly give way to composure. 'Of course,' he said. 'Tonight, or would tomorrow suit you? After work.'

She felt pride in his simple acceptance. It was typical of James, always anxious to help, without question.

'Oh,' murmured Emma. 'Secrets. Something to do with my birthday next week, perhaps—but I won't pry. Best to leave men and their secrets well alone, don't you agree, Annie?'

She wrinkled her nose conspiratorially at her hostess and reached for another fairy cake.

For the first time in his life Eddie Pearson knew ecstasy. He couldn't put a name to the sensation; he only knew that he had never felt so deliriously happy as he did now. The world was his; new joys and experiences offered themselves at every turn here in this beautiful part of Yorkshire, and the most wonderful were when he was alone.

It was fun in camp, of course, and he enjoyed taking his turn at peeling potatoes for supper or washing up the tin plates after. And it was fun talking with the lads long after lights out and sewing up the bottoms of Jackie's pyjamas so that he couldn't put them on, but the real joy was walking the fells alone, watching the dizzy waters of the stream break around the rocks and hurtle on downstream, and listening to the shivering, liquid song of the warbler hidden somewhere along the mossy bank.

This place was so unlike Hawskmoor with its barren moors and bleak, smoky landscapes as to seem like paradise. The heaven that Mother often talked about must be like this, he thought. Ash trees twined overhead, rabbits darted underfoot, and everywhere flowers—bird's eye, butter baskets, forget-me-nots, and the pervasive scent of wild garlic as his foot crushed it. Higher upstream there was the waterfall, and the delights of the cave hidden behind it, a secret, dripping cavern where the mind could conceive fantasies wilder than the fairytale books ever told. And beyond the waterfall there was the quarry with its long-abandoned workings. Here was paradise indeed.

Back in camp he wrote carefully on the back of the postcard depicting the waterfall—carefully, because it too would soon be mounted in his precious album.

Dear Mother, Having a lovely time here. This is the waterfall I visited today. Isn't it splendid? Please keep this card for me.

Your loving son, Edward.
PS Please give my love to Father.

As James Pearson emerged from the cobbled courtyard of Sykes' mill and mingled with the rest of the crowd of millworkers clattering home along Acre Street, he had much on his mind. As a rule he had no hesitation in telling Annie all about the affairs of the Amalgamated Society of Engineers, of which he was secretary, and of the problems the men often brought to him during the lunch break, but today was different. His heart was heavy at the prospect of what he had to tell her.

She was at the front door and came hurrying down the yard as she saw him. He noted that she was not wearing her apron, as she usually did, ready to dish up the supper as soon as he had washed. Her tired face looked pale and strained, and he reflected that a trip to Knott End might do her a world of good, as soon as time would permit it.

'James! Oh, James, I'm glad you're back!'

He took her arm and walked towards the door. 'Nay, listen, lass, I've something I must tell you first, before anything else. You'll not like it, I'm afraid.'

She grew visibly paler. 'Nor you what I have to tell you, love. Don't go in yet.'

She stopped on the doorstep, blocking his way. James touched her elbow gently. 'It's Iredale, lass,' he began, and heard her catch her breath.

'So you know? Emma Iredale is here now—she's in the living room, broken-hearted. Come in the scullery.'

He followed her inside and closed the scullery door behind them. It was going to be easier now that she knew.

'It's a terrible thing he's done,' he murmured. 'No wonder he wanted to talk to somebody about it. They told me at work about all the church funds that were missing, and him being treasurer it couldn't be anyone else. How the devil am I going to help him, Annie, me being a magistrate and all?'

Annie's jaw sagged and he saw her clutch hold of the edge of the scullery table. 'Church funds?' she whispered. 'You mean he stole them?'

James frowned. 'You mean you didn't know? What on earth were you going on about then? Why else is Emma so upset?'

Annie steadied herself and took a deep breath. 'I think you'd best sit down, love. I know I need to.'

She made to pull out a chair but James gripped her arm. 'Tell me—what is it? What's happened?'

Annie looked up at him with an expression of fear and disbelief. 'James—Emma came flying in here not twenty minutes ago, screaming, hysterical. It took long enough before I could get sense out of her. She came home this afternoon and found Edgar dead.'

'Dead?' repeated James, unable to take it in. 'Dead? I don't believe it!'

'And that's not all,' Annie added quietly. 'She found him hanging from the banisters. It was suicide, James.'

'Oh, my God! Poor Emma! Let me go to her.' Pushing past his wife, James hurried out of the scullery and across the hall to the living room.

111

SEVEN

If over the course of the next few weeks James found it necessary to spend a great deal of his time down at Emma Iredale's house, Annie could not find it in her heart to begrudge her friend. After all, Edgar Iredale's death had left the poor woman in a most unenviable position and she clearly did not have a very sound business head, so James's advice was invaluable. She would have welcomed help herself had she been unfortunate enough to be in such a plight.

But it was a pity Emma's need coincided with her own, for that nagging pain in her side was growing steadily worse. This week she had been forced to send her apologies to the Women's Committee and let the vice-chairman take the meeting in her place. But the hope that an evening's rest would see things right had been in vain, for tonight she felt dizzy and at times nauseous. She felt almost guilty when she confessed as much to James as they finished supper and Eddie went up to his room.

James scrutinised her face closely. 'Indeed,

you do look a bit flushed,' he remarked. It was the first time he had really looked at her in weeks, and the moment of attention gave her pleasure.

She ran a hand across her forehead. 'I don't think I've got a temperature,' she said, 'but I do feel hot. And I'm that tired all the time. I don't know what's up with me—it's not like me at all.'

He was regarding her soberly. 'Time of life, love. At your age women often get odd aches and pains, I'm told.'

She sighed. 'Aye, it could be that, I reckon.'

'Put your feet up once you've washed up,' he murmured, picking up the evening paper. 'I'll be off down to Emma's very shortly so you'll have a bit of peace. Go to bed early—I'll do my best not to wake you when I come in.'

Wearily she rose and began stacking the dishes. 'There's those envelopes I ought to be addressing,' she reminded him. 'They've to be done for tomorrow.'

He did not look up from the paper. 'Get Eddie to do them,' he murmured.

'Nay, he's his homework to finish.'

James sighed. 'Pity Harold's not here,' he commented, and that was his last word until he came out into the scullery some time later. Annie was leaning against the stone sink, trying to fend off waves of dizziness.

'Right then, lass, I'll be off. And by the way, don't forget I'll need a bag packed for tomorrow. I'll be staying in Harrogate overnight, think on.'

She forced a thin smile but as soon as the front door had banged shut behind him she gave a deep sigh. She'd forgotten the union meeting. Her arms ached with fatigue as she took the flat irons to the fire—his shirts had to be ironed before they could be packed.

The mantel clock was climbing steadily towards midnight before she had done. As Annie turned off the gaslight and climbed the stairs, she could not help feeling just a stab of resentment. Emma Iredale might well be in need of understanding and help, but she too would welcome a word of encouragement, just now and again.

'Are you sure there's no more papers, Emma? Nothing at all?'

James sat on an upright chair at the table, watching Emma's slim figure as she stood before her late husband's desk. Bills and invoices lay in neat piles in front of him, and Emma still clutched personal letters and cards in her hand. Her usually neat hair was slightly awry, and there was a vulnerable set to her shapely shoulders.

How young and defenceless she looked, and yet she must be the same age as Annie, he thought. Odd how some women had the happy knack of retaining their youth far longer than others. Poor little Emma. She did not have Annie's capable nature at all—a child in the ways of the world—it was his bounden duty to help, even if Iredale had not been a close friend. From the papers he had seen so far, it was clear the fellow was up to his ears in debt.

She cast him a helpless glance. 'I can't see any more, but why don't you search for yourself, James. You know what to look for better than I do.'

'Are you sure?'

She smiled thinly. 'Don't worry about my privacy, James. You know already how badly off I am. There's no one else I could trust.'

He was conscious of her grateful eyes fixed on him for the next hour or so while he worked out the figures. Calculations complete, he laid down the pen and turned to her.

'I won't beat about the bush, love. You were right. There's a debt of some twelve hundred pounds in all.'

Large liquid eyes stared at him. It was hard to tell where the black of the pupil ended and the darkest brown he had ever seen began. 'Twelve hundred? Oh, James!

Where am I to find that much money? It's impossible!'

He shook his head firmly, anxious to reassure. 'Happen not, love. There's the shop you can sell, and there's the house, if need be.'

'The house?' She was horrified. 'But where would I live then? I've no wish to go live with my sister in Fleetwood, and that's assuming she'd have me. Oh, James! What am I to do?'

She was wringing her hands and seemed near to tears. James took command.

'I'll tell you,' he said, rising from the chair with stiff movements. 'You'll make us a cup of tea, and then I'll be off home. It's getting late.'

Her hand flew to her mouth. 'Heavens, so it is. People will talk—we can't have that, can we? And you've to be off somewhere tomorrow, you said. How selfish I am, taking up your time like this.'

James pulled himself up to his full height. 'What are we in this world for, Emma, if not to help others in their time of need? Come on now, brew up for us, there's a good lass.'

'Dear James, however would I manage without you.'

She flashed him a smile before going out to the scullery and James sank into the comfortable chair by the fire, which presumably had been Iredale's. That smile was gratitude enough for his trouble.

Some weeks later Hal was just emerging from the classroom after a history lecture when Colville bumped into him, fair head bent low as he charged along.

'Oh, sorry, old man, just dashing off to a rugby practice. Heard the news, have you?'

Hal looked bewildered. 'News?'

'About the election—your Gregg friend didn't make it. Told you he wouldn't. Beaten into third place by the Conservative fellow. Must say, he was asking for it. Got to dash. See you at supper.'

Hal continued slowly on his way back to his room. Disappointing as the news was, Colville was right in saying that it was only to be expected—by all accounts Gregg was far from well and possibly even on the edge of a breakdown. Mother, and more especially Father, would be bitterly disappointed. That reminded him—he'd better write home tonight.

Dear Father, *he wrote in his neat copperplate hand,* I was so sorry to learn that Mother is unwell. It is so unlike her to stay in bed. In view of Mrs Iredale's situation, it seems to me an excellent idea to have her stay at the house to care for Mother until she is well enough to get up again.

I was also saddened to learn of Mr Gregg's defeat in the election. The country needs men with his passionate views, and I hope he will be successful at the next election.

Tell Eddie I have some lovely cards for him, all depicting British butterflies, and they will make a colourful addition to his collection. Am very busy just now as I have a thesis to complete before the end of term, but will write again very soon.

Your loving son, Harold.

The council meeting was over and most of the councillors had left the chamber. Alderman Lawson was still seated at the table, scribbling in the margin of his notes. Alderman Tunnycliffe was watching him curiously.

'What are you up to now, Lawson? More of your cunning projects?'

Lawson put down his pencil and straightened. 'Just a few calculations, that's all. Just working out what the borough is worth annually in rates.'

'What on earth for?'

Lawson's face spread into a slow smile. 'An idea I've nurtured for some years, that's all. Just how much it would cost to try to buy Hawksmoor.'

'Off the Hardcastles? They'd never sell—you're wasting your time. Any road, it'd cost a sight more than we could ever raise, and that's a fact. Daft idea. Waste of time thinking about it.'

'Happen it is, but I like to toy with the idea. I'm not the first, you know. German chap named Rothschild first came up with the idea some fifty years ago.'

'And the Hardcastles wouldn't sell?'

'No.'

'Told you so. They wouldn't now, neither. In any case, we've no German millionaire standing by with the ready.'

Lawson sighed. 'No, but the day may come. You'd be in favour of the idea, wouldn't you—getting the town for ourselves so we can make improvements and the like without always having to ask our feudal landlords?'

'Aye, to be sure I would. But the time's not yet, Lawson, nor even like to happen in our lifetime. Come on, let's be off.'

Lawson put away his pencil and rose slowly. 'If only we could find the man with the money, it could come about sooner than you think, Tunnycliffe. I'll not let my dream fade for lack of trying, that I can promise you.'

Vincent Gregg awoke, conscious of a heavy

pressure on his chest. Opening his eyes and waiting until the bleariness subsided, he realised the weight was that of Robert's arm, thrown affectionately across his body. Gregg groaned, remembering what had occurred.

Robert was still sleeping deeply, fair curls scattered about his head on the pillow. Gregg lifted the arm cautiously off his chest and moved it aside with the utmost care so as not to awaken the boy, then sat up on the edge of the bed. His head throbbed so much that he was obliged to rest it in his hands for a moment until his eyes could focus.

A chink of light showed through the drawn curtains on the far side of the bed. Making his way carefully around the sheets spilling from the rumpled bed across the floor he stumbled to the window, pulled aside the curtain and looked out across the lawns of Byram Hall. On the eastern horizon the rising sun was staining the sky and beginning to dissipate the early-morning mist. Dew-spangled grass and bushes emitted a freshness that was strangely at odds with his sense of distaste. He shivered, conscious of his nakedness, and turned away to find his shirt.

Robert moaned and stirred. Gregg stopped, shirt half-way over his head, and hoped devoutly that the boy would not wake. After last night, or what he could remember of it, things were going to be difficult.

'Vincent.'

The word was spoken softly, carressingly, and his heart sank as he pulled the shirt down and began buttoning it. He must endeavour to behave as naturally as possible, and not attempt to feign an affection he did not feel. Last night had come about partly out of drunkenness and partly out of his need for Robert's help, nothing more. But Robert was unlikely to see it that way.

'Come on, old boy, shake a leg,' he said brightly, but the effort made his head start to ache again. Dammit, if only he hadn't started in on that second bottle of whisky—but if he hadn't, he'd have been pursued by nightmares all night and he wouldn't have been able to fall in with Robert's desires.

'Come back to bed, Vincent. I want to talk to you.'

For a second he hesitated, but the boy's eyes were wide with pleading and he was smiling tenderly—he could not betray the trust in that look. Gregg sat on the edge of the bed and reached for his underpants, but Robert pulled him by the arm. He did not resist, letting himself be drawn down across the boy's lean body, but he could not bring himself to meet his gaze.

'You do care, don't you, Vincent? You meant what you said?'

He felt irritated, trapped. The boy was behaving just like a woman, hemming him in with emotional blackmail, and he could feel that odd sensation again of his face going numb. It had been happening a lot lately.

'You did, didn't you?' Robert repeated. 'You did mean it when you said you loved me? Tell me again, Vincent. It's very important to me.'

'Of course. I'm very fond of you.'

Robert's grip tightened slightly. 'Say you love me, Vincent. I know you do, for you were very tender. It was beautiful, Vincent, truly it was.'

'I'm glad. Shall we get dressed and go and eat now?'

'Tell me it was good for you too—it was, wasn't it? Do tell me again you love me.'

'Heavens, of course I do. I've always been very fond of you—haven't I shown it?'

Fingers caressed his arm and Gregg resigned himself. It wasn't all that distasteful really. He turned to smile down at Robert.

'It was a good night, Robert, and I enjoyed it. There, are you happy now?'

'More than anyone else you've slept with?'

Gregg laughed. He had enjoyed the favours of men as well as women, but Robert's anxiety to be reassured was more womanly than most.

'Yes, you goose. You're by far the prettiest boy I've ever known. Now will you get up?'

'Better than Trixie Anstruther too?'

Irritation surged again. The boy was not only jealous, which was infuriating, but he was probing too. Gregg stood up sharply, jerking free of Robert's grasp.

The youth flung back the bedcovers, revealing his slim nakedness, and crawled to the edge of the bed. 'Why won't you tell me, Vincent? I want to know! Why did you come here if it isn't me you love, tell me that?'

Gregg turned with a sigh. He must not let his irritation spoil his chances of success. 'Well, you're answering your own question, aren't you? Why else should I come if not to see you again? And I needed a place where I could feel at peace again after all that's been happening lately. Where better than with you?'

'After the disappointment of the election, you mean. Yes, that must have been dreadful for you. I'm sorry, I was forgetting....'

Gregg patted his hand before moving away from the bed. 'No matter, it's done now. But it took a fearful toll on my nerves, not to mention my pocket.'

He paused, and Robert looked up at him questioningly. 'Are you saying you need money again, Vincent, is that it? I gave you a hundred not a month ago.'

Gregg gave a short laugh. 'That's gone a long time ago, I fear. Wooing voters is a costly business.'

'So is drinking, and dining rich men's wives,' retorted Robert with bitterness. 'I know...I've heard.'

'You're jealous,' Gregg remarked quietly. 'You've really no need to be, you know.'

Leaning from the bed, Robert attempted to seize him, but succeeded only in grasping hold of his knee. 'Then tell me you love me, Vincent, tell me you love only me and you won't see that wretched Anstruther woman ever again, and I'll lend you whatever you want! Please tell me!'

Gregg pulled himself free, anger flushing his cheeks and making his head pound again. 'I can't, you fool! Don't you see, I have to keep in with people who may be able to help me—it's the way politicians operate—I can't make you promises I can't keep.'

Robert had let go of his knee and was crouching on the bed, the hurt and anger in his blue eyes giving way to hatred. 'You can't? You won't, you mean!' he spat.

'Then don't look to me for help. Go to those who are gullible enough to think you care about them—take them to bed and make love to them, but don't come near me again! Oh God!' he groaned, 'to think that only a few hours ago you were swearing your love for me, holding me close and kissing me oh, so lovingly....'

He buried his face in his hands and began to sob. Gregg, his back turned, knew he had handled the whole thing clumsily, but he could not bring himself to turn and face the boy, to try and rebuild the damage he had done. He could feel only distaste and a rising sense of nausea.

'Perhaps I had better leave,' he murmured.

Robert's voice was muffled, but there was no mistaking the words. 'Yes, go, and never come back! And never ask my help or try to see me, ever, I never want to clap eyes on you again.'

Gregg began putting on his trousers. 'I'll write to you, in time.'

'No! I want no contact with you! You deceived me!'

'Not intentionally.'

Robert's hands fell away from his face and his eyes glittered malevolence. 'You lied to me. You are a liar and a fraud. Get out of here, you bastard, and leave me in peace!'

As Vincent Gregg strode away down

125

the drive of Byram Hall he mentally kicked himself for his clumsy stupidity. He desperately needed money now more than at any other time in his life, and he had bungled his chance badly. Fresh plans would have to be devised, and quickly, if he were to avoid a bankruptcy case to add to all his other troubles. But with this godawful hangover added to a curious sensation of numbness and a feeling of being distanced from everything going on around him, logical thought was at this moment completely beyond his capability. Instead of turning into the lane leading to the railway station to catch the eleven-fifteen, he headed into the Railway Inn and ordered a double whisky.

A week later Robert's letter arrived.

No one in the world has ever mattered to me more than you, but you betrayed my love. Oh Vincent, I adore you, I worship you, but I am not blind to your selfishness and I cannot bear to share you with anyone else. Only swear to me that you are mine, and mine alone, and all I have is yours. There is nothing I would not do for you—lie, cheat, steal, even kill—but I must know that you are mine.

Write back if you can promise me this. Otherwise, let me hear nothing from you ever again in this life. No one can ever replace you.

Your loving Robert.

Gregg laid the letter aside with a deep sigh. There was no hope now of raising the kind of money he needed from Robert, not without swearing away his life and freedom. Better by far to end the relationship with the boy, sending back his letters in a bundle.

But no. Robert had forbidden him to write unless it was to capitulate to his demands. Leave the letters where they were, in the desk drawer. After all, they could come in useful some day. What was it the Countess had said about the value of the King's letters?

'Vincent, you are a very silly boy,' said the Countess. 'I've been warning you for long enough that you were getting in too deep. Now you can't pay your bills, you've lost your seat and the way you're drinking, you're heading straight for a nervous breakdown. Take my advice and get away from it all. Take a holiday, preferably abroad.'

'Can't afford it.'

'The same old cry. Well, I'll fund you for a trip to Spain—I have friends there who will put you up for a month or two.

Go there, forget all about problems here, and by the time you come back perhaps you'll have mastered this drinking enough to start afresh. How about it?'

He never could remember whether he answered or not, only that his head swirled and the world seemed to have removed itself beyond the seventh veil and was all very hazy and unreal. Dimly he recalled packing and leaving at night, the rent unpaid, and being aboard a tossing ship, but apart from feeling the heat of a blazing sun and seeing lizards crawling across his bed, the unreality of life seemed little different.

Eddie Pearson shivered in the attic and wished for the hundredth time that Mrs Iredale have never come to stay. Not that he disliked her—no one could dislike such a smilingly pleasant lady—but she had been given Hal's old room, which meant Eddie had had to go back into the attic. He'd lost the use of Hal's violin too. Father would not permit him to take it to the attic.

'It is your brother's property and must remain in his room,' Father had said, but he did not seem to object to Mrs Iredale using Hal's room.

Mother didn't really want her there either. Eddie had overheard her weak voice from the bedroom.

'There's really no need for her to come, James. I'll be up and about in no time at all, just you see.'

'It's no trouble to her at all, dear. She's an extraordinarily generous lady.'

'Don't think me ungrateful, love. It's just that—'

'And since we can do her a favour in return by giving her a roof over her head until she sorts things out, it seems to me a very practical solution all round,' Father had concluded, and Mother had said no more.

But that was weeks ago and Mrs Iredale had become so settled in the house she seemed to have taken over Mother's role. There was always a hot meal ready and a smile to welcome him home, a smile that seemed pinned on whenever Father was there and easily pocketed again. Father seemed content enough, with Mother still confined to bed. If only the weakness would leave her and she could come downstairs again, then maybe life would take on some of its old familiarity again....

But there was something to look forward to, with Hal due home from college next week. Hal would have to share the big attic bedroom with him, and there would be so much to talk about, so much to learn from Hal, so much to tell him about camping.

Hal was strangely quiet when he finally came home. Whether it was out of concern or consideration for Mother, Eddie could not tell, but his brother's reticence was disappointing. Staring out of the attic one afternoon at the green-domed clock tower, Hal remarked casually, 'Oh, by the way, Eddie, I'll be away for most of this vacation. I'm going to stay with a college friend in Harrogate.'

Eddie tried hard to disguise the disappointment that welled in him. 'Oh? Is it that Colville chap you told me about?'

Hal's tone was too casual, too offhand to be convincing. 'No, it's not. It's a girl, actually. Name of Lilian.'

Eddie was shocked, but most of all he felt betrayed. That his brother should choose the company of a college friend, and a girl at that... Oh, it was hurtful. Unable to find words, he picked his way down the stairs, crept past Mother's room and went on down to the living room. His slippered feet made no sound, and just as he was about to open the living room door he heard Father's voice speak softly.

'Don't worry, Emma. Just be patient. It can't be long now.'

Eddie opened the door and went in. Father was standing by the fireplace, his hands on Mrs Iredale's shoulders. Hearing a sound, she turned away abruptly and made a show of pulling the kettle off the fire.

'There, it's boiling. I'll make that tea now, Mr Pearson.'

There was something strange and stilted about her voice, and there was a peculiar air of tension in the room which Eddie could not understand. But in his disappointment over Hal it did not seem important.

EIGHT

It was a bitterly cold January day and snow lay deep on the cobbled streets as Eddie stumbled his way uphill towards the woods. Footprints ahead of him thinned out as he neared the farm wall with the stile that led to freedom. His own footsteps crunched with a satisfying sound as he trod the virgin snow, and he felt he could begin to shake off the anger which had been blackening his heart.

They must have known about Mother, both of them, Father and that Mrs Iredale with her perpetual smile—but they'd never told him. Not till the very end, that was, when it was too late to show Mother how he really felt about her, and when he'd only given her some skeins of silk for her embroidery for a Christmas present. It plagued his conscience that he could have saved up and bought her something which represented real sacrifice—but they hadn't told him, those wretched grown-ups with their passion for secrecy. Anger boiled in him again. They should have told him how sick she was—she was his mother, wasn't she?

But no, they'd kept it to themselves until the moment Mother had asked to see him. Eddie choked, remembering how unnatural she'd looked, as if she was already dead but for those eyes moving....

He kicked furiously at a mound of snow, recalling the frustration of being unable to help her. They told him at breakfast she was dead. They'd ordered the crêpe armbands and written the black-edged letters, then agreed that Mrs Iredale should go away after the funeral. Eddie had hoped she would never come back.

He cleared the crisp snow from a fallen tree trunk and sat, shoulders hunched, to watch the birds foraging for food. Mother lay deep under the snow now, and a tear welled under his eyelid and congealed there. He remembered watching them lower her coffin into the deep black hole, and felt again the eyes that watched him. Hal's hand had touched his shoulder briefly and the gesture had given him strength.

A blackbird, braver than the rest, hopped close to his foot, its glittering eyes surveying Eddie curiously. He dug in his pocket for a titbit, but found nothing. Two or three sparrows came to cluster hopefully around the blackbird.

'Sorry, birdies, I have nothing for you. I wish I had.'

He leaned on his red-chapped knees and watched as the blackbird gave up and hopped away, leaving the sparrows to wonder. Like my big brother, he thought; he too had gone away back to York and his friends.

He rose stiffly, conscious that his backside was damp and his knees stinging. If only he could have those long trousers he craved. All the other boys in his class had gone into long trousers except him, and Denton would not let the hurt heal.

'Yah, cissy boy! Still in short pants—whose mum doesn't want her little lad to grow up then? Whose his mother's baby boy?'

The insult hurt doubly because Mother was the one who would have coaxed Father into letting him have long pants if she was still here. Mrs Iredale wouldn't, even he'd lowered his pride to ask her. Not having any sons of her own, she'd never realise how important it was.

But she did think his damp trousers important. 'Just look at you, Edward Pearson! What on earth will your father say when he comes home? Get those trousers off and let me dry them out by the fire before he gets back, or you'll be in for it.'

He stood watching the steam rising from them where she placed them over the fireguard. Just like Mother's soul, rising to Heaven... He turned abruptly away and went to look out of the window. In the scullery he could hear Mrs Iredale clattering pans.

Birds were scratching about in the yard, one of them a blackbird pecking and then looking up again anxiously. Eddie felt a start of pleasure. He was certain it was the same bird from the woods.

'Oh, you little beauty,' he murmured. 'You followed me home. You knew I needed a friend.'

The day had been stiflingly close. Vincent Gregg took a walk along the rock-strewn beach of the little fishing village, scarcely aware of the shawled women sitting chattering in voluble Spanish on the jetty wall.

He was aware, however, of hunger gnawing his stomach. The cloudiness in his brain was clearing enough for him to register that. Too much of the local vino, that was the problem, but it was cheap and potent and it served both to dull the ache of hunger and to blot out memory at the same time. But having just awoken from the afternoon siesta, he was now all too conscious of the hunger pangs.

Nearing the end of the beach, he climbed up on to the roadway and made his way uphill towards the main road of the little town, leaving behind the mist now beginning to glimmer over the sunset-sparkled water. The locals were already starting to gather on benches outside the cafés, laughing and joking as they swigged the first of the evening's wine. It was all right for them, he thought moodily; with a hard day's work completed they could settle down to enjoyment with carefree consciences. But he, Gregg, what had he achieved? Nothing. Precisely nothing. Just like every other day since he came here. All the time he'd been in Spain, he'd behaved exactly as he had been doing in London. And far from dispelling his depression, these months in the sun had served only to heighten it.

There had been still a ray of hope, a glimmer of optimism last year, after that disastrous election, but where was it now? He could still remember vividly how, as the car drove him down the street away from the town hall after the election result, his supporters, loyal even in defeat, had crowded around the car and cheered. He could still recall his stirring words to them.

The day is coming when socialism, the hope of the world, the future religion of humanity, will have wiped out Liberalism and Toryism from the face of the earth... Stick to your flag... Don't let our colours be stained.... Stick to the gospel that first inspired your heart and you will live to rejoice in a victory that none can gainsay....

That hope, that determination, were still not dead in him, but the spiritual strength to carry on had been missing. During his absence the unemployment problem in Britain had worsened and the industrial might of the Germans was making people talk of the German menace; the working man back at home was, if anything, worse off than ever. Now he was beginning to feel the stirrings of new energy, but as always, money was the problem.

A display outside a fish restaurant caught his eye. A huge mound made up of a living lobster, crabs and langoustes, still wriggling although fettered in position, formed a fascinating, mouthwatering spectacle. He watched, entranced, the cooling spray of seawater playing across the moving shellfish.

'Buenas dias, señor.'

Señor Fredrico, the *propietario* himself, stood outside his restaurant to enjoy the air. Behind him Gregg could see a few of the red-check covered tables were already occupied, and a delicious aroma of shellfish and garlic mingled with tobacco smoke drifted out into the still air. His stomach rumbled in expectation.

Fredrico, noting Gregg's evening clothes and sensing a potential customer, moved forward. 'The lobster is especially fine today, señor. I can highly recommend it—with our special garlic sauce, you will find it a feast fit for an emperor. Come inside, sit down and Maria will bring you a bottle of our finest vino.'

Gregg hesitated, only half-understanding the man's swiftly-spoken Spanish but fully understanding his drift. He might look the prosperous visitor despite the rather crumpled appearance of his suit, but there were few pesetas remaining in his pocket. The Countess had been liberal, but so had his spending.

Maria, plump and smiling, was already pouring the wine. He watched the ruby liquid spilling into the glass and yielded to temptation. By the time the lobster was cooked he had already consumed most of the bottle of wine. Fredrico was right; the lobster was delicious. Still hungry, Gregg ordered a side dish of mixed shellfish and calamares. How he was to settle the bill did not begin to concern him until his hunger was satisfied, and then his ingenious mind began to work.

A quick reconnoitre of the remaining

pesetas in his pocket with his fingertips told him he had about half the amount of money he needed. The lobster was not yet quite consumed. Suddenly Gregg spotted a large, lazy beetle crawling across the tiled floor at his feet. Making sure he was unobserved, he put his foot on the insect, felt it crunch, and then lifted the shell and slid it unobtrusively under the uneaten lobster.

'Hey, caballero,' he called. A waiter came running. 'I cannot eat this!' Gregg exclaimed, pointing dramatically to his plate. 'What kind of establishment is this, serving up vermin to the customers?'

The waiter stared, uncomprehending. Gregg rose unsteadily and made for the door. 'It is disgusting. I shall pay only for the wine.' He tossed some coins on the table and turned to go. 'I shall not eat here again, nor recommend this place to my friends, I promise you. Tell *your propietario,*' he called back over his shoulder. The waiter, recognising one word, threw up his hands.

'*Si, el propietario, señor,*' he exclaimed, and disappeared into the kitchen area. Gregg wasted no time. He strode out into the darkness and away down the street, slipping down the nearest alleyway. Behind him he could hear voices pursuing him, voices raised in anger. Glancing back, he caught a brief glimpse of Fredrico's portly figure stumbling after him, but a sharp turn in the alley cut him off from sight. Gregg started to run and did not slacken his pace until there was no more sound of the voices and he was far enough away from Fredrico's to feel safe.

Slowly he retraced his footsteps across town towards the apartment. Indigestion was beginning to plague him now. Violent exercise so soon after a huge meal evidently did not agree with him, especially since his stomach was more accustomed to drinking than to eating these days. It was no use. Poverty was obliging him to have to live off his wits again, just as he had done in England. He might just as well go back home, where there were still some who cared about him and where there was work to be done. And go back home soon—before the rent fell due, since he had already spent it. Misery in a familiar land was far preferable to misery in a strange one.

The commissionaire bent to open the door for him as he approached.

'*Buenas noches, Señor Gregg,*' he murmured.

'*Buenas noches,*' replied Gregg, and under his breath he added, 'and *adios.*'

Gregg had been back in London for

only a matter of weeks when he chanced to meet the Countess out shopping. To his embarrassment he saw that she was accompanied by Robert Hardcastle, but it was too late now to escape. She hailed him with delight.

'Vincent, my dear! I heard you were back in town but didn't know where on earth to find you. Where have you been hiding? Come, let's all go into Fortnum and Mason's for a cup of tea and you can tell us all about what you've been up to.'

She had seized his arm and was already manoeuvring him towards the door of the store, and he knew that no excuse was possible. Robert, after his first startled stare, was conscientiously avoiding meeting his look. There was no choice but to fall in with her.

In the elegantly furnished tea-room, he took care to take the seat opposite the Countess so that he did not have to encounter the boy's gaze. Glancing at him surreptitiously while the neat little waitress took the Countess's order, he noted that Robert seemed paler and more drawn than he remembered.

He leaned across to pat the Countess's jewelled hand. 'Really, Countess, you're just as imperious and impossible as ever! Don't you realise that I am on my way to a most important appointment and that I shall be incredibly late if I stay and gossip here with you?'

She widened heavily mascara'd eyes and pouted. 'But my dear, I haven't seen you in ages! We must have a really long talk, I insist!'

Gregg rose with a smile. 'Tomorrow, Countess, I promise. I'll call on you at eleven, if I may.'

Her expression brightened. 'Very well, if you promise to turn up. My curiosity won't bear the suspense any longer than that. At eleven sharp, promise.'

'I'll be there. Now I must run. Goodbye, Countess, and good day to you, Robert.'

The Countess watched his tall, lean figure as he made his way out of the tea-room and then she turned her attention to the younger man.

'You didn't have much to say,' she remarked drily. 'I though you and Vincent used to be close friends.'

Robert's blue eyes stared at the bird-of-paradise-patterned wallpaper behind her fashionable hat. 'None closer,' he murmured.

'Have you seen him since he got back from Spain, then?'

'I didn't know he was back until today.'

'Oh yes, I saw he'd been writing articles in the *Clarion*. You haven't been keeping in touch, then?'

'No. Ah, here's the tea.'

The Countess studied his expression as the waitress placed the silver teapot and a plate of fondant iced cakes before them. He was clearly unhappy, and she wondered if Gregg's sudden appearance had anything to do with it. Busying herself with folding her gloves neatly, she waited until the waitress had left. Then she began to pour the tea.

'You're very fond of him, aren't you, Robert? But don't let him fool you—he's a charmer, gets on with everyone, men and women alike, you know. Women especially. They all fall madly in love with him. He doesn't set out to charm them—he just can't help it.'

Robert looked at her sharply. 'You think I'm jealous? I'm not, you know, really I'm not.'

She smiled comfortingly. 'I know. I'm not nosing, but don't forget I'm old enough to be your mother, my dear, and I do care about your welfare. You can trust me.'

He sniffed and took the cup of tea she offered. 'There's nothing to confide, I assure you. But we were close, Vincent and I....'

'I know.'

'There was between us the kind of affection that can only grow between two men....'

143

She nodded. 'I know what you mean.'

He was gazing into space above her head as he murmured. 'A love deeper, perhaps, than that between a man and a woman—well, on my part, anyway.' He jerked his attention back to the moment. 'But that's in the past. It's all over now.'

'Perhaps as well, my dear,' the Countess murmured. 'We all know Vincent and his foibles. Full of good intent and idealistic above reproach, but no one will ever hold his attention for long.'

She sighed deeply, sipped her tea and relapsed into thought for a moment. 'There was a time when he seemed like a meteor, a dazzling ray of hope for the socialist cause, but I think he's burnt himself out now. Oh yes, he'll go on believing in his beautiful dreams, but I fear he hasn't the moral fibre to carry them out.'

'No,' murmured Robert.

'Too self-indulgent,' she continued. 'Given to tastes one would expect rather from an aristocrat than a man from the Liverpool slums. He's heading for bankruptcy, you know. Pity. A wonderful man, but in a world of his own, our beloved Vincent.'

Robert picked up the plate of cakes and held it out. 'How about one of these little fancies, Countess? Might I suggest the pink one, for it exactly matches your hat.'

Recognising the dangerous ground she

144

trod, the Countess accepted Robert's lead. 'How thoughtful of you to notice, my dear, but then you always did have an eye for colour and shape, a true artist's eye. Have you ever thought of becoming an artist? You really should, you know. Such talent should not be allowed to go unrecognised.'

A pink flush of pleasure crept across his cheeks, and the Countess poured herself a second cup of tea.

'Vincent, my dear!' Trixie Anstruther held out her arms in welcome. 'I'm so glad you found time at last to look me up—allow me to introduce you to Maurice Chabelin. Maurice, this is Vincent Gregg.'

Vincent eyed the handsome young Frenchman judiciously. His presence indicated that Trixie's husband was away again, and he could spoil everything. *'Bonjour, monsieur,'* he said civilly, holding out his hand.

'Monsieur le Comte,' Trixie corrected him.

'I beg your pardon,' said Gregg. The Frenchman smiled.

'No need to apologise, Monsieur Gregg. Madame, I will take up no more of your precious time. So kind of you to receive me.'

'Not at all,' said Trixie graciously, holding out a hand for him to kiss. 'Do call and see me again soon.'

'You can be sure of that, Madame.'

As soon as the Frenchman had gone, Gregg took Trixie by the shoulders. 'Let me look at you—heavens, you're as beautiful as ever,' he murmured. She laughed and broke away.

'Come and sit with me on the settee and tell me all you've been up to since I saw you last,' she invited, and as Gregg sat down she regarded him closely. 'You don't look well,' she commented. 'And I'm told you're deeply in debt.'

He hung his head. 'Bad news travels fast.'

'On the verge of bankruptcy, in fact.'

'Yes.'

She sighed deeply. 'You know, of course, that as a declared bankrupt you won't be received in polite society?'

'Yes.'

She clicked her tongue in irritation. 'Don't just keep saying, yes—what are you planning to do about it? You can't just keep going on aimlessly, hoping things will work out. What will you do?'

Suddenly the clouds vanished from his face and the sunniest of smiles emerged. She marvelled at how handsome he still was, despite the harsh effects of his heavy drinking. 'Let's not talk of depressing matters any more,' he said. 'I want to feast my eyes on your beauty—that's cure enough for any man.'

Firmly she blocked his hand as it approached to caress her. 'And there's one thing more I want to know, Vincent.'

'What's that, my dear?'

'Robert Hardcastle. I've never seen a soul looking so miserable. Did you break his heart too before you went away?'

'What nonsense you do talk! What on earth gave you that silly notion?'

She shrugged exquisitely gowned slim shoulders. 'Oh, I don't know. Call it intuition, if you will. But I know he did have a crush on you.'

'Years back. All over long ago. Oh, Trixie, if you knew how I'd longed for you all these months! Have you missed me—just a little?'

She gave him a coy smile. 'Why on earth should I?'

'I think you did—just a bit.'

'Whatever gives you that idea?' Green eyes opened wide.

He tipped her mischievously under the chin. 'You were careless, my love. You asked if I broke Robert's heart as well. As well as whose, I wonder?'

He was smiling down at her, his teasing smile sending shivers down her spine. She half-closed her eyes. 'Ah, you are too clever by half, my friend,' she murmured.

147

'You always said you preferred intelligent men,' he reminded her. 'I remember you saying a man could stir you more easily with his mind than with his body.' He leaned close, so close she could smell the brilliantine on his hair. His voice was caressingly low and seductive. 'Tell me you've missed me, Trixie. Tell me you're glad to see me again.'

She laughed softly. 'You know I'm always glad to see you, Vincent, but I'm old enough and wise enough to know you have a reason for coming to me now. What is it?'

His fingers were stroking her arm, so gently the touch was no more than a breath on her skin. 'Do you need me to tell you, Trixie? Do you need to be told that I desire you, I want you, so urgently that it hurts?'

He was pressing her backwards on the settee, leaning over her and touching his lips to her neck. Trixie felt the blood pounding in her head and let herself melt into his embrace. Then suddenly she thrust him away.

'Stop it, Vincent—let me go. I know what you're after, and I'm not going to be used.'

He stared at her in amazement. 'What are you talking about, my kitten? I'm not using you. Perhaps I was getting a little carried away, but you've only your beauty to blame for that.'

He could see her expression was set as she rose from the couch. 'Come, you haven't offered me a drink yet,' he bantered in an effort to restore the atmosphere. 'It's not like you to be so remiss. Shall I mix you a cocktail?'

She turned to face him. 'Where are you staying, Vincent?'

'At the Court Hotel. Would you like me to take you there for dinner?'

'Can you afford to pay?'

He threw back his head and laughed. 'How like a woman! We could dine well, then take champagne to my room....'

'And then you could make love to me. Is that it?'

He stood up and came to stand close to her. 'If you were to give me half a chance,' he murmured huskily in her ear.

'I knew it!' She turned to glare at him. 'You have no money. You want to compromise me—and what for? Do you think I don't know? Do you think I'm absolutely stupid? I can see through your little game, Vincent Gregg, and I'm not going to fall for it, see? I wasn't born yesterday!'

He stared at her, thunderstruck. 'Game? I don't know what you're talking about, truly I don't. All I want is to take you out to dinner....'

'And then to take me to bed—in a public place where we'll be recognised—and why? So that you'll be in a position to blackmail me!'

He took a step forward. 'No! Oh no, I wouldn't do that to you for the world, I swear I wouldn't! You misjudge me, Trixie!'

Her eyes glittered contempt. 'Do I? Then it's only in one detail—it's my husband you plan to bleed in return for keeping your mouth shut. You know he's one of the richest financiers in London, and you're bankrupt. You want to put your socialist principles into practice with a vengeance!'

He was standing helplessly spreading his hands. 'I don't know what you mean....'

'Oh yes you do! Capitalists shouldn't monopolise wealth—it should be shared with the poor—isn't that what you're always preaching?' Her lips were curled in a sneer. 'Well I'm damned if my husband will pay out to you, Vincent Gregg, to keep you in idleness! Find another gullible fool to pay your debts, for I'm hanged if it will be us!'

'Trixie—please—you misunderstood....'

'I understand all too well! Get out of this house, Vincent Gregg, and don't ever set foot in it again—do you hear me? I never want to clap eyes on you again, and I'll make certain none of my friends do either. Now get out!'

It was a very dejected Gregg who emerged from the villa and crossed the rainswept square that evening. There was hardly the price of a cab-fare in his pocket and he faced the prospect of a long wet walk back to the lodging house on the modest side of town. It afforded him ample time to consider that he had pretty well exhausted all the possible sources of help he had been banking on. The Countess, Robert and now even Trixie had turned their backs on him—it really was too unkind.

Blackmail, Trixie had said. Strange, that. It reminded him of the Countess and her letters from the King long ago. Funny how readily the notion of blackmail came to the minds of some people.

NINE

Eddie Pearson sat on the edge of his bed, angrily kicking the toes of his newly polished boots against the counterpane of Hal's bed. It seemed bitterly unjust, heartless in the extreme, that no one but himself seemed to remember that today was the anniversary of Mother's death.

They were too wrapped up in the hectic business of living, that was the trouble. Father, having been successful in standing as Labour candidate for the ward, spent his time flying hither and thither on council business nowadays as well as on Church and union affairs. And Hal... Eddie snorted. Hal had gone all soft, spending precious vacation time writing endless letters to that Lilian girl, and now, to make matters worse, getting Father to let her spend a few days here with them.

She was downstairs now, chattering brightly to Father about politics and similar boring things, clearly impressing him with her knowledge and clear-cut views. Hal sat by, smiling like an idiot, and Eddie could have kicked him. It was hopeless trying to talk to him about wild flowers or cycling trips these days. He'd gone dull and boring, just like the other grown-ups.

'Eddie! Come on down, tea's ready!'

With a sigh he took off his boots and put on his carpet slippers. Father and Hal would never notice if he'd kept his boots on—nobody had bothered since Mother died—but that Lilian was getting very bossy. She'd been here too long, that was the trouble. He wondered how on earth his brother put up with her.

But she had her redeeming features, he decided as he came down the attic stairs and the savoury smell of kippers rose to meet his nostrils. His father, seated by the fire and still dressed in his work clothes, glanced up from the paper as Eddie took his place at table.

'Homework finished, Edward?'

'Yes, Father.'

'All correct?'

Eddie flushed. 'I think so. I got answers, anyway.'

Father came to the table and Hal took the plate of kippers from Lilian with a smile, passing it to his father. 'But have you double-checked, Eddie? That's the secret, checking everything.'

The boy felt his cheeks crimsoning even more. They were both playing up to the visitor, and he was the victim. Anger gave him the courage to say what was on his mind.

'It's a year ago today since Mother died,' he said quietly. Father seemed to hear only that Hal had made a slip.

'Your brother's name is Edward, Harold. You know how I dislike abbreviations.' Father's voice was stern, and it was heartening to see it was Hal's turn to blush.

'Quite right, Mr Pearson,' said Lilian. 'I hate to hear people call me Lily or even worse, Lil. Lilian has a distinctive ring about it, don't you think, an air of authority.'

'Indeed it has,' Hal agreed quickly. 'But what you say is what gives you authority, Lilian. You never venture half-considered opinions like so many women.'

She inspected the piece of kipper on the end of her fork before answering. 'No, I try to weigh up a matter carefully before adopting a stance. That's only the sign of any intelligent mind, don't you think?'

'Quite so,' said Father.

Encouraged, Lilian went on. 'I mean, I thought over all the important matters of our time very seriously. That's why I am convinced that my views on pacifism are the right ones, and on suffragism and socialism.' She glaced at Hal and at his plate. 'You should eat up the skin of that baked potato too, you know, Harold,' she remarked. 'It's very good for you.'

Eddie tried again. 'It's Mother's anniversary,' he murmured, but no one paid any attention. He did not know whether they had heard.

Lilian ignored him and turned her attention back to his father. 'So you can see why I was so pleased about your family backing Mr Gregg in the election that time. He represented all the views I hold dear.'

'And lost his seat so that he was no longer able to voice them,' Mr Pearson returned.

'Oh, but he should try again!' Lilian said with enthusiasm. 'The cause needs men like him.'

'I hardly think so.' Father's voice was quiet but his tone was firm. 'He will never get a seat here again.'

'Oh, no?' said Lilian. 'How can you be so sure?'

Father laid down his knife and fork. 'I know I speak for others in the Colne Valley when I say that. Oh yes, he was a very exciting speaker, and he captured all our hearts and gave us hope. But he showed he couldn't live up to his ideals. He's self-indulgent and lazy, a heavy drinker too, and that doesn't go down well with our people. You're a stranger hereabouts,

Lilian, but I can tell you that Hawksmoor folk are a thrifty, hard-working lot. They're very Nonconformist—Wesley was a great influence on our lives—and they don't approve of lazinesss. And it's not only the electorate—why, even Mr Snowden, who sponsored him into the House, turned against him, remember. Moderation, that's the thing, and moderation is a word Mr Gregg does not appear to have in his vocabulary. That's why he'll never be able to gain local support again.'

Silence fell around the table. Eddie knew that for Father to deliver a speech as long as that it was evidently a subject on which he felt strongly. Hal knew it too. Only Lilian went on, anxious to redeem herself.

'He still works for suffragism,' she said quietly. 'The suffragettes are very glad of his support. Mrs Glasier, Mrs Pankhurst, all of them appreciate his efforts.'

'To be sure,' said Father, and Eddie was relieved to hear the mollified tone of his voice. 'And so he should. Women have a great deal to contribute to society, and it would be helpful if some, at least, had the vote. At the age of thirty, perhaps, when they have achieved a little worldly wisdom.'

Eddie saw Hal glance quickly at the girl and knew he was signalling her to hold her tongue. Father's last words were clearly meant to put her in her place. But Lilian had not done yet.

'The time will come when women will be truly appreciated,' she murmured. 'It may take a crisis to give us our chance, but it will come.'

Father glanced at her sharply. 'War, you mean? Oh, you surely don't believe all this claptrap about the German menace? Sabre-rattling, my dear. The rich, the industrialists, getting worried about the competition in trade, that's all. And in any case,' he added slyly, 'since you share Harold's views as a confirmed pacifist, what do you think you could do in wartime to make women indispensable?'

Lilian's cheeks burned scarlet, and Eddie was pleased. 'There's lots women could do,' she said hotly. 'And I'd have no problem with my pacifist views—I would join a nursing corps and do my bit that way.'

'Very commendable,' said Father, rising from the table and resuming his newspaper. 'Nice kipper that, Lilian, I enjoyed it. How long did you say you would be staying in Hawksmoor?'

Eddie felt a surge of joy. After that, Lilian would have no choice but to put a limit on her stay. The sooner the house got back to menfolk only, the better.

Lilian left a couple of days later. Harold mooned around for two days more and then decided life was not too bad after all. He'd be going back to college soon for his final term, and then he'd be looking for a teaching post.

'There'll be lots of revision to do before the exams,' he told Eddie. 'I can do a lot out of doors, sitting on the grass. With Lilian—she'll be revising too.'

Hal was about to pack his books to return to college when Father announced that he was going to stay with friends in Knott End for the weekend. When he returned he sent Eddie to fetch Hal down from his bedroom.

'Now,' he said solemnly as his two sons stood before him, 'As you know, life has not been easy for us since your dear mother died.'

Hal hung his head. Eddie followed suit, but his heart was glad that at last Mother's name had been spoken.

'It has obliged us to have to carry out work for ourselves which is not strictly speaking men's work.'

True, thought Eddie. That hole he'd darned in his blue sock last week was still making him limp, but he'd known there'd be no new socks before his birthday.

'Cooking, cleaning, laundry, shopping— that's all really a woman's province, but

158

there's a limit to what Mrs Charnock can do for us. And it's expensive.'

Funny, thought Eddie, but he'd never thought of that. It hadn't occurred to him that Father had to pay the fussy old neighbour for all those apple pies and meat patties she brought round. He stood expectantly, hands clasped behind his back just like Hal, waiting for Father's solution.

'So I've come to a decision,' Father went on ponderously. 'We need a woman's hand around the house, of that there is no doubt, and I have found the very lady—and she is willing to oblige.'

Eddie heard his brother's quick gasp. 'You mean...?'

Father nodded. Eddie stared from his face to Hal's and wondered.

'Yes,' said Father. 'Mrs Iredale.'

For a moment there was silence. Eddie was puzzled. Mrs Iredale had not seemed the kind of woman who would do someone else's cooking and cleaning. His father put his hand on Hal's shoulder.

'I hope you will understand, Harold, that this is necessary to me.'

'Yes, Father.' Hal's voice sounded muffled.

Father took a deep breath. 'The wedding will take place next month. You will, of course, come home from college for the occasion.'

Eddie stared blankly at his father. 'Wedding?'

His father's smile was thin. 'Yes, Edward. You will have a new mother. Mrs Iredale and I are to be married.'

It was a long, hot summer and if Eddie felt that Mother's memory was betrayed by Father's hasty remarriage, the feeling was gradually jostled out of his mind by other pressing matters of life. Like leaving school, for instance. Father decided that his younger son should follow him into Sykes' mill and train to be an engineer.

'Secure job, that,' he told Eddie. 'So long as there's machines, there's work for engineers.'

Eddie thought of the deafening clatter of the weaving sheds in the great, gaunt mill he passed on his way to school, and tried to explain that the thought of living amongst them every day of his life appalled him. Father just didn't appear to understand.

'Why, your best subject at school is arithmetic and geometry, and there's lots of mathematical calculations to be done in engineering, lad. You take after me; your mother always said so. We'll have you down there next week and get you indentured, we will. Five years from now when you qualify, you'll thank me for this, Edward, you see if you don't.'

Postcards from Hal came all too rarely nowadays, but the next one made it plain Father had taken it as a matter of course that Eddie would welcome the apprenticeship.

I was very pleased to learn that you have chosen your career in life. A sound choice, it seems to me, and I hope you study hard to pass all the necessary examinations. Lilian and I are working conscientiously for our Finals.

Eddie sighed and pushed the postcard loose inside the album. He had little interest these days in keeping it up to date. Everyone seemed to take it for granted that engineering was good for him, so there seemed little point in telling them he'd much rather be a street-sweeper or a lamplighter or a knocker-up with a long pole. It must be rather fun to wake people up, tapping at their windows while it was still dark of a morning. More fun than greasing oily engines and coming home all dirty to your tea, anyway. Father got some rotten jobs to do, and maybe worst of all was when one of his men would come to the house with a splinter of steel in his eye and Father, taking a tiny pair of tweezers, would have to probe it out. Eddie squirmed.

There was so much he could do with his life, left to his own devices, thought Eddie. Why, at fifteen, young Hugh Wagstaff had been signed for the Hawksmoor rugby team—Eddie could still remember how they'd displayed the lad's birth certificate in the programme—and at seventeen he'd gone on to play for England.

But inevitably the day of indenture came. Dressed in his best Norfolk jacket and cap, Eddie stood before Father's critical stare. Father nodded.

'Aye, you'll do,' he said at last. 'Reckon he looks a credit to me, Emma?'

Eddie did not turn for her approval. She came round him to peer closely at his neck and collar. He looked at the floor, trying to squash down the feeling of resentment. He was thankful he was now as tall as she was, and she could no longer pat him on the head.

'Yes,' she murmured, 'neck scrubbed like I told you, ears clean. But here, let me wipe that sleep out of your eye.'

He could not help pulling away as she seized the corner of her apron and, licking it, began to scrape at the corner of his eye.

Father grunted. 'He'll do, right enough. Come on, lad, or we shall be late.'

She stood on the doorstep to watch them go down the yard towards the gate.

'Remember to keep your head up, Edward,' she called after them. 'Look confident even if you don't feel it.'

Eddie fell into step beside his father and for a time they walked in silence. Father cast him a sidelong glance. 'Never heed, lad,' he muttered. 'She means well—she only wants you to be a credit to us, me being foreman and all.'

'I know.' Eddie had heard for himself the conversation in their bedroom. She did mean well, telling Father how she'd washed his son's Sunday shirt specially for today, it being so important a day. She agreed with Father that Eddie should be not an ordinary or bound apprentice, but an indentured one. Eddie could visualise her in that room, sitting at Mother's dressing table as she spoke and using her ivory-backed brush to smooth her greying hair. Mother's hair had had touches of grey in it too, silvering the tips of the dark brown like sunlight on a dark waterfall. Mother's hair had been long and thick like Sally Parkinson's, so long she could just sit on it. Mrs Iredale's hair was nowhere near as long and had a thinness about it that seemed somehow to match her personality.

No, she wasn't a bad woman; you couldn't really dislike her, Eddie thought, but he could not bring himself to think of her as anything other than Mrs Iredale. He knew she was Mrs Pearson now, but that was Mother's name, not hers. Father had suggested Eddie should call his new wife Mother, or even Step-mother, but to Eddie she was forever Mrs Iredale. To avoid complications, he called her nothing at all.

They turned in at the mill-yard gate, their boots ringing out on the cobbles. The clatter of machines from within the gaunt grey walls was deafening. Father gritted his teeth.

'Now let me do the talking, lad, when we get into Mr Earnshaw's office. I know best what to settle for.'

In the dusty office off the main weaving shed, a bright-eyed little man sat at a desk. After the first curious summing-up of his fraying collar and the black stump where his front tooth ought to be, Eddie mentally withdrew from the business being conducted. They were planning his life, but he could feel only a sensation of drowning in the terrible noise of the machines, and he wished with all his heart that he could be far away and alone up in the silence of the woods, left out of the dizzying business they called earning a living.

'Well, I think we're agreed,' said Mr Earnshaw at last. 'Start Monday. All right, Edward?'

164

Eddie started. 'Sir?'

He felt his father's elbow give him a sharp nudge. 'Mr Earnshaw is asking if you agree, Edward—five shilling a week, fifty-one hours, start Monday.'

'Oh—yes,' Eddie stammered. 'Thank you, sir.'

It was on the homeward journey that Father spelt out the details, his voice stern. 'I could tell you were off on that silly day-dreaming of yours again. You really will have to learn to concentrate, my lad, or you'll not keep that job. You don't know how lucky you are, getting a position at Sykes'.'

'Oh I do, Father, and I'm grateful.'

His father grunted. 'There's a lot of studying, think on. One afternoon a week at the technical, and then three nights a week as well. Five years' hard work ahead, but it'll be worth it in the end, you'll see.'

Five years. It sounded like a lifetime. He'd be twenty by then, a man full grown and on ten shillings a week. But still not fully qualified, his father told him, not till he was twenty-one, and a year after that he'd finally get the full rate of four pounds a week. Four pounds! The prospect of such wealth one day went some way towards dispelling the gloom and trepidation he felt.

Emma showed her pleasure by giving her husband a peck on the cheek and toasting crumpets for tea as a treat.

'So nice you've got both the boys settled, James,' she remarked. 'We'll have more time for ourselves now you can stop worrying over Edward's future. Oh, I saw that Mrs Denton in the Co-op today and we were talking about Sykes'. Her lad's been working there for some time now. He'll no doubt be in the same shop as your Edward.'

Eddie groaned. He thought he'd seen the last of his persecutor when Denton left the board school to start work last year, but now it seemed as if Fate was playing tricks on him. Suddenly Monday was no longer a day to look forward to....

Vincent Gregg descended stiffly from the train. The journey from London had been a long and stuffy one on this hot summer's day and he desperately needed a drink. He emerged from the colonnaded entrance of Hawksmoor railway station into the sunlight and headed across the square to the George Hotel.

The bar was quite full, merchants having finished their business for the day, at the Cloth Hall mostly. Taking his whisky to a corner seat, Gregg sat down to survey the other drinkers to see if there was anyone he knew. One he recognised by sight, a Liberal alderman by the name of Dawson or Lawson or something, but he avoided the man's look. Now if he'd been a socialist it would have been different....

Another whisky, and then he'd feel better. Let's face it, he told himself, no one in respectable London society wanted to know him any more. Here, in Hawksmoor, he'd been a hero. Even if party members did not prove as enthusiastic as they used to be, there would still perhaps be the prospect of welcoming arms. There'd been that delectable little Mrs Longden, for instance. And that other little one, that friend of hers who'd been widowed in a tram accident—either of them would be sure to offer solace for a world-weary soul. He needed rest and peace, comfort without demands. Ladies, as he had discovered long ago, were the most likely creatures to listen and provide.

Another whisky, and then he would set about finding out if Mrs Longden was still as tractable as she once had been.

Hal was home from college and waiting eagerly for the postman every day. It was not only from Lilian that he desperately wanted news, but also from the college authorities. Any day now the degree results would be announced, and Eddie held his breath too.

The letter came at last. Hal was in transports of delight. 'I've got a second, Eddie!' he whooped, dancing round the living room, the letter in his hand. 'I'm a B.Sc now! I'm a graduate!'

Emma smiled. 'I'm so pleased for you, dear. And I know your father will be delighted. Where is he, Edward? He didn't come home with you tonight from the mill?'

'Union meeting. He said he wouldn't be long and to keep his tea hot.'

Father simply nodded approval when he learnt the news. Eddie could tell from his expression that the thought of failure for his son had never crossed his mind.

'Good,' he said shortly. 'Pity it wasn't a first-class degree, though.'

Hal showed no sign of disappointment at Father's reaction. 'I must write and tell Lilian at once, and find out how she's done,' he said, and rushed upstairs to his room. Eddie surveyed his father's tired face thoughtfully. No matter how kind Father could be, he had that strange attitude towards his family—however well they did, they could always have done better. There was no satisfying him, and Eddie wished with all his heart that just for once in his life he could do something to make Father smile and nod approval.

'Will there be a ceremony?' Father asked later that evening. 'For the graduation, I mean?'

'Oh yes, Father,' Hal replied enthusiastically. 'Two tickets for the family to come and watch.'

'A proud day that will be, when the first Pearson gets his hood and gown. Your stepmother and I will make sure to be there,' said Father.

Eddie could not explain the sinking feeling in the pit of his stomach or the angry feeling of resentment against the Iredale woman. All he knew was that Hal had been his hero all these years, and now he was being left out of his brother's triumph, and it was unfair. They were going to celebrate without him.

'You're looking a bit down,' Hal commented.

'I'm all right. Just wish summat would happen, that's all.'

'A man should beware lest his dreams come true,' Father remarked drily.

Emma Iredale glanced up from sewing a button on Hal's shirt. 'What's up, Eddie? Tiring day, was it?'

He mumbled some reply. Father spoke abruptly.

'Leave him be, Emma. He'll get used to it. All that noise and clatter is a bit moithering at first, but you have to get used to it. Eddie knows he's a long way to go yet.'

Eddie lay that night in the stuffiness of the attic bedroom with the deeply breathing figure of Hal beside him and recalled the words. Yes, there was a terrible long way to go yet, and he wondered if he could ever survive it. Manhood, and with it freedom, came too slowly. He fingered his chin as he did every night, hoping to find there at least enough hairs to make it possible to ask Hal if he could borrow his shaving brush. But just like last night and the night before, there was nothing.

Oh, if only something would happen, something exciting to lighten the boring, mind-splintering succession of days, months, years ahead in the mill. Something earth-shattering and unexpectedly different... The thought lulled his mind into sleep.

At breakfast Father's face was pale as he read the morning newspaper. At last he laid it aside.

'Germany has invaded Belgium,' he muttered as Emma handed him a cup of tea. 'Britain has declared war on Germany.'

The cup clattered in the saucer. 'War?' she echoed. Eddie saw his brother's face whiten.

170

'Aye, lass,' Father said, and there was infinite weariness in his voice. 'There's no choice for any of us now. We're at war with Germany.'

TEN

The drawing room of Sir Marcus Hardcastle's London flat was littered with hatboxes and swathes of tissue paper. Lady Hardcastle, still in outdoor clothes, stood before the mirror, twisting her head this way and that to survey the pink hat she wore. Suddenly the door burst open, and a scarlet-faced Sir Marcus stood there, breathing heavily.

'Alicia! Where in heaven's name have you been? I've been asking the servants every half-hour for the past three hours, and all I got was, "She's gone into town, sir." What on earth kept you?'

'Shopping, dear. Just look....'

'For three hours? I needed to talk to you, and where the devil were you? Shopping! Three bloody hours!'

Lady Hardcastle stared at him in amazement. 'You needed me, Marcus? Good heavens!'

He clicked his tongue in irritation and sank into an easy chair. 'Don't be flippant, Alicia. It doesn't suit you, and especially when it's a matter as serious as this.'

She laid aside the pink hat and came

towards him, repressing the impulse to remark that in twenty-five years he had never before said that he needed her. His tone indicated something far too unpleasant for that.

'What is it, Marcus?'

His head sank into his left hand. 'There's an almighty war going on,' he muttered.

'I know. All kinds of shortages threatened, they say. That's why I just had to go up to Bond Street today.'

He looked up, his ruddy face registering incredulity. 'To stock up—on hats?'

'You never know—Millichip's might not be there by next Ascot and Henley. But what was it you wanted to tell me?'

'It's Robert....'

Lady Hardcastle paled suddenly. 'Robert? Oh, my God! He hasn't had an accident, has he?' The pink hat fluttered, forgotten, from her fingertips to the floor.

Sir Marcus groaned. 'Worse. He's enlisted.'

Lady Hardcastle shrieked, her fingers flew to her mouth, and for a moment she swayed. Her husband watched her anxiously, fearful lest she have one of her famous fits of the vapours, but she rallied admirably. She sank into the plush armchair facing him and gathered up the Pekinese lying asleep there before she spoke.

'Are you sure, dear? Are you certain he isn't having a little joke with you? You know he's always had this whim for playing practical jokes on people—remember the time he had us all believing that the servants had gone on strike and we'd have to prepare our own dinner? And then there was the time he put the dead rat in—'

'No, Alicia.' Sir Marcus shook his balding head firmly. 'This is no joke. The recruiting officer was here this afternoon, and he confirmed it. The boy is to report to the training camp on Friday.'

'What does that mean, Marcus?'

He sighed. 'Marching, drilling, learning to use arms. Taking orders and that.'

His wife gasped. 'Taking orders? Surely he will be an officer—giving orders, not taking them? And using a gun? Oh no, Robert could never kill! The whole idea is preposterous. He can't possibly go.'

'You don't understand, Alicia. He's got to go.'

'Nonsense. In that training camp they might make him train in wet grass or out in the rain. You know what a bad chest he has. No, he can't possibly go. What do you mean, he's got to? Don't be so heartless, Marcus. If he's got his heart set on it, talk him out of it. He's probably only done it because everyone he knows is doing it. He's been taken in by those posters everywhere—you know, "Your country needs you". If you don't talk him round, I will.'

'Listen, you silly woman!' Sir Marcus' voice was shrill. 'There's no choice about it now—he's signed up. He's signed his name. He's of age, and his signature is binding.'

'Well, buy him out. You've bought your way out of things before now.'

Her voice was cool, her manner practical as she stroked the Pekinese's ears. He realised she had great faith in his power to control life's problems, but this time he and his money were powerless and the fact angered him. He had no one to rail at but her.

'You can't swaddle the lad any more like you've been doing all these years,' he rumbled, 'making a right namby-pamby out of him. You'll have to resign yourself to it, lass. Your precious son is going to fight for his country, and that's that.'

She considered for a moment. 'Well, at least you could make sure he is giving orders and not taking them. I hate to think of him messing about in muddy fields, specially now the winter is coming on. Buy him a commission, Marcus. Then he'll have a batman to do all the horrid jobs for him at least. Go on, it won't break

175

you to do him a favour.'

Sir Marcus rolled his eyes at the ceiling. 'Can't you understand, woman, that there's nothing I can do! Officer or not, he'll have to do his training like everyone else. Good thing is, though,' he added begrudgingly, 'he'll be with a decent regiment—same as Lord Anstey's son'll be in.'

Lady Hardcastle brightened. 'The Honourable Rupert? Oh well, that's all right then. I know for a fact that Mirabel Anstey wouldn't let Rupert go anywhere that was undesirable. If it's good enough for the Ansteys.... Oh, by the way, Marcus, did I tell you that Mirabel won a prize at Mr Cruft's dog show with her Benjie? She says Pekinese was by far the most popular dog entered this year. I should have entered Pooky, after all—I told you I should.'

Sir Marcus groaned and gave up. Alicia's world was governed by Ascot and Henley and the London season and what all the right people were doing. It was useless to expect her to understand that Rupert Anstey, Honourable or not, was just as vulnerable to cold steel as Tommy Atkins.

Vincent Gregg lay in bed and stared at the crack in the ceiling above him, trying to wipe out from his mind the naked figure of the woman lying next to him. He didn't even know her name, he thought bitterly.

She rolled over and smiled, and the sight of the mascara running down from the corner of her eye disturbed him. 'You awake, love?' she murmured. 'Fancy another cuddle before you go?'

'No.' He swung his legs out of bed, conscious now of the acrid smell of stale sweat in the little room. God, that drink should have reduced him to this! She lay watching him dress, one slim arm curled under her tousled head.

'Got a wife to hurry back to?' she enquired, and there was a hint of a smile at the corners of her lips.

He made no answer as he buttoned his trousers and reached for his bow tie. He bent to look in the fly-blown mirror on the dressing table as his clumsy fingers tried to fasten it.

'Or a job? Got to get to the office? You don't look the type who's got to go to work, you don't,' she remarked, throwing back the sheet and pulling herself upright. Through the mirror he could see the shapely curve of her young breasts as she sat on the edge of the bed, chin cupped in hands, to watch him. He could at least see what must have captured his lustful eye, in whatever bar he had picked her up last night. He wondered whether he had satisfied her before oblivion claimed him.

She evidently read his mind. 'You were

great, love, the best in a long while,' she murmured. 'Sure you don't want another cuddle before you go?'

'No thanks. Got to hurry,' he grunted, jerking the tie into something like the right place and picking up his jacket from the floor. As he brushed it down with his hand he added uncomfortably, 'How much do I owe you?'

Throwing back her head she gave a full-throated laugh, then stood up and came to him, putting her arms about him and holding him close. He did not resist.

'You don't remember, do you? You gave me money last night, soon as we got here. You don't owe me nothing. Fact is, I owe you, but you said keep the change.'

'Then keep it.'

'From a fiver? You sure?'

Bright eyes looked up at him in disbelief. He nodded. Even through his jacket he could feel the warmth of her body, but she stirred nothing in him. Maybe it was the shabby room, or the smell, or the dishevelled bed, but whatever it was, he was anxious to be away from here.

She stood back, looking up at him with birdlike curiosity in her bright eyes. 'One thing puzzles me, though,' she said. 'You being a gent—and I know you are, from your clothes and the posh way you talk and the way you throw money about—so why are you hanging round pubs like you got nothing better to do? Why ain't you in the Army like everyone else your age?'

He reached for his overcoat. 'You got a good body,' she added thoughtfully. 'You ain't sick, so why you still here and not in France, eh? Still, I ain't grumbling. A nice young toff like you makes a nice change from old men and boys.'

As Gregg walked along the drizzle-grey street, welcoming the cold freshness of rain on his face, he tried to push from his mind the picture of those old men and boys he had followed into the arms of an unfussy tart. He wanted to forget the depths he had sunk to, the squalor and uncertainty of his precarious way of life.

He needed direction, a goal, instead of this continual aimless drifting. France. Yes, why shouldn't he join the Army? Pacifism was all very well, but that had been an ideal of his youth, long before he had tried to warn the country about the growing menace of German militarism. His warnings had fallen on deaf ears, but that was no reason to stand sneeringly aloof from the fight now.

The Army, yes, that was the answer. He had no one to answer to for his change of heart, no one in the world.

It took Eddie some time to get over the feeling that he, somehow, by wishing for something dramatic to happen, had personally brought the war about. But as summer dwindled into autumn and then into winter, his guilt began to dissipate. After all, nothing much seemed to be happening as far as the war with Germany was concerned. True, there had been a recruiting officer in Hawksmoor and some of the lads in Lindley like Eric Broadbent and Tommy Drake had enlisted and been seen parading about the village in their smart new uniforms before vanishing to join their regiment. But otherwise there seemed to be little happening, and everyone said it was only a skirmish and would all be over by Christmas.

It seemed too far away to be real, anyway, but what was happening here in Hawksmoor was very real. Hal was home for good now, having got himself a teaching post in Venn Street school. He talked incessantly about his colleagues and pupils and the importance of doing his job well so that he should come up to scratch when the inspectors came.

'It's so important, Eddie, with pay depending on results like it does. I don't know, what with preparing lessons, going to Labour Party meetings again and the cycling club, I've me time filled and no mistake.'

His dark eyes glowed and Eddie revelled in having his brother back to share his room and his confidences. He was no longer alone. He had an ally.

Hal lay back on the bed. 'And it's fair grand to be bringing money home instead of being a drain on Father's pocket. Doesn't it make you proud to hand over your money every Friday night?'

Eddie nodded, mindful of that very first wages packet he had borne home with such pride, and of Father's words: 'Now think on, lad, you hand over that packet to your mother unopened. It's for her to decide how much she'll give you back for spending money.'

How proud he would have been to hand it to Mother and watch her warm, slow smile. As it was, Emma Iredale had not been unreasonable.

'How would it be if you gave me three-and-six a week and kept one-and-six for yourself?' she had suggested, and from that time on he had religiously passed over the money every Friday; but he opened his wage packet and withdrew his own money first. Somehow it seemed less disloyal to Mother's memory as Emma's slim fingers tipped the coins out of the packet and secreted them in her various jars labelled *rent, coal, gas* and *food.*

Hal, lying with hands behind his head, suddenly began talking again. 'You know, Eddie, you ought to come out with me sometimes. You'd enjoy the Labour Party meetings. There's a real grand chap called Arthur, lively and full of ideas and a great sense of humour. You'd like him, and the others.'

'No time,' said Eddie. 'I've got technical two nights a week, remember. And I'm stuck with homework the other nights. Only Sunday left, really.'

Hal sat upright suddenly. 'Then you could come to the Clarion club with me. It'd do you good riding out in the countryside.'

'No bike,' Eddie replied succinctly.

But Hal was not easily deterred. 'Arthur was saying the other day that he'd got an old bike in his shed he wanted to get rid of. He'd let us have it for a shilling or two —we could do it up. What do you say, Eddie?'

Eddie's heart leapt. A bicycle of his own—and Hal for company! 'Do you think we could? I mean, I haven't got much money.'

Hal waved away the protest. 'I'll see to that—call it your birthday present.'

It was a sorry-looking affair when Hal brought it home. Emma Iredale threw up her hands in horror.

'You're not to bring that in over my clean floor,' she protested. 'Whatever do you think you can do with a thing like that? It's covered in rust!'

Hal remained cheerful. 'Surprising what a bit of emery paper and a touch of oil and paint can do,' he replied. 'We'll make a new bike of it in no time.'

Eddie was delighted with his new acquisition, and it gave him added pleasure that his father watched with approval as he worked on it. Even Emma Iredale gave grudging admiration.

'Why, it looks something like now,' she commented. 'It looks quite respectable.'

Suddenly Eddie felt that his world was filled with sunshine. His work at the mill, though long and exhausting, was proving by no means as boring as he had expected. He'd grown accustomed to the noise and he was not, to his relief, in the same shed as Denton, whose jibes he had only to suffer during the breaks. And the mathematical work involved in learning engineering processes proved stimulating. He was enjoying the challenge of making the figures work.

He was a man now, bringing home money for his keep, gaining confidence in his job and now, with Hal for company and the prospect of freedom to roam the countryside, life was opening up for him. He was not aware that his contentment manifested itself to others until one day Sally Parkinson caught sight of him as he crossed the mill yard towards the weaving shed.

'What's up with thee, Eddie Pearson?' she called. There was a teasing ring in her voice and a smile on her pretty face. 'You look like you've lost a halfpenny and found sixpence. You're in a right way to being a good-looking lad if you're not careful.'

He felt himself colouring hotly. 'Nay, I'm just happy with life,' he answered gruffly. She laughed and tossed her head as she turned to walk back into the weaving shed.

'Then I wish a bit of it would rub off on me,' she called back, and then she was gone.

He felt a glow of pleasure as he finished the day's shift. She was a nice girl, Sally Parkinson, and he was glad he'd stopped Denton from messing up her pretty hair that time in the Band of Hope all those years ago. Then a bright idea struck him. Why not invite her to sit with him while they ate their snap tomorrow dinnertime? But on second thoughts, perhaps he'd better not. Those friends of hers would never cease their twitting remarks, and what Denton would say didn't bear thinking of.

Lilian came to stay at Easter. When Sunday dinner was over, Eddie made ready to go down to the Clarion club as usual. He wheeled his bicycle out into the yard, where Hal was standing in the sunlight talking to Lilian.

'Are you coming to the club?' Eddie asked.

Hal looked startled. 'Not today, Eddie. I thought I'd take Lilian for a walk up Lindley Moor edge. Show her the view across the valley towards Halifax and the old ancestral home.'

Eddie cocked his head. 'Crag Heights, you mean? It's not our home.' He bent to fasten on his cycle clips.

Hal gave a nervous laugh. 'In a way it is—it was our great-grandfather's home and Father was brought up there. It would have been ours if Great-grandfather hadn't married his housekeeper. I just thought Lilian would like to see it.'

'Indeed I would,' said Lilian. 'I could do with a blow of fresh air after that big dinner. Never mind the club today, Harold. Let's be off before the sun changes its mind.'

Eddie hesitated, then threw a leg over his bicycle. 'Right then. I'll tell Arthur you'll

185

be back as usual next week, shall I?'

'I shall see him at the party meeting on Wednesday, anyway,' said Hal. 'Enjoy yourself, Eddie.'

Hal watched his brother's lean figure as he rode off down the cobbled street, then turned to Lilian. 'The time's not far off when he'll prefer the company of an attractive young lady too on a sunny afternoon,' he remarked. 'Come on then, let's be off.'

Lilian glanced up at the sky. 'There's rain-clouds coming in, Harold. Happen we shouldn't go that far, after all.'

They had barely reached the corner of the street before the first raindrops began to fall. Lilian drew the collar of her jacket closely about her throat.

'Would you rather we went back, love?' Hal asked.

She shook her head. 'I want to talk to you. Let's go somewhere we can find shelter.'

Drawing her arm through his, he led her into the recreation ground. As they walked the length of the gravel path towards the wooden shelter, rain began to spatter heavily on the leaves of the oak trees overhead. Once inside the shelter, they sat down on the wooden bench.

The sky was darkening. 'Eddie will get soaked,' Lilian remarked.

'Not he. He's got his mackintosh.'

Rain drummed on the roof and Lilian huddled closer to him. 'You wouldn't think clouds could thicken up so quickly,' she murmured. 'It's black out there now.'

He put his arm about her shoulders. 'April shower, love. It'll soon be gone, you'll see.'

'It's like the clouds of war,' Lilian said thoughtfully. 'Just a few at first and then gathering in intensity. Oh, I wish the war was over, Harold.'

'It soon will be. It can't last long. Everyone says so.'

She looked up at him, contempt in her eyes. 'Surely you're too intelligent to believe what everyone else says—just because they want to believe it? We know the real confrontation is yet to come—and it will, Harold, it will—and what are we doing about it?'

He looked down at her in surprise. 'We? What can we do, Lilian? We're pacifists, remember. We can have no part in this struggle.'

She shrugged herself free of his arm. 'Fighting isn't the only way of doing our bit. But it is our duty to help our country in whatever way we can.'

He smiled. 'A sudden burst of patriotism, Lilian? I see the posters have had their effect on you.'

She was staring thoughtfully down at her shoes. 'I had a letter from James Colville the other day.'

'Really? What was his news?'

'He's enlisted. Wasn't going to wait for the Registration Act to go through.'

Hal felt irritated. 'What Colville does is no concern of mine. He never shared our views. He's not of our class, remember.'

'What's class got to do with it?' Lilian retorted angrily. 'It's living up to one's conscience, maintaining one's ideals—that's what matters.'

'Exactly.'

'And my conscience says I should do something for my country, not sit idle.'

Hal's voice was quiet but firm. 'I will not enlist, if that's what you're suggesting, Lilian. I will not go against my conscience for anyone—even you.'

'I wouldn't expect you too, you know that.' Her voice sounded sullen, petulant even.

'I've talked by the hour with Arthur about this—'

'Oh, Arthur, Arthur—do you think I care a fig what Arthur thinks? Why, the Labour Party itself has put aside pacifism to join the Government.'

'The ILP has, yes. That doesn't mean all socialists have to accept their view.'

'Happen not. But the fact of the matter

is, Harold, that the Government is going to introduce compulsory conscription very soon, and there's not a damn thing you can do about it. You'll have to join up then.'

Harold got up abruptly and walked to the edge of the step. He could feel the cold rain on his cheek. 'I won't,' he said quietly. 'That's one thing I'll not do.'

'What choice have you got?' Her voice was cold and menacing as doom. 'They'll send you to prison if you refuse.'

He felt the fire that rose from his belly, and when he spoke his words glittered with determination. 'I don't care what they do, Lilian—they'll never make me fight, and that I swear. Arthur and I have agreed. We'll protest—they can't deny us that right.'

'And after that? If they don't listen? And they won't, you know that. What will you do? Let your father suffer the disgrace of seeing you sent to gaol? Is that what you want, Harold?'

He turned on her savagely. 'What would you have me do? Desert my principles? What are you planning to do, Lilian? Forget everything we once swore we stood for?'

'I'm going to join a nursing corps. The Scottish Women's Hospital committee need volunteers. They're setting up a new field hospital in Northern France.'

'Oh, that feminist lot.'

'You needn't sneer. They're doing fine work. But what will you do, Harold?'

He was gazing out over the rain-sodden field and his reply came softly over his shoulder, so softly she had to strain her ears to catch it.

'I only know one thing for sure. No power on earth is going to force me to spill blood. I'll fight every authority there is, Government or police, but I will not fight, so help me. I'll go on the run first.'

ELEVEN

Alderman Lawson sat in the arbour in a corner of his garden, a rug drawn over his knees, trying to focus his attention on what Alderman Tunnycliffe was saying.

'A good meeting on Tuesday. Pity you missed it.'

Lawson frowned, trying to recollect which council sub-committee meeting Tunnycliffe was referring to. 'Oh, Land and Properties,' he murmured. 'I really wasn't up to it, still trying to shake off the last of this bronchitis attack. Should be back on Monday, all being well.'

'Only important matter was the purchase of Crowther's house and the land it stands on. Committee passed it.'

'What do they plan to use it for?'

'Nurses' home, probably. Not enough room at the infirmary. And there's the land—fifteen acres of it in all—that'll come in useful.'

Lawson nodded. 'Good idea. Far-seeing policy that. Whose idea was it?'

Tunnycliffe spread his hands as if in apology. 'Well, it was Councillor Pearson's, actually. He put up a strong case for it.'

Lawson nodded again. 'Good man, that Pearson. Sound thinking, even if he is only a working man. Solid, reliable sort. Pity he's not one of ours. Any other news?'

Tunnycliffe leaned back, stretching his arms above his head. 'I think that about wraps it up as far as council business is concerned. Did I tell you I'd had a letter from my nephew?'

'The one at the Front?'

'He was. He's at a base hospital in Kent right now, recovering from a wound—nothing serious, he says, just a piece of shrapnel that ploughed across his scalp. He'll be back at the Front very shortly.'

'Glad to hear it.'

'Know what he told me? He said as all the fighting stopped last Christmas Day and all the soldiers, Tommies and Jerries alike, all came up out of their trenches and shook hands with each other.'

Lawson stared at him in disbelief. 'Stopped fighting? Put down their arms, do you mean?'

'So he says. They all celebrated together, he said. Had a good laugh and sang together, swapped little gifts even, showed each other photographs of their families. Hard to believe, I grant you, but he says it happened, and our Ernest is no liar.'

'I saw nowt about it in the papers,' Lawson grunted.

'Nay, well, I don't expect the Government liked it overmuch. They'll see it doesn't happen again, I'll be bound. But they were back to fighting again the minute Christmas was over, he said, same as if it had never happened.'

Lawson snorted. 'I reckon that head wound affected his memory.'

Tunnycliffe looked affronted. 'I told you, our Ernest doesn't tell lies. Why, he says he kept a piece of chocolate one of the Jerry soldiers gave him—he were going to bring it home, but he got that hungry one day when the rations didn't come up that he ate it.'

'I'm sure he did.' Lawson gave a dry laugh.

This time Tunnycliffe chose to ignore him. 'But wait while I tell you who brought the rations up to the trenches, Lawson. According to Ernest, the driver was a Private Gregg.'

Lawson stared. 'Who?'

'Private Vincent Gregg, Lawson. None other than our famous MP as was for the valley.'

'Gregg? But he was all for pacifism, spoke thousands of times against war, wrote about it time and time again in the papers. I don't believe it.'

'That's what our Ernest said. Gregg's out there with the lads in all the muck and mud, fighting as a common private. You can hardly credit it, can you?'

Lawson drew the rug up about his ample waist. 'I'm glad to hear it. Why, he was forever on about war being only the capitalist's weapon for expansion and materialistic gain. A way of diverting working men's attention away from their problems—problems caused by the likes of you and me, Tunnycliffe—that's what he claimed.'

'Well, you have to admit the war came at just the right time, what with all the strikes we'd been having all over the country. I reckon we might have had a revolution on our hands before long. At least the men have something else to think about now, fighting for their country.'

'Aye, happen so,' remarked Lawson. 'Well, all I can say is, there's hope for us yet if a die-hard socialist like Gregg can see the error of his ways and do the decent thing when he's needed. Time was when that man was a blasted menace to us, but not any more. Now, what else is coming up?'

'Well, there's education committee on Tuesday.'

'What's on the agenda?'

'Oh, purchase of new books, extension

for lavatories at Beaumont Street school, and appointment of a new schools inspector.'

Lawson gave a dry little cough. 'New inspector—ah yes, that's important. I'll make sure I'll be well enough to get to that meeting. Better get back inside now, though, before it gets any cooler out here.'

The clock on the schoolroom wall was showing five minutes to four. Harold Pearson rubbed the seven times table off the blackboard, flicked the chalk dust off his gown and turned to his class.

'Now, put your slate and chalk away in your desk and sit to attention.'

There was a clatter of desk lids and then forty attentive faces stared at him expectantly. There was no need to announce the next event to them for they knew the day's routine by heart.

'Stand.'

Boots clattered against iron desk legs. Forty children stood stiffly to attention.

'March.'

One by one each aisle emptied as they walked into the main assembly hall, where the headmaster stood waiting on the dais. Harold took his seat at the dust-covered piano. Only a moment more... He struck the first chord, and heard the deep intake of breath.

Now the day is ended.
Night is drawing nigh,
Shadows of the evening
Steal across the sky.

Another day over. He felt a deep sense of relief. 'Good afternoon, school,' said the head.

'Good afternoon, sir,' chanted a hundred voices.

'Dismiss.'

They marched out in orderly style, but once outside the door there was a rush of bodies, a thunder of boots on bare floorboards, followed by the shrill sound of excited voices outside in the sunlit playground. They were glad of their freedom at last, thought Hal, and so was he.

But he could not leave the building yet for there was still much to be done before the inspector came next week. All the texts on the classroom walls must reflect the diligence not only of the pupils but of their teacher. Since handwriting played such an important part in the curriculum, he must write out laboriously, yet again, the perfect formation of each letter of the alphabet, large and clear, for the children to copy, over and over again, until even the most eagle-eyed inspector could find no fault.

What Hal was to earn would be decided by the inspector's findings.

Bent over his desk to peer closely at his work, trying hard not to let the pen nib splatter ink, Hal did not hear the headmaster enter the classroom. He became aware that he was being watched, and looked up sharply.

'I beg your pardon, sir,' he said, stepping down from the raised desk. The head waved his hand.

'Don't let me disturb you, Pearson. Just wanted to give you a word of warning. Don't listen to any of the tricks your colleagues may advise you to adopt, that's all.'

'Tricks, sir?'

'Don't pretend they haven't told you. I'm not green, you know. They all try it on, but it's foolish. The inspectors have seen them all before.'

'I'm sorry, I honestly don't know what you mean, sir.'

The head clicked his tongue in irritation. 'Telling the children to put their hands up whether they know the answers or not, that sort of thing. He knows you'll only call on the child you know can answer correctly. Honesty is the best policy, Pearson; face up to the consequences like a man.'

Hal watched his portly figure as he swept out, wondering how many years it took for a black academic gown to acquire that greenish hue. He sighed deeply, and began to put his pens and inkwell away in his desk. All too soon it would be morning again and the children would be reassembled in the hall singing

Jesus bids us shine
Like a candle in the night.

He hung his gown away in the store cupboard and went out. As he passed through the assembly hall he noted with a wry smile the text nailed to the dingy wall: *God is Love.*

Outside in the cobbled street he hesitated, reluctant to go home to Lindley yet and be faced with the choice of whether to go straight up to the attic bedroom and start on preparing tomorrow's lessons or to listen to Stepmother's recital of the day's happenings. He was in no mood to listen to her complaints about Mrs Charnock or some other neighbour, complaints always delivered with a shy, nervous smile as if to temper their bitterness. Instead, he decided, he would take a stroll through the park.

Summer flowers bloomed in profusion in the neatly tended flowerbeds, filling the air with a sweetness which helped to drive the choking sensation of chalk dust from his lungs. There were mostly women in the park, pushing perambulators or dragging toddlers by the hand. At this time of the afternoon most people were still at work. Hal took a postcard from his pocket, then flung down his jacket and lay full-length on the grass beneath a tree. The card showed a view of a delightful old chateau, under which were the words *Abbaye de Royaumont.* So remote, so far away as to arouse envy; he turned it over.

Dear Hal, *he read in Lilian's neat hand,* This lovely old place has been empty since the nuns left it ten years ago. Glorious grounds—you'd love it. Trenches nearby, but fighting lines are 30 miles away. Can sometimes hear the gunfire.

They say there will be a big battle this week and we will get the wounded straight from the trenches. By the way, if you put 'On Active Service' on the envelope when you write to me, you won't need to use a stamp.

Hope you have decided by now how you may best contribute to the war effort—you just can't sit on the sidelines and leave it to others.

Love from Lilian.

He stared up into the canopy of leaves

overhead and wondered why it was that Lilian's words had the power to cast a shadow over his day. It couldn't be that she nagged his conscience, could it? His conscience was clear—war was anathema to him. Arthur and he and all the other fellows at the Labour Party were all of the same mind—nothing on earth would induce them to respond to the call to arms. Arthur had already begun formulating hazy plans for what they should do when conscription was introduced and if their appeal for exemption was turned down.

'We'll pretend we haven't received the conscription papers,' he said, 'or if we're pushed we can just vanish on our bikes. It's easy—ride off to some quiet place up the moors and lie low.'

Just how to explain absence from work Arthur had never suggested, but he would be sure to have some answer. Despite his small, wiry build he was a shrewd and cunning fellow. His quick dark eyes and deft movements somehow reminded Hal of a ferret, courageous and undeterred. Arthur never wavered in his beliefs, and neither would Hal, however Lilian might taunt.

Arriving home, Hal turned in to the yard and was surprised to see his father sitting sunning himself outside the door on one of the kitchen chairs.

'You're home early, Father.'

'Aye. I had to take this chap to the infirmary after he'd had a mishap with one of our machines. Nasty cut—too much for me to manage. After that, I reckoned it was too late to go back, it being near enough finishing time.'

Shielding his eyes against the sun, he looked up at Hal. 'Fancy a walk up the moor before supper?'

Emma, busy peeling potatoes in the scullery, made no objection and the two men strode away up the village street. It afforded Hal great pleasure to see the warmth and respect with which the villagers greeted his father, the women standing on their doorsteps awaiting their husbands, and the men who doffed their caps and greeted him cordially. A churchwarden, foreman at Sykes' mill, union secretary, councillor and magistrate—it took hard work and unceasing effort for Father to earn respect like that. Hal felt proud to be a Pearson.

They made their way out of the village and uphill across the fields, climbing stiles and drystone walls until they reached the moor. Purple heather filled the air with soft scent and both men remained silent, as if allowing themselves to be drugged by the peace around them. Father leaned against a low drystone wall and gazed out across the smoke-covered valley in silence. Hal knew he was recalling his youth.

'Fine house, that Crag Heights,' he remarked, nodding towards the ivy-covered mansion standing sentinel on the moor's edge.

His father merely grunted.

'I bet you enjoyed living there, servants and all.'

His father pointed to a pebble-strewn track leading from the house, down the steep slope to the valley below. 'See that track? Used to ride down there every day to the paper mill where I started work. Never mind servants, lad. I worked hard.'

'Rode on horseback, did you?'

'Aye, Grandfather lacked for nothing.'

Hal mused for a moment. 'Strange to think that the Pearsons had money once,' he murmured.

His father shook his head. 'Nay, not the Pearsons, lad. He were a Stott, think on. Stotts have lived hereabouts for many a century, he used to tell me. I loved to listen to his tales. I used to think he were so old, yet he couldn't have been any older nor I am now.'

Hal smiled. Fifty was old in his view. 'The Stotts weren't always well off, were they?'

'Not until Grandfather James made brass out of dining rooms for navvies, and put it into that paper mill, they weren't. Sheer hard work it were, nowt else.'

He turned to face his son. 'Know what he used to tell me, Hal? He were born at the time the weavers were trying to stop machines being brought into the mills, smashed 'em up rather than let 'em be set up.'

'The Luddites,' murmured Hal.

'Aye. Do you realise that was a hundred years ago, Hal, and my grandfather were alive then. It makes you think.'

'A great deal had happened in that time,' agreed Hal. 'So much progress—new machinery, dyestuffs, and heaven knows what else. The Luddites would never recognise Hawksmoor now if they could come back.'

'Seems a long time, a hundred years, so much happening, and yet in another way it's no time at all when you recollect that somebody you know was living then.'

Hal smiled. 'You're proud of your family, aren't you, Father?'

'And not without reason. Stotts have never been an ambitious lot but they've always been fighters. I've never given it much thought before, but I reckon I am proud.'

Fighters. Hal felt his cheeks redden. 'Are you saying you're ashamed of me, Father? Are you saying you think I ought to fight?

Because I won't, you know. I can't.'

'Nay, I'm not saying that at all. We've all got to do what we feel is right.'

'I will fight for what I believe in, Father, but I won't fight someone else's battles, specially when it means spilling blood. And this is someone else's battle, not ours.'

'How do you reckon that?'

'It's the capitalists exploiting the ordinary man, you know that.'

'And who are these capitalists, Harold?'

'Millowners, landowners—the Sykeses, the Harcastles of this world. We've no time for the likes of them, men of no principle using and abusing the likes of us. Why should we be cannon-fodder, only to further the cause of our enemies? It doesn't make sense.'

'Do you see Sykes and Hardcastle as our enemies? Just think on, Harold—I, and thousands more like me, wouldn't have a job but for men like Sykes who put their money into what they believe in.'

'Happen you're right, Father. But what about the landowners like Hardcastle? What right have they to live off all that land they own, not doing a stroke of work? Doing nothing for their country, they aren't, only taking from it.'

Father sighed and turned to look out over the valley again. 'I couldn't agree with you more about them not having the right to own all that land—by rights it should belong to us all. But I tell you this, young Robert Hardcastle is fighting in the trenches right now.'

Hal could feel anger rising in his throat. 'You're not going to let go on this, are you? But I won't have you flinging Hardcastle at me like he was some example I ought to follow. I know about young Hardcastle, and I can tell you he's not what you'd want of a son.'

'Oh? I didn't know you knew him.'

'I don't, but Colville knows him well and he told me.'

Father stood upright and took a deep breath. 'Let's walk down to that big rock and sit down. There's summat I want to tell you. I hadn't meant to, but I reckon now's the time.'

Puzzled, Hal followed him to the jutting outcrop of rock on the moor's edge. He watched him flick a patch clean with his pocket handkerchief and then sit down. Hal squatted beside him, resting his elbows on his knees and waiting for his father to speak. For a time there was silence but for the cry of birds wheeling overhead. Suddenly Father turned his head, holding Hal's gaze with his penetrating blue eyes.

'How would you feel,' he asked quietly, 'if you were told that that Hardcastle lad was your own kith and kin? Would you feel any differently then?'

Hal's breath caught in his throat. 'Robert Hardcastle—related to me? That's impossible!'

The corners of Father's lips turned up in a wry smile. 'You'd think so, wouldn't you? But I came across an old diary a while back.'

'Whose diary?'

Father's gaze shifted out to the distance and Hal watched his lean profile intently. It was unlike Father to talk at length, nor was he a man to joke.

'When I was a lad, living at Crag Heights, Grandfather once gave me a box of dusty old papers from the attic which he said had once belonged to my mother. Usual stuff women collect—theatre tickets and programmes and dance cards and that. Then there was this diary. I couldn't make it out as a lad—writing were too faded and spidery.'

He paused for a moment, deep in recollection, then went on. 'It was dated 1825. Name and address, Susannah Hardcastle, Langley Hall. That's where the Hardcastles used to live, you know.'

'Yes, but how did it come into the family? And what has it to do with us?'

Father hesitated as though undecided whether to go on. 'The way Susannah tells it, her brother seduced one of the parlourmaids. She had his child. They never married.'

'So what does that prove?'

'Susannah says that she was still paying maintenance for the child, long after her brother's death, because she felt it her duty. The mother died and the money was being paid to the child's aunt. She names the child, Harold. It was Tamar, Grandfather James's cousin and later his wife.'

Hal frowned. 'Are you saying that my great-grandmother was a Hardcastle bastard? That we've got Hardcastle blood in our veins?'

'So it seems, Harold. There's no reason to disbelieve it. Susannah is hardly likely to have acknowledged the child's right if she wasn't convinced in her own mind. Neither would she want to admit to the shame of it if it was untrue.' He looked his son full in the face. 'So you see, lad, like it or not, you and young Hardcastle have a common heritage.'

Hal groaned. 'I almost wish you hadn't told me.'

'Nay, well, happen I'd have done better to leave well alone. I've never told anyone before, and I'd be obliged if you'd not mention it neither. I just thought it might temper your views a bit, that's all. It did mine, I can tell you. I could never say black's black and white's white again like I did as a youngster. There's many a shade of grey in between, think on.'

The sun was dipping low over the western skyline. Father rose stiffly and stretched. 'Come on, lad, we'd best be off. Emma'll have that supper ready by now, and she's not a woman to be kept waiting.'

TWELVE

Night lay black over the French fields, and Vincent Gregg could see little on his return journey to base camp except for what the lorry's headlights picked out in front of him and occasional flashes of gunfire behind him. He stared through the rain sleeting across the arcs of light, caught momentarily like white bullets before ploughing into the morass of the country lane.

He could feel the wheels grinding and slithering in the mud as the engine struggled to overcome the evil conditions. He was cold and hungry and his eyes ached with fatigue.

But it was worse by far for those back there in the trenches. He had seen them, white-faced and shivering in sodden uniforms, huddling together for warmth. It was cold here in the unheated cab of the lorry, but for those poor devils it was far more terrible. One man, squatting alone in a corner of the mud-filled trench during a lull in the fighting, had lit a scrap of paraffin-soaked rag in a tobacco tin and was doing his damndest to thaw out frozen, chapped fingers over its flickering warmth.

It gave Gregg pleasure to recall how those white, dispirited faces suddenly came to life at the sight of him. For a brief moment the anxiety of waiting for the order to go over the top was forgotten as they clustered about him.

'What you brought us this time, chum? Bully beef and hard biscuit again, eh?'

'Or have we struck lucky and got some chocolate this time, mate?'

'Have you got any letter for us? It's weeks since I heard from my girl.'

Those letters meant a lot to the men, and he envied them. No one in England wrote to him. No one cared. It was almost as though he had never existed. The Countess was dead. Trixie Anstruther's activities were probably restricted now her husband was no longer able to travel abroad. It amused Gregg to reflect how Trixie would have enjoyed the company of officers home on leave from the Front. And Robert—well, their friendship had withered and died after that night which should never have happened....

And Mother. Gregg sighed. She would undoubtedly have written to him, despite advancing arthritis, if only he had kept in touch with her. It was his own fault entirely. In those last years before the war he had been too immersed in his own problems to visit her, too reluctant to let her know how her precious son had sunk far below her cherished dreams for him. She would be proud to know he was fighting for King and country, but even if he were to break the long silence and send a letter to her now, in what terms could he possibly write? He could not destroy the gentle creature's illusions about mankind by telling her of the horrors and disgusting degradations of war. Nothing else filled his mind these days but the horrifying reality of it all. War was terrible and inhuman, but it was real, and here, and now. It saturated both his days and his fitful nightmares.

At last base camp came in sight. Gregg turned in at the perimeter gate and the sentry came forward to challenge him, then, recognising him, waved him through. Outside the stores hut he squelched to a halt and switched off the engine. Tired as he was, he was reluctant to join the others in the billet yet. Closing his eyes, he laid his arms across the steering wheel and put his head down.

For some moments he remained thus, sleep almost claiming him, then suddenly a voice startled him.

'Soldier!'

He jerked upright, and through the cab

window saw a uniform bearing the insignia of a lieutenant. He stiffened. 'Sir?'

'You Gregg?'

'Yes, sir.'

The young officer nodded. 'Move over, Gregg. I want a word with you.'

Surprised, Gregg shifted across to the passenger seat but he voiced no question. One did not question an officer even if he were as young and fresh-faced as this one. Lieutenant Colville, he knew, had not been at the camp long but he seemed a decent enough fellow, quiet and authoritative enough to command the men's respect. Gregg surveyed him thoughtfully as he took off his cap and settled himself in the seat.

Colville turned to look at him. 'You do the provisions run regularly, Gregg?'

'Yes, sir. For the past three months.'

'And you also collect supplies from the station?'

'Yes, sir.'

The younger man settled himself back and eased his tie from his throat. Outside in the darkness and the rain nothing moved. Colville stared at the rivulets of rain pouring down the windscreen. For a time there was silence. Gregg grew curious. Whatever the fellow had to say, he wished he would get on with it so that he could get back to his bed and sleep.

Colville seemed to come back to life. He dug into his pocket and brought out a packet of cigarettes, tapped them, and then held the packet out to Gregg. Gregg looked at him in surprise.

'It's all right,' Colville said with an easy smile, 'we're off duty. We can relax.'

Tentatively Gregg took the cigarette though he would far have preferred his pipe, which lay waiting in the billet. He watched the flame as Colville held the lucifer to each cigarette in turn. Gregg cleared his throat.

'If I might make so bold as to ask, sir....'

'No need to stand on formality, Gregg— as I said, we're off duty. And I already know something of you—it's not as if we were complete strangers. Your background is not unlike my own.'

Gregg looked at him in surprise. 'I'd have thought yours was a far more privileged one than mine, sir.'

Colville smiled. 'Not identical, I grant you, but we both had the benefit of a good education. If I'm not mistaken, you were an MP once, the darling of London society too—for a time.'

Gregg's gaze shifted away. 'Ah, that was a long time ago.'

But the man was not to be deterred. 'Life wasn't easy for you, Gregg, after

213

society turned its back on you, as I recall.'

'Perhaps with good reason,' murmured Gregg.

'Falling on hard times is hardly what I would call a good reason. It happens to many of us. I read of your problems—your illness, your bankruptcy, and how everyone, even your own constituents, turned against you.'

Gregg was uneasy. The fellow was reminding him of events he would prefer to forget. 'Might I ask why you wanted to speak to me, sir?'

The younger man eyed him speculatively. 'I'm coming to that. You could do yourself a favour. Make a change from the rough justice you've had. Do us both a favour. How would you like to be assigned to special duties?'

Gregg looked at him, perplexed. 'What kind of special duties?'

This time it was Colville's gaze which flickered away for a second. 'What would you say to making use of your responsibilities in such a way as to feather your own nest a little? I might add, you would be doing yourself a favour in more ways than one.'

Gregg's reply was wary. 'Just how do you mean?'

'My gratitude could extend itself to

214

events after the war has ended. I have contacts....'

His voice trailed away significantly. Gregg studied his open young face and marvelled. He could guess at what he was hinting, and thought it ironic that such deviousness could parade under such an innocent exterior.

'If I understand you correctly, sir, you are asking me to connive with you—'

'Collaborate,' Colville corrected him.

'In diverting supplies from where they are intended to go,' continued Gregg.

Colville looked him directly in the eye. 'And how would you react to such a proposition? I am sure extra money would not go amiss with you—and the prospect of better things to come in civilian life?'

Gregg's reply was icy. 'You're suggesting that we deprive those lads out there of their due rights? The thought to me is anathema. I'll have nothing to do with it.'

Colville sighed. 'I don't think you should reply in a hurry, Gregg. Take your time. Think it over, bearing in mind what future benefits it could reap for you. Your honest Tommy Atkins won't miss out on much, I promise you—blankets never reach him out in the trenches anyway, and precious few cigarettes.'

Gregg stared at the mud-caked floor of

the cab. 'I couldn't let down my fellow men, Mr Colville. I've fought for the underdog all my life and I'm not going to stand by and see him cheated now.'

Colville threw back his head and laughed. 'You're an idealist, Gregg, living in a fool's paradise. I've heard your speeches—and splendid speeches they were too—but it's all ideaology, man, a perfectionist's dream. Can't you see that? That isn't the way the world turns.'

Gregg muttered at the floor. 'I spoke for the masses, who could not speak for themselves. They believed in the same principles as I did—one for all and all for one. They believe in it still, and I won't betray them.'

Colville's young face reddened with anger. 'You really swallow that, don't you? And yet where was your precious fellow man when you needed his vote to get you back into the House? A fat lot they cared about you then. They turned their backs on you—the common man had no more time for you than the society women you bedded. They all betrayed you.'

Gregg glared at him. 'You have no right to speak to me like that, officer or not.'

'Because you don't want to hear it. But it's the truth I'm saying, and you know it. Where were they all when you needed them? Where was Trixie Anstruther? Where was Robert Hardcastle?'

'Robert? You know him?'

Colville gave a dry laugh. 'I knew him well once, in my schooldays, the prissy little nancy boy. I tell you, if I'd kept the letters I had from him... But still, as I was saying, where was he when you needed his help? Oh, yes, he told me all about it. But above all, where was your precious Tommy Atkins? You've got it all wrong, Gregg. You're too much of an idealist to see what's in front of your nose. It's the men who think and act for themselves who get ahead, the entrepreneurs of the world. It's dog eat dog in this life, each man for himself. I've had to learn that the hard way, and so will you, in time. Stop wearing your conscience on your sleeve, man, and do yourself a favour for a change.'

Gregg turned away to stare out into the night, unwilling to hear. For a few moments there was silence, then Colville put on his cap, stubbed out his cigarette and reached for the door handle.

'Well, as I said, think about it. There's no need to answer now. The mayor down in the town is expecting a consignment on Thursday night. I need a driver, a man I can trust. If it's not you, then that's your loss for I can easily find someone else. But I know I can trust you. Think about it.'

He opened the lorry door, swung out

his legs and dropped down into the mud. Gregg's mind was in a turmoil. He parked the lorry and headed back through the driving rain to the billet.

The lads sharing his billet were grouped around the warmth of the wood stove, smoking and laughing at some joke. He made towards his own bed at the far end of the hut and threw off his coat. More than anything, he wanted a mug of hot cocoa and a quiet smoke and then sleep. He opened the door of his cupboard and took out pipe, matches and tobacco tin, then sat on the edge of his bed. He was savouring the thought of rubbing the tobacco, filling his pipe and taking those first, luxuriating breaths....

He looked down into the tin in amazement. It was empty, and yet he knew it had been full that morning. He stared at the tin for a moment and then let his gaze travel down the length of the hut to the group around the stove. The laughter stopped, and one by one they began laying aside their pipes.

Hoarsely Gregg found his voice. 'My tobacco tin—it's empty,' he said. 'Any of you know anything about it?'

He could feel the unease in the air. They began shuffling towards their beds.

'Not me, mate.'

'Didn't know as you had any.'

'But someone must know,' he protested. 'I know I left it full this morning.'

'Get 'em to pass a Bill about it in the House,' one of the men grunted, and their laughter gave Gregg a chill feeling. They were lying, he knew, and he felt hurt. They were closing their ranks against him, making him feel the outsider. Anger rose in him.

'Now come on, stop fooling about,' he said fiercely. 'One of you must have taken it, and I want it back. Now.'

They all stared at him, but no one spoke as they continued to undress. There was nothing he could do in the face of their silence conspiracy. 'Lights out' sounded and the room plunged into darkness.

For long seconds he fumed in the dark, and then a quiet voice spoke.

'Share and share alike, that's what you've always preached, isn't it? Well, someone done it for you.'

It was the next morning that Gregg discovered that the silver smoker's knife given to him by the Countess in celebration of his election win, all those years ago, was missing.

On Thursday night a heavily laden lorry pulled away from the camp down the rutted lane towards the nearby town. Fitful shafts of moonlight breaking through the clouds illuminated the set features of Private

Vincent Gregg at the steering wheel.

Young men and bicycles sprawled on the grass outside the Clarion cycling club hut. Hal sat, arms hugging his knees, listening to Arthur. The sun was beginning to sink behind the corrugated iron roof and it was growing chilly in the lengthening shadows. Arthur was pacing up and down, his dark features set in a frown, running his thin fingers through windblown hair.

'Like I were saying, they came yesterday, my calling-up papers, and I tell you this, I'm not going.'

'Aye, so you've always said in the past, Arthur, but now it's happened, what can you do, other than appeal?' one of the lads remarked.

Arthur turned on him angrily. 'Do? I'll tell you what I'll do—I'll burn my calling-up papers, that's what I'll do.'

'Nay, you can't do that. They'll have you for that.'

Hal had never seen Arthur's face look so venomous. 'I bloody well will and all—and what's more, I'll do it where everyone can see me. I'll do it on the steps of the town hall. Aye, I will—tomorrow morning, when folks is on their way to market. That's what I'll do, and you can come and watch.'

Stunned silence met his words, and Hal could only feel an uneasy sense of admiration. Arthur was a marvel, never sacrificing his principles even if his own safety was at stake. He could do no less than support such courage.

'Nay, we'll be at work,' someone protested.

'But I'll be with you,' Hal interposed, and was gratified to see Arthur's fleeting smile.

'Right. Here comes Cedric up the hill now—we can get the bikes put away.'

The last straggler of the day's outing grunted to a halt and jumped off his machine. 'Bloody steep hill that,' he panted. 'Sorry I were late. Have I missed owt?'

'Nowt as matters,' snapped Arthur, then turning to Hal he added, 'Ten o'clock, then, outside the town hall. And bring some lucifers, lad, just in case mine get wet.'

'He never did!' exclaimed Emma, looking up from the blanket square she was knitting for the troops. 'Well, I never! Who'd have thought that of a friend of yours, Harold? I hope as how you'll not do the same with yours when they come.'

'They've come,' replied Hal quietly. 'They came in the post this morning.'

Eddie looked up from the book he was reading. 'What's come, Hal?'

221

'My calling-up papers.'

Eddie laid the book aside. 'Have they? Are you to go off in the Army now, then?'

Hal eyed his brother solemnly. 'You know my feelings about that, Eddie. No, I'll not.'

Emma looked concerned. 'But your father....'

'He's signed lots of forms for them as don't want to go,' Eddie cut in. 'I know, because I've brought them home from the mill for him before now.'

'That's right,' murmured Emma. 'Them as wants to appeal as conscientious objectors, that is. They need a magistrate's signature on the paper.'

She looked up at Hal. He shook his head.

'Nay, I'll not ask him to sign mine.'

Emma sighed with relief. 'Happen that would be as well. It could be very embarrassing for James, his son being a CO. I'm glad you're mindful of your duty, Harold.'

Hal sank wearily into a chair. 'I'm afraid I'm not making myself clear. I shall register as a CO but I'll get someone else to sign my papers. I just want to avoid any argument with Father.'

Eddie frowned. 'Why, Hal? I mean, why won't you go? I'd give anything to have the chance to be a soldier, go abroad and all.'

'No you wouldn't. You'd hate bloodshed too. You cried when your pet mouse died after that cat got it.'

'But there's times you have to kill, Hal. You'd kill a man if you saw him shooting Father, wouldn't you?'

Hal got up irritably. 'Oh, shut up, Eddie. Someone's been mouthing the same old argument and you repeat it without even thinking. Well, I've thought and better thought, and I know what I believe. Nothing on earth will shift me. I've made up my mind to go to the tribunal.'

His voice was snappish and cold and Eddie was anxious to restore peace. 'What's tribunal, Hal?' he asked equably.

Hal perched on the edge of the table. 'It's a sort of court, but not with a judge or magistrate. There's the mayor, I think, and an army officer and the vicar and one or two more. If you think you have good reason not to go in the Army they listen to what you have to say, and then decide.'

'And you'll tell them you don't believe in killing?'

'Yes.' Hal's answer was low but there was no mistaking the firmness in his tone.

Emma sighed. 'You know your father has just decided to join them reservists, the Hawksmoor Volunteers, don't you?' she said quietly.

'I know. He must act according to his conscience too.'

For a few moments there was silence in the little parlour but for the slow ticking of the clock over the draped mantelshelf, then Emma laid aside her knitting and rose stiffly.

'Come on, shift yourself, Hal, so I can lay the table before your father gets back. Eddie, go down the cellar and fetch me that jelly off the stone slab, there's a good lad.'

As Eddie pulled back the chenille curtain covering the cellar door he heard Emma's troubled voice. 'Eh, Harold, I hope as how you know what you're doing. It'll not be easy for us all, for your father especially, if it gets known as you're a conshie. It'll not be pleasant at all.'

'One step at a time, Stepmother. I've not been registered yet.'

The stone-flagged cellar struck chill into the bones after the warmth of the living room, and Eddie shivered. He had hated cellars ever since that time Denton had taken him down into the crypt of that mission chapel and told him that bodies were buried there. He avoided looking down at Emma's well-scrubbed flagstones, just in case.

He picked up the white earthenware dish lying on the stone table and looked at the crimson smoothness of the jelly. It was like red wine in a chalice, or blood....

Blood. War. He thought of wounded men stretched on operating tables, and shivered again. He must fight off such feelings of cowardice, for if the war lasted long enough he too might be called upon to do his bit. And it might still be on in two years' time, when he was eighteen—after all, it had lasted two years already.

But he wasn't alone in his apprehension. For the first time he realised that Hal was no hero either. All these years he had revered his brother as his idol, and now....

A voice from above startled him. 'Eddie! What you doing with that jelly? I shall know if you've had your fingers in it.'

He picked up the dish and started towards the stairs, but for no reason he could think of the prospect of jelly for tea followed by a walk in the recreation ground with Sally Parkinson held no excitement. His heart felt heavy.

Arthur was waiting for Harold outside the Labour Party rooms.

'Well? How did your tribunal go, Hal?' Hal shook his head. 'No good. I've got to go in. Deferred till the end of the month. How did you get on?'

'Same. But listen, I've found someone as can alter the deferment paper—change the date on it, no trouble at all. Real clever it is, no one can tell the difference.'

Hal stared at him. 'Change them? Where?'

'In Lancashire—not far—we can ride over on Sunday. It's two sisters I've heard of. Couldn't be easier.'

'But if they do, can't they tell—the authorities, I mean?'

Arthur shrugged. 'They've got the same kind of ink, seemingly, and they can wipe it out somehow and put another date in later. We could go on like that indefinitely.'

Hal felt uneasy, but in the light of Arthur's further persuasive arguments that evening, it seemed a reasonable risk to take, especially in view of authority's obduracy. Any course was justified when capitalism and militarism tried to make a humane man forget his humanity.

THIRTEEN

On Sunday mornings James Stott Pearson felt proud to be seen sitting with his family around him in the same old pew they always occupied, but this sunny Sunday morning it was different. He was only too well aware of the eyes fixed upon them as he ushered Emma into the pew and Harold and Edward followed.

He could see bonneted heads bending to murmur into neighbours' ears, knowing their words were masked by the muted, majestic swell of the organ. He could see the embarrassed looks as their eyes caught his and the quick way they looked away. And all the time Harold seemed blissfully unaware that he was the cause of all the stir. James sighed.

Edward was fidgeting with his cap. James murmured to Emma.

'Ask Edward what's up, and tell him to sit still.'

She inclined her head towards the boy, exchanged some words, reached into her bag, then slipped him something.

'Forgot his threepenny bit, that's all. I've lent him one.'

James frowned. Manhood and the responsibility of going out to work did not seem to be making the lad as reliable as he ought to be. He did his work well enough, by all accounts, but his mind seemed to be elsewhere half the time. Maybe he too was feeling the pinch of having a brother who was known throughout the village as a conshie. Maybe he was getting taunted at work about it, too. James himself was—indirectly, to be sure—but the taunting hurt, none the less.

Emma gave him a nudge and he saw her eyes indicate the front pew. He followed her gaze. Old man Sykes, top-hatted and carrying his silver-headed cane, was heaving himself to his feet and turning to face the congregation, just as he did every Sunday. James watched as the old man's gaze travelled over the pews, taking careful note.

'What are you looking for?' enquired Alderman Lawson as Sykes lowered himself again with difficulty.

'Just checking on my foremen,' grunted Sykes. 'They know as I expect 'em all to be at Sunday morning service. Sets a good example to the rest.'

'I see. And what if they choose to lie in?'

'Then they've me to answer to when

they get to the factory tomorrow morning, that's what. I can't afford to have idle devils bossing my men. They know.'

'Are they all here then?'

Sykes snorted. 'Aye, they're all here, but there's one as I wish wasn't. Pity, as he's one of the best. You know him, and all.'

'Who's that then?'

'Councillor Pearson. His lad's a conshie.'

'Oh, my God! Such a splendid fellow too, even if he doesn't always vote our way. Poor devil—what a slur.'

'It's monstrous, if you ask me! He ought to make that lad see sense—it's his duty to fight for his country. Teaching is all very well, but it's not getting down to it.'

'My sentiments precisely. Downright cowardice.'

Sykes eyed the alderman from under bushy eyebrows. 'You got sons, Lawson?'

'Ah, no. Three daughters.'

Further conversation was cut short by the arrival of the vicar and a crescendo of organ music as the congregation rose.

By the end of morning service Eddie had spotted what he sought—a glimpse of Sally Parkinson's pale blue bonnet on the far side of her portly father and the pink flush of her pretty face beneath. His heart leapt and the discomforts of a too-tight collar and the choking smell of camphor from someone's hoarded Sunday-best suit were forgotten.

She was here! Now, with luck and if he could elude his family, he could snatch a word with her, maybe even arrange to see her later. A walk with her, alone, would make his weekend complete. He could face anything tomorrow at work, jeers and insults and all, if only he could share a moment of heaven with her.

As the service ended and people began to file out, he let Father, Hal and Emma precede him. Outside in the sunlight Father did not, as he usually did, linger to talk with acquaintances, but made straight for the lychgate. No one greeted him. Eddie could see curious glances as the family trooped down the gravel path. He paused and bent to adjust his shoelace.

He was still fiddling with it when the Parkinsons came by. Sally dropped back behind the others.

'Wilt meet me in the rec at seven?' He coloured deeply, certain his whisper must have been heard by the whole congregation.

Sally blushed, and walked on by. 'Aye, I will.'

At least he didn't have to make excuses for going out these days. In any event, after tea the family all seemed too preoccupied with their own affairs to question him.

Sally never looked prettier than when she joined him outside the shelter, rosy and smiling, just as the clock tower struck quarter past.

'Sorry I'm late, love,' she panted. 'I had to patch me father's work trousers ready for morning. Still damp they were too—they take ages to dry after me mam's washed 'em, they're that thick.'

'Never mind—you're here. Where'd you like to walk this evening?'

It didn't matter to him where they went. It was enough that Sally was at his side, chatting happily to him or listening intently. She was the only one who listened to him as if his views were worth hearing, and he loved her for it. His supreme moment of happiness came when he walked her home to the corner of her lane.

She looked up at him shyly. 'That were nice, Eddie. I do enjoy your company, I really do. You can kiss me goodnight if you like—here.'

She indicated her cheek, and with thumping heart Eddie bent and kissed it. Its softness and the sweet smell of her skin delighted his senses, and he felt his knees shaking.

'You got lovely skin,' he muttered. 'Soft, like the kitten I wanted to keep once, but I couldn't have it.'

'Why ever not?'

He shrugged, trying to brace his trembling knees. 'Oh, Mrs Iredale said we couldn't have a cat. Its hairs would stick on her plush cushion covers, she said, and me dad wouldn't like that. I had to give the kitten back.'

'Shame,' murmured Sally. 'You ought to have a pet to love.'

'I had a spider once. I used to talk to it.'

She didn't seem impressed. 'I'm sure you could find a more cuddly creature to stroke, Eddie, if you really tried, that is.'

His breath caught in his throat. Did he understand her correctly? She was smiling up at him shyly from under her lashes.

'I mun go in, for it's getting late. Kiss me goodnight again, Eddie.'

She held up her face again. As he bent to her cheek she turned her lips to meet his and his brain spun. Her lips were warm and tender. Joy rippled through him, and then a sense of triumph. He seized her about the waist and swung her around, delighting in the sensation of how small and light she was and then suddenly, with a giggle and a wave, she was gone.

As Eddie walked home to Hollin Row there was a spring in his step and joy in his heart. He felt himself a man, strong and superior. He wanted to protect and cosset her, live for her and through her, for ever. A new determination entered his soul, steel-like and invincible; he was going to study and learn like a man possessed, earn the qualifications to make him a fully skilled engineer so that then he would earn the fortune that would enable him to give Sally a life of luxury. Life now had a purpose.

He was still toying with this new glory in his life late that night in his room. Hal still hadn't come home. Clarion cycle runs seemed to be getting longer than ever these days, but Eddie was glad of the privacy to think about Sally. Emma Iredale's voice drifted up the stairs.

'Is Harold back yet, Edward? I've not heard him come in.'

'No, he's not.'

'You still burning the gas? Time you put the light out, Edward. We're not made of brass.'

Dutifully he turned off the gas, watching instead the flickering shadows on the wall cast by the candle he had lit as he always did, usually to read or review his postcard album. He rolled over on the bed and watched the candle's flame, and a thought struck him. A bonfire, yes, a bonfire of all his childhood things, that was what he would have. A symbolic fire, burning his childhood and welcoming his newfound manhood. The idea appealed to him. He could get rid of all those comic papers he had hung on to only because the Iredale woman disliked them, and that wretched cigarette card collection she'd given him because some relative of hers was throwing it out, and the odd theatre programmes of plays he'd never seen—they could all add to the blaze.

All, that was, except those items other people might consider to be rubbish but which to him were treasures he would never surrender to anyone, not even to Sally Parkinson. Like a broken-toothed comb, a double-headed halfpenny, a pencilled note now barely legible and three bent hairpins. They all lay in the biscuit tin decorated with emblems for the dead Queen's Golden Jubilee, the tin he kept tucked away in the back of his cupboard because it too, like its contents, was one of his few remaining mementoes of Mother.

Lilian put the thermometer back in the jar and looked across the high hospital bed to the ashen-faced nun sitting, hands clasped, beside the patient.

'His fever's cooling now, Soeur Marie. I'd get some sleep, if I were you, before the next lot come in.'

The little Sister of Charity sighed. 'With God's grace and your patient care, Sister

Lilian, he'll live after all, then. I am so glad. I hate to see a boy die so young. He can be no more than eighteen.'

She bent her head in prayer just as she had been doing throughout the whole of the previous night, then made the sign of the Cross and moved away to the next bed. Lilian fought to ignore the waves of fatigue which threatened to engulf her and walked briskly across the stone-flagged cloister to the little chapel that served as the office. Her patients were for the most part still unconscious from anaesthetic after the surgeon's valiant efforts. Time now to catch up with some of the essential paperwork.

Sister Edna bustled into the office. 'Hear the gunfire?' she asked. 'One of the ambulance drivers says there's a terrific bombardment going on at the Front and we can expect a load coming in tonight for sure. Field stations have a lot in already—they're going down like ninepins on both sides.'

Lilian groaned. 'Oh, God, when will the carnage stop, Edna? Folks at home have no idea of how hideous it all is out here. It breaks your heart to see these lads.'

Edna nodded, reaching across her for more iodine from the cupboard. 'Beats me how they put up with it. It's not just the wounds, though God knows they're bad enough, but all these boys brought in crippled with rheumatism as well. They'll never walk again, some of them.'

Dipping pen in ink, Lilian wrote name after name in a neat list, imagining, as she always did, how those mothers would feel when the War Office published their sons' names among the wounded. Relief, perhaps, that at least they were alive and not among the list of valiant dead. The roll of honour now was grown so large that one began to question....

'By the way,' Edna reminded her as she was about to go out, 'don't forget we've got that officer coming up from Chantilly this afternoon, about those extra beds you requisitioned.'

Lilian glanced at her fob watch. 'I'd almost forgotten. God, I'm tired. Make us a cup of tea, will you, Edna? With luck we've just got time.'

It was mid-afternoon when the officer finally arrived, accompanied by a thick-set sergeant twice his age, for the lieutenant looked no more than twenty or so. Lilian could feel no surprise, for the war seemed to throw up boys in the most unexpected positions of authority. She held out a hand in greeting, but the young man ignored it and saluted.

'Lieutenant Hardcastle, ma'am, at your service,' he said gruffly. The sergeant stood at ease, hands behind his back, his gaze lifted towards the vaulted ceiling.

'You came about the beds, I believe,' Lilian said crisply. 'I need six more, and just as soon as you can get them here. No time to lose.'

He reddened and looked startled. 'I don't think you understand,' he said uncertainly, 'it's not quite as easy as that.'

'Easy?' Lilian retorted. 'What do you mean—easy? I have dozens of wounded men out there, and as many more likely to arrive at any moment—do you think it's easy for them? I might get fifty more tonight, and I ask for only six beds.'

'To put where?' His young voice was terse. 'You say your wards are full already.'

'Some of my patients will be leaving tomorrow, but I still need more beds. I'll put them between the others if need be, but for heaven's sake get them to me, Lieutenant.'

He consulted the list in his hand. 'According to my records, you have been supplied with ten beds already since the beginning of the month, Sister—'

'And may need as many again before the end if this slaughter goes on,' Lilian cut in. She could feel her patience beginning to fray at the young man's intransigence.

'How do you allocate your major wards, Sister?'

She tried hard to keep her tone equable. 'One for amputations and shrapnel wounds, one for rheumatism.'

His young eyebrows arched in surprise. 'Rheumatism? You can't be serious, Sister? Do you mean to tell me there are men in bed, pulled out of the battle on grounds of rheumatism? I find that hard to believe. How can you be sure they're not just malingerers?'

Lilian exploded. 'Malingerers? Those men in there—have you seen them? Crippled by months of standing knee-deep in water in the trenches, never on dry land by day or night for weeks on end? My God, Lieutenant, have you no idea what it can do to a man?'

She thought she detected a flicker of a smile about the sergeant's lips, but the officer merely shrugged.

'I've seen my father racked by it for a day or two in the winter, but he soon gets over it. Lots of people suffer from it in Yorkshire, where I come from, but it's not a killer, Sister. Not like wounds from mortars and shells.'

Her eyes narrowed. 'Isn't it? I wonder how long it is since you left Yorkshire. I tell you this, Lieutenant, I come from Yorkshire too, and I've never in all my born days seen the kind of agony these men go through. I wonder, if you could suffer for a day the pain that they do, would you still say they were malingerers? I doubt it, Lieutenant. Your experience of battle conditions is very limited yet, I fear.'

The sergeant's face was contorted in an effort not to laugh out loud. The young officer looked uneasy and changed the subject.

'What part of Yorkshire do you come from, may I ask?'

'Halifax. And you?'

'Hawksmoor. Not far away.'

Lilian stiffened. She was damned if she was going to let this cocky creature establish common ground with her. 'Hawksmoor, eh?' She could not help the sneer. 'Then I can tell you for certain, Lieutenant, that you do not know rheumatism like your men from the Yorkshire regiments do. Ask them about rheumatism, those of them lying out there in the ward. Malingerers, indeed!'

Confusion showed on his ruddy face. 'I didn't mean to underestimate their pain, Sister, for I have experienced pain for myself. Why, I remember being thrown from my pony once, right into the middle of a thorn bush. Jolly painful that was, I can tell you, lacerated from head to foot, I was. The scars were with me for months after.'

Lilian could see her own feeling of scorn

reflected in the sergeant's eyes. 'Really, Lieutenant,' she remarked, and it gave her pleasure to see his discomfiture. 'Then I'm sure I can rely on you to see we get our beds as quickly as possible. We'll put them in sheds if need be, for we have already made use of *baraques* on occasion when we've been overcrowded. You will see to it, won't you?'

There was a distant boom of gunfire, and Sister Edna hurried into the office. 'Soeur Marie wants you,' she said sharply. 'The first ambulance has just arrived with tonight's wounded, and a sorry mess they are, too. Several more are following.'

'Right, I'm coming.' As Lilian hurried out after her the lieutenant rose to his feet.

'Come along, Sergeant, get a move on,' he snapped. 'Back to base camp at the double. Supplies department will be going to the dogs without us to keep an eye on things.'

Along the length of the cloisters a line of stretchers lay on the flagged floor, bearing blood-soaked bodies writhing and moaning in pain. The boom of guns echoed along the corridors, and outside tyres crunched on gravel, heralding the arrival of yet more ambulances. Lilian was bending over a corporal with half his arm shot away when Lieutenant Hardcastle and the sergeant passed her on their way to the abbey entrance, but she did not see the young officer avert his gaze and reach into the pocket of his uniform jacket for a handkerchief.

At the pillared entrance the sergeant eyed him with curiosity. 'First sight of action, sir?' he queried. 'Turned you up a bit, has it?' From the nearest ambulance uniformed orderlies were already unloading a makeshift stretcher on which a soldier lay immobile, clutching in his hands a mound of his own entrails.

'Get the car started and let's get out of here,' Hardcastle stammered, but the sergeant was ready to catch him as he stumbled and fell, retching, against the marble pillar.

'Have you not had no white feathers sent to you then? Nor no poison pen letters about your lad being a conshie? No sarky comments nor nowt?'

Mrs Charnock's crumpled features registered disappointment as she poured tea for her neighbour. Emma Pearson sat upright, clutching her purse in her hand.

'No, nothing like that. Folks hereabouts wouldn't be so cruel,' she said tartly, but Mrs Charnock had not given up yet.

'Oh, I don't know. That Mrs Gardiner's had no peace since her lad vanished so's they wouldn't get him. Nasty letters like what I've never seen before. I didn't think folks would use words like that, but they do when their blood's up, seemingly. They hate conshies, they do, and they'll let 'em know it.'

'They're called conscientious objectors, Mrs Charnock, and they have a legal right to do it, you know.'

'When other lads are fighting and dying? You try telling their mothers that. I hear as conshies get the sack for it and all.'

'So you've heard,' Emma remarked drily.

'About your Hal losing his teaching job, you mean? Well, I did hear a rumour....'

'And no doubt passed it on.'

Mrs Charnock bridled. 'What do you mean, Mrs Pearson? I told no lies, I'll have you know. I'm not one to spread untruths.'

'But you find pleasure in talking about others' misfortunes. In future I'll thank you to talk about your own affairs and leave my family out of it.' Emma dipped into her purse and withdrew a coin. 'Here's the sixpence I owed you. Good day to you, Mrs Charnock.'

The older woman followed her to the door. 'You've not finished your cup of tea,' she muttered. Emma made no answer, and as she walked back up the yard to her own door Mrs Charnock leaned out to call after her.

'Your family, is it? One you married into, think on, when you lost your own. James Pearson was too good a catch for you to miss.'

The sound of a slamming door was Emma's only reply. Later that night in the privacy of their bedroom she recounted the incident to her husband.

'I didn't tell her, James. It would have been all round the village by morning if she knew Harold was missing. But she's bound to find out sooner or later.'

James sighed as he climbed into bed beside her. 'Best let matters take their own course, love,' he advised. 'There's nothing we can do about it. But in the meantime, do as you've done—say nothing, and let Harold work things out his way.'

He did not expand on the subject, but she knew what he was thinking. Harold was best out of the way so that they need neither explain nor apologise for his actions. Nor, if they remained in ignorance of his whereabouts, could they betray him. His deferment had run out and the authorities were looking for him.

James was breathing deeply as if almost asleep. Suddenly he spoke. 'By the way, Emma, I forgot to tell you. They're sending a deputation out to France to see what conditions are really like. A couple of the millowners, a barrister, the mayor and that, and they've asked if I would like to join them.'

'To go to France? But why you, James? And won't it be very dangerous?'

'They won't let us go too near where the action is, don't worry. The union asked me to represent them. It's an honour, don't you see? To show their respect.'

'Very nice, dear.' It was an inadequate reply and she knew it, but how could she voice the thought she knew was already in his mind? James did not need it to be pointed out to him that there was a strange irony in his being selected for honour for his lifelong work for the union at the very time that his firstborn son was on the run like any common criminal.

FOURTEEN

Eddie emerged from the dusty machine shop into the sunlit yard of the mill, unfastening his snap tin as he went. He seated himself on the stone wall as he always did on fine days, to watch the world go by while he ate his dinnertime sandwiches of potted meat or cheese. Today Emma Iredale had packed him one of her tasty Cornish pasties as a treat.

Other apprentices and mill girls came to sit on the wall, laughing and teasing as they unwrapped their sandwiches. Sally was not amongst them, but soon he saw her close friend Mavis emerge from the weaving shed, pulling off her cap and shaking her hair free in the sunlight. He scrambled up to go across to her.

'Isn't Sally with thee?'

'Nay. She said I were to tell thee as Mr Henshaw sent her into Hawksmoor to fetch more paper for the office. She hoped as she'd be back before dinner hour were up.'

Disappointed, he sat down again and continued to munch the pasty. Maybe he should feel unhappy, he thought, what with

Hal being gone from home for so long and no word from him, but how could he be unhappy after last night?

In his mind's eye he could still see clearly the pale oval of Sally's face in the moonlight and hear her gentle voice.

'I'm right fond of thee, Eddie Pearson. Tha'rt a grand lad.'

Oh, Sally, my little love, he thought, if you only knew how my heart sang when I heard those words! Everything else in the world had been driven from his mind since she had taken over his life.

'Are we—are we going steady, like?' he had asked hesitantly. Her lovely smile was answer enough before she spoke.

'Aye, we are, lad. We're walking out, thee and me, Eddie Pearson. We're going steady, aren't we?'

A knot of apprentices from his shop were sitting on the wall nearby, whistling at the girls as they passed and roaring with delight when one of them glanced back and gave them a saucy smile.

'Eeeh, tha'rt a little cracker,' shouted one.

'I'd like to meet thee at back of the loading bay of a dark night,' shouted another.

The tallest of the group glanced across at Eddie and jerked his head in the direction of the girl. 'Not a bad armful, is that one, eh? I wouldn't mind getting a leg across that, would you?'

Eddie ignored him. The lad inched up closer. 'Dost hear me? Or haven't you had a girl yet, is that it?'

Eddie still held his tongue. Their talk sickened him, the same raucous, suggestive comments day after day. And truth to tell, he didn't understand some of what they said.

Another of the apprentices joined the tall one. 'Who, Pearson? He's never had his leg over nowt, him. He doesn't know what it's all about, dost tha, lad?'

'Nay, come off it,' said the first, 'he's been going out with that mate of Mavis's, that bonny little lass from the weaving shed for weeks—tha doesn't mean to tell me he's not had a go at her? I know I would have done, long afore now, her with a backside like that and all.'

Eddie felt the colour flooding his cheeks. 'Shut up!' he snapped. 'Don't talk filthy, and especially about a lass like Sally Parkinson. I'll not have it.'

The apprentices hooted with laughter, and the tall one flicked breadcrumbs off his overalls. 'I reckon as tha's a bit put out, Pearson, because tha's not had it,' he drawled. 'Well, if she won't, there's plenty more as will, isn't there, lads? See that dark one over there, the one with the ringlets?'

His tow-haired sidekick glanced across the millyard, grinning, then his grin was suddenly replaced with a disbelieving look. 'Mavis Butterworth, dost mean? Nay, surely not. She's been walking out with George Parkinson for a year or more. Going steady, they are.'

The factory hooter sounded the end of the dinner break and the tall youth stood up languidly. 'That's as may be,' he said, shoving the remains of his meal into his overall pocket, 'but what I tell you I know for a fact.'

Eddie could see the way the younger lad looked up with admiration in his eyes, and he and the leader fell into step side by side as they headed back towards the machine shop. He knew what they intended, but they could not hurt him. They could not make him feel a novice in the ways of the world nor spoil Sally's purity for all their suggestive crudeness and leering hints. He could feel only scorn and a protective anger that they should touch Sally's dear name with their filthy tongues.

He would marry her one day, he knew it as surely as if they had already declared and sealed their love. He was certain of it, and he knew Sally was too. With her gentleness, her warmth and sincerity she delighted his soul.

By six o'clock, when the hooter signalled

the end of the day's work, rain was pouring down in a relentless stream. She was waiting for him at the factory gate as she always did, her pretty face lighting up at the sight of him. Even in her drab old working dress and clogs and that threadbare shawl hugged tightly about her head she was still the loveliest creature he had ever seen. Even with rain slashing at the cobblestones and dribbling down the back of his neck his whole world still glowed with a golden radiance. There was magic in just being near her.

And more than that. She roused in him sensations he had never known before. His whole being surged with tenderness and love at the sight of her, but her nearness caused a fire in his belly which sometimes frightened him in its intensity. He longed to be able to tell her of this new world she was opening up to him, but the words would not come.

They walked along the length of Acre Street together, side by side but not daring to touch hands. Dozens of pairs of clogged feet clattered alongside them, homewards towards tea and family. Neither of them spoke until they reached the corner. She looked up at him, earnestness in her clear blue eyes.

'I'm off to the Band of Hope tonight. Art coming?'

An hour together in the dark bandroom with only a flickering lantern to betray them. 'Course I will. Meet you outside the door.'

Emma Iredale was bending over the range dropping dumplings into the beef stew as he came into the living room.

'Is your father with you?'

'No. I've not seen him.'

She sighed and straightened up, wiping the flour from her hands on to her apron. 'I wish he'd hurry. Harold's back.'

'Hal is? Where is he? Is he all right?'

She nodded, but the corners of her lips were tight. 'He's fine. He's up in the bedroom. But no one's to know he's here. Think on, Eddie—we could be in serious trouble if anyone found out.'

'I'll not tell. I must go up and see him.'

'Aye, well get them muddy boots off first.'

Tossing his jacket on the hook at the back of the door and his boots on the scullery floor, Eddie ran upstairs, two at a time, to the attic. Hal was sitting gloomily on the edge of his bed, still wearing a damp jacket and boots. He looked pale and pinched.

'Hal! It's grand to see you! Are you well? You look a bit tired.'

He sat on the further bed opposite Hal

250

and searched his face anxiously. The light seemed to have gone out in his eyes.

'I'm well enough. Listen, Eddie, I had to come back. I didn't really want to, knowing how Stepmother frets that someone will tell. But I've got to get a message to Arthur. It's important, Eddie, and I knew I could trust you.'

'Me?' Eddie felt bewildered. He hardly knew any of them, these friends of Hal's, and he didn't much care for the look of Arthur. But if Hal needed his help....

'I've written a note. If you can get it to him, either at the Labour rooms, though that's risky, or to his house—the police aren't after him at the moment, they won't be watching.'

He held out a folded sheet of paper. Eddie took it hesitantly. 'It's all right,' said Hal. 'It's nothing illegal. It's only to tell him that Frank Duckworth needs to get home—his mother's ill, so he's been told, and there's no one there to see to her. He's worried sick, stuck where we are up on the moors.'

Eddie tucked the note in his pocket. 'I'll see he gets it—I know where he lives, down Chapel Hill.'

'And don't tell anyone, specially not Father or Stepmother. She thinks I've come back for more clothes. Soon as it's dark I'll be on my way.'

'Whereabouts are you staying, Hal?'

His brother shrugged. 'It's never the same place two nights together—we can't afford to stay in one place too long. Folks take a dreadful risk letting us stay. We've got to keep moving on.'

'But how do you know where to go? How many is there?'

'There's me, and Frank, and Percy Booth and a couple more you don't know. We know the safe houses, as we call them, people who sympathise with us. And there's signals to tell us when it's safe. Police are everywhere, asking questions.'

'Then how do you know when it's safe, Hal?'

'Like I said, signals. You know how everybody has Union Jack flags up nowadays? Well, they lower the flag to half mast if police are about. That sort of thing. Last night, for instance—we had to sleep in a shepherd's hut on the moors in the end. Damn cold it was too, I can tell you.'

'Where was that then?'

Hal rose slowly from the bed and went to the window. From this vantage point he could see the copper dome of Sykes' clock tower, now turning green with verdigris. 'Nay, I'll not tell you that, lad,' he murmured. 'The less you know, the safer it is for everyone....'

Eddie jumped up and came to stand

beside him. 'Don't worry, Hal, I'll see that Arthur gets the message safely—I promise.'

His brother turned and looked down at him. 'You know, Eddie, I sometimes wonder,' he said absently.

'Wonder what, Hal?'

'Whether it's all worth it, all this running and hiding and secrecy. Our money's running out, too. I don't like it. The others found it fun, at first anyway, dodging the police and keeping one step ahead of them, but with me it was a matter of principle. But now, well, look where it's got me. If it wasn't for the cause needing us to distribute the pamphlets and continue the struggle....'

There was such sadness in his eyes that Eddie felt a lunge of pity for him. It must be terrible to have lost such a good future as a teacher, and equally terrible to know that you had brought humiliation to your parents—they could no longer hold up their heads in the village. But still, if a man was doing what he really believed in....

Hal picked up his cycle clips from the bed. 'It's beginning to get dark,' he muttered. 'I'll have some of that hot stew Stepmother promised and then I'll be on my way.'

He strode off down the stairs, lifting his head to sniff the aroma of succulent meat.

Eddie could see a damp patch on the bed where Hal had been sitting. By the time he followed his brother downstairs he had already forgotten about the note for Arthur and was feeling the familiar sensation of excitement he always experienced when he was going out to meet Sally.

Arthur found the note on his doormat and wasted no time. As soon as night fell he hurried round to the Duckworths' little back-to-back cottage in Primrose Street.

'Have no fear, Mrs Duckworth,' he assured the sick old woman, 'I'll see as your Frank gets safely home soon as ever I can.'

The message from Arthur was waiting at the next safe house when Hal, Percy and Frank rode up there on a windy night: *Harold Pearson will accompany Frank into Hawksmoor and keep an eye on him. I'll be in Liverpool until Friday. Keep the flag flying.*

'What's he doing in Liverpool?' asked Frank.

'Didn't he tell thee? He's joined the Seamen's Union,' replied Percy.

'Oh,' said Frank, then added after a long pause, 'Whatever for?'

Percy took a deep sigh. 'Tha weren't listening when he told us. He's fixing for some of us to get on board ships going to

America, that's what.'

'Oh aye, I remember now.' There was another pause. 'I don't want to go to America. I want to stay here, where I were born and raised.'

'Aye, I know. So do we all, Frank, but if it's that or go to jail, which wouldst rather do then?'

Frank studied the floor and made no answer. All the lads were fed up, he knew, but for him the whole business of objection had lost its meaning. All he knew was that Mother was sick, and more than anything in the world he wanted to be left in peace to care for her.

'It's all right, Frank,' Hal murmured reassuringly, 'I'll get you home tonight, I promise.'

Clouds were drifting across the face of the moon as Vincent Gregg stood by the perimeter fence waiting for Lieutenant Colville. He could smell the young officer's approach before he actually appeared, the scent of a Passing Cloud hovering in the air.

'Evening, Gregg,' said Colville. 'Care for a cigarette?'

Gregg took it without a word. He had learnt the system now. It was for the officer to command, for him to obey. After all, he was doing quiet well out of it....

Colville inhaled deeply, blowing out a cloud of smoke with evident appreciation. 'Not tonight, I think,' he said at last. 'Moonlight is a damned nuisance.'

'Yes, sir.'

For a time they stood in silence, and Gregg found pleasure in the camaraderie they shared. For the first time in many years he was experiencing a sense of peace, and there was irony in the fact that it took a war to give him peace.

'Seen a newspaper lately?' Colville asked.

'No, sir.'

Colville flicked his ash into the mud. 'Seems Lloyd George has set up a political fund—at least, that's what he calls it. Just a clever cover, if you ask me.'

'Cover for what, sir?'

'Raising funds by selling off peerages. Oh, he won't call it that. But it's surprising how all those wealthy fellows who are donating thousands suddenly receive titles. Political fund be blowed. He's lining his own pocket, if he's got any sense, and there's no flies on that little Welshman.'

Gregg was turning over this information in his mind, wondering why Colville should consider it significant, when the young officer spoke again.

'Of course, he won't be able to do it openly. Must have someone handling it, very discreetly, on his behalf.'

'A middleman, you mean.'

'Exactly. Wonder who the lucky devil is. He'll be getting his rake-off, that's for sure.' Colville sighed and threw the end of his cigarette in the mud. 'God, Gregg, sometimes I wish I was back at home instead of stuck out here. Still, I suppose our day will come. In the meantime we must do what we can.'

'Yes, sir.'

'So we'll see about getting that delivery through tomorrow night instead, if this rotten French weather permits. All right for cigarettes, are you?'

'Thank you, yes.'

'Well, there's a bottle of armagnac in it for you next trip. You'll enjoy this one, I promise you—tasted it myself tonight and it's a cracker.'

'I'll look forward to that.'

Colville gave him a searching look. 'Yes, you have a gentleman's tastes all right, Gregg. What the devil you're doing as a private, I'll never understand, but that's your business.'

Gregg hesitated before answering. 'Time was when I considered it my duty....'

'But times have changed, I see. Well, how about my recommending you for corporal? As my batman, of course?'

Gregg smiled. The man had a curious

way of obviating any problem, even this one of them having to meet in secrecy. If life were ever foolish enough not to conform to what Colville expected of it, then he would make it.

'I should be delighted, Lieutenant Colville.'

'Good. Then that's settled.'

He squelched away in the mud, leaving Gregg to watch the drifting clouds alone.

Arthur was shivering with cold when he left the railway station that night and set off along Hawksmoor's main street. But at least if his jacket was thin and his body cold, his heart was warmed by his success. Two more of the lads were safely out of the country now, with luck on their way to the start of a new life in a thriving young country.

More than anything, he would have liked to stop off at the Unicorn for a drink, but resisted the temptation. Too risky, his face being as well known as it was. What was more, there was precious little money left in his pocket. Turning up his collar and putting his head down against the biting wind, he marched on. There were few people out on the streets on a night like this.

At the top of Chapel Hill two figures stood by the railings. One was a policeman.

Arthur's first instinct was to turn off down Southgate—but then he realised that the other figure looked familiar—yes, it was Frank Duckworth. Arthur's nobler instincts prevailed. He could not leave daft Frank to cope with the law alone.

'Good evening, officer,' he said amiably. 'What seems to be the trouble?'

He saw Frank's startled look. The police officer glared at him. 'No concern of thine, young man,' he said tersely. 'I'm just carrying out my duty.'

Frank found his voice. 'He's taking me in, Arthur. He's just arrested me.'

'Nay, surely not, officer,' said Arthur.

'Sergeant, if you please.'

'Hasn't he told you he's got a sick mother—at death's door, in fact?' said Arthur smoothly.

'That's no concern of mine,' replied the sergeant. 'I've me duty to do. Come along now, Duckworth.'

'As a police officer, aye,' said Arthur, 'but we must never forget our duty as Christians.'

The sergeant looked startled. 'How dost mean?'

'Well, charity and all that. You can't rob a dying woman of her only son now, can you?'

The officer looked nonplussed. 'Aye, well happen it's a bit hard on the lad,'

259

he agreed, then remembering his position he added, 'but I can't let him go, whether or not. It's not for me to take that into account. He mun tell the magistrates that.'

'Magistrates? Dost think millowners and the like'll care about a poor lad and his ailing mother? Nay, officer—I mean, sergeant—that's expecting a bit much.' Arthur's voice had never wooed a girl more sweetly than he coaxed the police officer now. Frank was listening open-mouthed.

The sergeant came out of the spell first. 'Now come along,' he said to Frank, 'let's be having you. I mun get thee down to the station afore my shift finishes. Come on now.'

'I'll strike a bargain with thee.' Arthur's voice came softly in the wind. The sergeant turned.

'Eh? What's that?'

'You let Frank go and I promise I'll bring thee three conshies in his place on Monday morning. Dost agree?'

'Three?'

'Aye. Think how proud they'll be of thee in the force. It could even mean promotion for thee.'

The sergeant scowled. 'How do I know tha'll not cheat me—I'm not daft, tha knows. I wasn't born yesterday.'

Arthur turned so that the light of the

gaslamp fell on his face. 'You know me, sergeant. I'm Arthur Pogson. I'm a man of my word if nothing else.'

The sergeant peered closely. 'By heck it is,' he murmured. 'I ought to be taking thee in and all.'

'But you're too wise to do that,' urged Arthur. 'You can see the sense in waiting till Monday and taking three of us in, can't you?'

The sergeant studied his face for a moment, then looked at Frank. 'Not him, tha means?'

'No. Me and two others. We'll come to the station without fail first thing, and you can arrest us. It's a promise, sergeant, on my word of honour. Just let me take him to his sick mother.'

The sergeant hesitated for only a second, and then his hand fell away from Frank's shoulder. 'Go on then. I haven't seen thee,' he muttered. As Arthur led the bewildered Frank away, the sergeant's voice followed them. 'But just thee turn up on Monday morning, think on,' he called. 'Thy life'll not be worth living if that lets me down, I can promise thee that.'

Frank scurried to keep up with Arthur's quick stride down the hill. 'Thanks, Arthur,' he mumbled. 'I thought I were done for then.'

'Think nowt on it, lad.'

261

'Wilt tha really give thyself up on Monday for me?'

'Tha heard me say so.'

'But what about them others? Wilt turn them in too?'

'If they're willing. I think I know two as'll be glad to pack it in.'

'Tha does? Who?'

'Harold Pearson, for one. And I think Percy's had enough too. I'll speak to them tomorrow. Now let's get you home.'

Eddie and his stepmother had been sitting listening all evening to Father's vivid account of his trip to France. Eddie could scarcely keep his fingers off the brass shellcase Father had brought.

'I picked that up from the battlefield,' Father said. 'It had actually been fired.'

'By our men or the Boches?' Eddie wanted to know.

'I really don't know. But that reminds me—I have another memento for you, Emma, a little ring one of the hospital sisters gave me when we inspected a field hospital. Here.'

She took it from him, but there was no excitement in her eyes. Eddie knew why. 'Very pretty, dear,' she commented. 'Is it silver?'

Father shook his head. 'The sister said the men make them out of the metal from shells while they're lying ill in bed. It keeps them occupied, but they're of no value, I'm afraid, apart from their significance. The men call them "boches" too.'

Emma laid the ring aside and took a deep breath. 'I'm afraid I have something to tell you, James. Eddie, you'd better go to your room.'

Father looked at her sharply. 'What is it? Tell me.'

She sighed. 'It's Harold. They've caught him. He's to go on trial next week.'

Father gasped. 'Caught him? Is he at the police station? I must go to him at once!'

'No, James, you can't. You could be sitting on the bench next week yourself.'

'Me? Sitting in judgement on my own son? Oh no, Emma, they couldn't do that! I'm sure they wouldn't do that!'

Eddie eased himself unnoticed out of the room. It was too painful to see Father's face, white and anguished. Somehow one's whole world went topsy-turvy when one's father made no effort to hide the tears in his eyes.

FIFTEEN

From three different areas near the Somme, a corporal, a nurse and an officer wrote back home to England.

Dear Mother, *wrote Vincent Gregg,* I'm sorry I haven't written to you for so long but life has been hectic. You remember I told you when I enlisted—well, here I am now, somewhere in France. I hope your arthritis is not proving too painful during this winter. Don't worry about me. My job consists mainly of driving a lorry carrying provisions to the troops at the Front. I am fit and well—probably fitter than I have been in years—and I am sleeping well.

You would be proud if you could see how handsome I look in my uniform. Just as soon as I get home leave, I shall come and visit you so that you may see for yourself.

France under present circumstances is not a pretty place. How I long for the fresh green fields and streams of England. I look forward to the end of the war and getting a regular job.

I promise I shall make you proud of me again, Mother.

Meanwhile Lieutenant Robert Hardcastle was penning a letter home to his father.

The war is an atrocity, *he wrote,* a blasphemous and heinous indictment of mankind. They say that this is the war to end all wars, and I pray to God that it is so.

Tell Mother not to be too anxious about me. Assure her that I am wearing woollen underwear and that my work keeps me mainly at a base camp far from the trenches. My duties are sometimes onerous, but I am fortunate in being blessed with a splendid sergeant, a chap by the name of Pursglove. Reginald is a sound fellow and I would not be without him for the world.

In the abbey crypt, Sister Lilian dipped her pen in the inkwell and wrote with characteristic directness.

Dear Mr and Mrs Pearson, Thank you for your letter and for the packet of tea, which arrived safely yesterday. I thoroughly enjoyed drinking a cup of my favourite brand again before going to bed.

I was sorry to learn that you had not heard from Harold lately. No, I have no news of him either. We have not been in correspondence since I made it clear how disappointed I was in him. I did not even know he had left home until your letter came.

I cannot say I enjoy my work here, for the casualties are terrible; but I do feel that I have discoverd my vocation. When this dreadful war is over I should be well qualified to apply for a position in nursing at home. I think now that I shall never marry but make nursing my career instead.

She paused, chewing the tip of the pen thoughtfully. That said it all, she thought. No need to elaborate, to explain that she could never marry Harold. There had been a time when she would gladly have married him, but not now. She could never marry a coward.

A horn sounded, and above the roar of gunfire she heard the sound of lorry wheels crunching on gravel outside. Another consignment of casualties. Flinging down her pen, she pushed the unfinished letter into the drawer then hurried out of the office to receive the new arrivals.

The little tea-shop in the high street was

crowded, but James Pearson sat staring at the red-checked tablecloth oblivious to the other customers. He had taken the day off work to be as near Harold at this time as he could be. The town hall was just in the next street. At this very moment perhaps Harold was discovering his fate.

Emma arranged her gloves and handbag neatly on her lap and leaned forward. 'They make a lovely pot of tea here, you know. I often pop in when I'm shopping. Do you fancy a nice cream cake to go with it?'

He grunted. The last thing he felt like doing was eating. His mind and his stomach would continue to churn until he knew the outcome of the hearing.

'Come on now,' said Emma. 'It's no use fretting. It's just a mercy you didn't have to be there too.'

'I wish to God I could be,' James muttered. 'The boy's having to face it alone without any of his family.'

Emma leaned across and patted his hand. 'He knows we're with him in spirit, love. And he's not entirely alone—there's Arthur and them with him.'

'They can't help—they're all in the same boat.' James relapsed into silence.

Emma withdrew her hand and sighed. 'Yes, it's all a great pity,' she reflected. 'If only he'd gone in the Army straight away, our name wouldn't be splashed all over the papers. Such a shame for you, love.'

He looked up at her from under his eyebrows and she could see the irritation etched in his face. 'It's not that that's bothering me—I can put up with that. It's Harold I'm bothered about—you know how strongly he feels about his principles. I can't see him giving in easily, and especially with that Arthur Pogson there.'

'I always thought you liked Arthur,' Emma said mildly.

'I did—I do. I just feel that with him being such a firebrand and being a friend of Harold's and all—oh, I don't know, Emma. I don't know what to think any more.'

The waitress, pert and pretty with her bobbed hair and neat white cap and apron, came to take their order. Seeing James's abstracted look, Emma took the initiative.

'A pot of tea for two, oh, and a plate of those little fancy cakes too, please.'

When the waitress had gone, Emma tried again to reassure her husband. 'Harold's not entirely alone, you know, love. It isn't as if he didn't know you'd like to be there. He knows we're waiting here to find out what happens. He knows we'll be down there as soon as it's all over.'

James took out his hunter watch and

looked at it. 'Half an hour to go yet,' he sighed, then glanced back over his shoulder. 'Where's the waitress with that tea?'

'She'll be here in a second.'

When the tray arrived, Emma poured the tea and chatted brightly. 'You'll enjoy this, love—it's the same brand we drink at home. You remember, I sent a packet of it to Lilian.'

Instantly she regretted mentioning Lilian's name. James had been hurt to the quick by her letter when the girl said she never intended to marry now. He had recognised it as a direct allusion to Harold and how he had failed her. Never once had James complained that his son had failed him, but James was not a man who was given easily to showing his true feelings....

Suddenly Emma became aware of trousered legs at her side and followed them up to the face.

'Harold! Good heavens! So soon?'

James half-rose from his seat then, recollecting himself, sat down again.

'Take a seat, son,' he said quietly. Harold tossed his coat carelessly on the coatstand and came to sit with them. His face was pale and wore a slightly bemused expression.

'Well, how did it go, lad?' his father asked. 'I didn't think it would be over yet. I planned to be at the door when you came out.'

'I know. I'm grateful.'

Emma signalled to the waitress, who came across. 'Can we have another cup, please?' she said with a charming smile, and then turned her attention to her stepson. 'Well now, Harold, tell us all about it. We've been dying to know. Your father hasn't been able to touch one of these fancies yet.'

She was pointing at the pretty pink and white iced cakes. Harold was not listening. He held his father's gaze in a silent interchange.

'Well,' said Emma, 'if you two aren't interested, I shall help myself to another.'

The waitress brought the third cup and Emma began to pour tea.

'It's all settled,' said Harold quietly. 'I'm to go in the medical corps.'

His father's gaze did not waver but for a moment he did not speak. 'And Arthur?' he asked at length.

'He's been sentenced to two years in Wakefield Prison. So was Percy.'

James took a sip of his tea. 'Are you satisfied with that, Harold? Going in the medical corps?'

Hal sighed deeply. 'Yes, I reckon I am, Father. At least it's not combat duties. I won't have to carry a gun. I'll be helping my fellow men, not killing them.'

James nodded and straightened. 'If you're content, then all's well. When are you off?'

'I'm catching the ten o'clock train tomorrow.'

'Right. Emma, pour us another cup of tea, will you, love? This one's gone a bit cold.'

No more was said, but Emma could see the tension drain away from her husband's face. He was a fine man, was James Pearson. He didn't care a tinker's cuss about public opinion, just so long as he and his sons could walk with pride, knowing they had lived up to their consciences. A strong character, this man, and she congratulated herself for the hundredth time for having had the wit to marry him.

In the private back room of Madame Celia's gown shop Lady Hardcastle stood, arms extended, while Madame Celia stretched a tape measure around her waist. In a shadowed corner Madame's assistant was noting down the measurements in a small red ledger.

'And did I tell you I had received another letter from my son since I last saw you about the green watered silk?' Lady Hardcastle remarked. 'Such a good boy—writes home every week, you know.'

'I hope he is well, Your Ladyship,' the dressmaker said with difficulty, her mouth full of pins.

'Mercifully, yes. But he tells me conditions in the trenches are terrible. Doesn't complain, you understand—Robert is far too much of a man to complain. A real stoic.'

'You must be very proud of him. Thirty-two, Rose.'

'Indeed I am,' her ladyship sighed, 'but then I suppose every mother who has a son fighting bravely for his King and country has a right to take pride in him.'

'Yes indeed, Your Ladyship. Forty-two.'

Lady Hardcastle turned slightly to survey herself in the long mirror. 'Though I say it myself, I do feel that I am in good shape for a woman of my age, wouldn't you agree? My measurements can be hardly any different from what they were on my wedding day.'

'Nape to waist, thirteen. Quite so, My Lady. Would you care to choose the material now?'

'But I've already told you I wanted the moiré.'

'Yes, My Lady, but you hadn't quite decided between the saxe blue and the magenta. Perhaps you would care to look at them both again by the window?'

Lady Hardcastle sighed and glanced at her fob watch. 'Really, Madame, I cannot spare the time. I've promised to help out at the meals kitchen at twelve—one must do one's bit, you know, especially in these hard times. One must pay no heed to the risks.'

'Risks, My Lady?'

Lady Hardcastle shuddered. 'Fleas, my dear. And worse. So sad really—one would think they could be issued with soap and taught how to wash properly. Still, it's a hazard one has to face if one is to help one's fellow human beings.'

'Surely no more of a risk than your son has to face, Your Ladyship.'

Lady Hardcastle regarded her dressmaker in horror. 'My Robert? Exposed to fleas? Oh, my God! I never thought of that!'

Madame Celia turned away quickly lest her smile be seen. 'Rose, fetch out the blue and magenta moirés again for her ladyship, will you?'

'No need,' said Lady Hardcastle. 'I have decided. I shall have the mustard yellow. It will go with Pooky's Sunday bow perfectly.' A moment's pause, and then she added reflectively, 'Fleas, in heaven's name! Poor Robert, having to run the same hazards as my dear little Peke. I can keep Pooky away from other horrid dogs, but my son....'

'When would Your Ladyship care to call again for the first fitting?' Madam Celia enquired. Her client was regarding her with curiosity.

'You have a soldier son, don't you?' she enquired. 'What is he, private or sergeant or something? My son has a sergeant who just adores him.'

'Yes, My Lady. My son's a captain, in an ordnance corps.'

Her ladyship nodded. 'Oh, well done. Robert's a lieutenant, of course, but then he had the advantage of public school. Tell your boy to keep at it. Encourage him, and I'm sure he'll do well too.'

She did not notice the dressmaker's mouth open and close before she turned aside, for she was still deep in her own thoughts. 'Oh, by the way, has Mirabel been in lately? She wouldn't have chosen my yellow moiré too, would she?'

'No, My Lady. You're quite safe with that.'

'Good thing too. It wouldn't go with that red hair of hers—it is still red, isn't it?'

Madame Celia's eyelashes fluttered. 'I really can't say that I noticed at the time.'

Lady Hardcastle's eyes widened. 'You didn't notice? But you can't possibly have missed it, no one could!'

'Ah well, she was wearing a close-fitting hat, and she didn't stay very long. She was telling me about her son's mishap.'

Lady Hardcastle was all attention. 'Rupert? What happened to him?'

'You haven't heard, My Lady? He was rather badly wounded at the Front, I fear.'

'At the Front? Where? Oh, the poor boy!'

'His leg, apparently. It was shattered by shrapnel and had to be amputated. Her ladyship was very distressed about it. I understand he's been cited in dispatches for bravery.'

Lady Hardcastle could not hurry home to Sir Marcus fast enough. 'To think of it, Marcus, Rupert with his leg shot away, and our poor boy still out there in the thick of it! What are we to do? Can't you speak to the War Minister or something?'

Sir Marcus put down his newspaper irritably. 'No, I can't. And damn it all, Robert's only in a base camp, you know, not in the front line. He'll come to no harm. Now stop fretting and get on down to that soup kitchen or whatever it is.'

'No harm?' repeated his wife. 'Well, that just shows how much you know, Marcus. I've just found out that he's in terrible danger—those privates and things are poor people, Marcus—he could get fleas!'

Sir Marcus groaned and picked up his paper again. 'Then he'll have to be deloused, just like that precious dog of yours, won't he?' he muttered from behind the paper. Lady Hardcastle gave him a withering look and swept out of the room.

Eddie had been there at the station with Father to see his brother off. Emma had not, but then, he thought, perhaps that was just as well in the circumstances. There had been no tears, no fuss; just a strong, silent handshake before the train steamed laboriously out of Hawksmoor Station into the promise of a bright spring day.

Father and he had spoken little about Hal on their way back to Lindley. It was tacitly understood that the parting was inevitable and must be faced with fortitude. He knew they would both miss Hal, although he had been at home so little lately, and he felt a gap in his life. Hal, his hero for so many years, far away in a foreign land—life would seem very strange. But Eddie was totally unprepared for the next vicissitude life had in store for him.

A warm spring evening and Sally close in his arms in the shadow of the church, and Eddie's world was perfection. It was only in hindsight that he realised that Sally's manner had been rather different that evening, just the slightest bit strained.

'I like this old church, don't you, Sal?'
he murmured contentedly. 'That spire—it
always makes me think of a finger reaching
up to heaven, know what I mean?'

'Aye, it's nice,' she agreed.

'The sort of church that'd be nice for a
wedding—nice lych-gate and all.'

'I suppose so, if anyone were thinking
of getting wed,' she answered coolly.
Her disinterest, her complete lack of
enthusiasm, were the first signs he had
spotted that all was not well.

'What's up, lass? Not going off me, are
you?' He held her at arm's length to survey
her expression, to await strong denial.

'What makes you think that?'

It was not said teasingly but with an
uncomfortable, almost defensive air. He
felt uneasy.

'There's summat up, lass,' he said
quietly. 'What is it? What's bothering
thee?'

'Nowt. Why should there be?'

He tilted her chin with his fingertips.
'Come on, tell us what's up. I know you
too well, Sally Parkinson, I can see you're
not yourself. What is it?'

She hung her head so that he could
not see her eyes as she answered. 'It's
me mam. She's been on at me.'

'What about? Me?

She nodded, still not looking up. 'Aye.

She wants me to finish with thee.'

'Finish with me?' He was stunned for a moment. 'But I thought she liked me.'

'She does—well, she did. It's not thee, love, it's Harold.'

'I don't understand. What's Hal got to do with us?'

But already the truth was beginning to dawn before she answered. 'It's because of him being in all the papers, Eddie. No one in the village has a good word to say about him. Me mam—nor me dad neither, come to that—wants me to have owt to do with thy family.'

He was staring down at her, horror and disbelief choking him. This couldn't be his Sally talking, speaking so coolly about breaking with him just because of what her parents thought.

His voice came out in a croak. 'But he's gone in the Army, Sal. He's gone off to camp today. He is a soldier now.'

She shrugged. 'Aye, but he had to be forced to—folks still talk, tha knows. Pearson's is not a good name hereabouts now.'

'Not good enough for you to be linked with, is that it? After all the time we've been together, Sally. Is that all it means to you?'

He could hear his own voice, the pleading in his tone mixed with anger.

She still did not raise her eyes to meet his. She was looking down at the tree roots protruding from the muddy earth, and her stance somehow put him in mind not so much of a saddened or disappointed creature as of a sullen child. He felt angry.

'So are you going to take it at that, Sal? Are you going to let them stop us meeting? Don't you care enough about us to fight?'

She looked up at last, and with a sudden sense of fear he recognised that there was no warmth in her clear eyes. 'What's to fight about?' she asked. 'I've no wish to be on bad terms at home. I just wanted to tell thee as I couldn't see thee again, to explain as it's not thy fault, Eddie, really it isn't. Tha's a nice enough lad, but it's got to end. I mun get back now.'

She turned to go, and for a moment he stood, mesmerised, as he watched her slim figure walking quickly towards the lych-gate. Shock and a sick feeling of despair held him powerless, and then suddenly he sprang to life. He could not let her go like this.

He ran after her, catching up with her on the gravel path. 'Sally—please, tell me you don't really want to do this. Tell me we meant something to each other?'

She paused and looked back at the hand

he held out in supplication, but she did not take it. A faint smile came to her lips, but whether of concern or pity he could not tell.

'I told thee, it's not thee, Eddie—it's because of thy brother.'

Desperation seized him. 'We shall be friends still, though, shan't we? You'll eat your snap with me at dinner break still?'

Slowly she shook her head. 'Nay, I'll not do that, lad. I can't let folks see me with thee no more. Goodbye, Eddie.'

Then she opened the lych-gate and was gone, leaving him standing there alone and helpless like a child in the dark.

In the darkness of his room that sleepless night, many confused and agonising thoughts tormented Eddie's mind, but by morning one thought had crystallised clearly. It was Hal who had brought about his misery and ruined his world. But for Hal and his damned stupid principles, Eddie would still be secure in Sally's love. Damn and blast him! No man had the right to destroy his brother's happiness just to ensure his conscience was placated.

It was a cruel blow to discover that the hero of all one's boyhood years was only a fallible creature with feet of clay.

SIXTEEN

Harold Pearson was not finding army life at all congenial. After a short spell of basic training in medical matters, he found himself aboard ship and then suddenly ashore again in the midst of an inferno which could have originated in the nightmares of a twisted mind.

Not that he was directly involved in the wholesale massacre currently taking place along the length of the river Somme, but every day he was obliged to drive out in one of the fleet of ambulances to retrieve the left-overs of humanity resulting from the day's battle. At times he found the sights so grisly and the suffering so unspeakable that he could not help reflecting that man could not be sentenced to a worse fate in any English prison. He could almost envy Arthur and Percy, shut away from it all in Wakefield...

Even when, sickened and exhausted, he was at last able to crawl into his bunk in the old farmhouse, it was only to re-enact in dreams the horrors of the day. And on waking he was obliged to face the scorn of his fellow soldiers. They never addressed their comments directly to him, for they seemed to have some kind of tacit agreement amongst themselves to send him to Coventry. But they made sure their scorn was audible none the less.

'What's up with him that they had to force him to come out here, then? Mother's boy, is that it?'

'Not him, he's just a bloody coward, that's all.'

'Some poor devils of parents are stuck with bastards like him. Fancy having to tell your mates that you've got a conshie coward for a son.'

'Couldn't handle a rifle if he tried, that one. He'd probably shoot hisself if he did.'

'That'd be no loss to nobody. Might be a good thing if he did—save us having to shoot the bolshie bugger.'

It was a waste of time trying to explain to them that it was a matter of principle with him, that he was willing to do his bit but not to take up arms. They would never understand, even if he could get them to listen. Only Father had granted him the courtesy of letting him do what he felt was right, and possibly that was only because he was his father. No one else understood. Certainly not Eddie, for he was too young, nor Stepmother, though she at least did take the trouble to write to him. Her last letter told him titbits of local news.

> You probably remember that common Denton family from up East Street—well, their boy came home last week with a very nasty wound in his hip, I think, and everyone put bunting out to welcome him home. Quite the hero he is now. Whoever would have thought that of a Denton? And I had a nice letter from Lilian saying how much she liked the tea I sent her....

Lilian—he remembered wistfully how well he had once got along with her. If only he could talk to her about how he felt—but was she still as idealistic as she used to be, he wondered, or had war in all its bestial horror wrought a change in her too? It was too late now to try to rebuild that once perfect intimacy between them.

So there was no one he could write to, to pour out his torment. Instead, his only recourse was to poetry. For long hours, closing his ears to the taunts flying around the billet, he struggled to pen the images he hoped would help to expunge the horrors of war from his mind.

The once-ripe fields of verdant France,
Now steeped wine-red with our spilt youth....

But it was no use. Each time he closed his eyes to sleep, the images returned—the headless corpses, the disembowelled but still breathing boys who by rights ought to be playing football in an English field, not spraying death and reaping it in return. It was all such a monstrous waste and a desecration of all that he had ever held dear. As the days slipped by, Hal felt his faith in man and in God slipping away too. Life seemed futile.

When the order came to move, the sergeant wasted few words. 'Infantry men move up to the front line, medical orderlies await orders. Shift yourselves, lads, we'll be off in ten minutes.'

They gathered their belongings in silence, ignoring Hal's watchful eyes. He guessed what was going on in their minds. At last they were ready, only waiting for the lorries. One stared at him balefully.

'We could all be carrion meat by tomorrow, and he's the lad who'll still be walking about when we're gone,' he mutterd.

'Neither use nor ornament, him,' said another.

'Aye, picking off what's left, no doubt. That sort's not above taking a ring or two,' rasped a third.

Noting their malevolence, Hal hung his

284

head, making no effort to defend himself. It was fear that spoke in their words, not malice.

'Aye, that's him,' murmured the first soldier, 'a ruddy vulture, that's what he is. But even vultures get shot sometimes. He's not safe from bullets, no more than the rest of us.'

'Ah, shut up, Harry,' the small fellow exploded. 'Who's talking of dying? Not me, I tell you—I've got a bonny wife back in Blighty, and I'm going home to her. So shut your mouth and don't go putting morbid thoughts in folks's minds.'

'That's right,' agreed the burliest of the group, slinging his rifle over his shoulder. 'We're going home all right, lads, but like Harry says, I'm not so sure about him. If a Jerry shell doesn't get him, it wouldn't surprise me if a Tommy bullet did. And what's more, no one'd care.'

The sergeant appeared at the door. 'Right, lads, let's be having you. Time to mount up—lorry's waiting.'

One by one they filed out past the sergeant, leaving Hal sitting alone. The sergeant said stiffly: 'And you—the ambulance crew is waiting. Get moving.'

Hal rose quickly. 'We're following you?'

The sergeant shrugged and turned away. 'Don't know. Last thing that bothers me is where you lot are.'

Outside, the ambulance was standing in the rain. An officer, huddled in his trenchcoat, came hurrying to speak to the driver.

'Cover the western end of the attack. Take all casualties to Royaumont. Now get going.'

Emma Pearson sat stiff-backed at her dressing table, hairbrush poised over her head while she surveyed her reflection in the mirror. Her husband stood patiently by the bedroom door.

'There's less than an hour to go, love. We can't afford to be late for the mayor's reception.'

She sniffed and put down the brush, taking up instead a jet necklace, which she began to fasten about her throat. James came forward to help.

'Here, let me do it for you.'

'Never heed. I can do it for meself.'

There was in her tone an air of resignation, of martyrdom almost. James sighed. Women. They were inexplicable creatures, but he wished she would get it over with, whatever the mood was, so that they could get to the reception on time. These things were important, but it was no use trying to explain that to a woman, especially when her feelings were hurt.

'Now look, Emma,' he began patiently,

286

'I've already explained. It was just a dream, that's all. Don't go trying to make more out of it than there is.'

Thin shoulders shrugged, ruffling the black feathers on her bodice. 'It means nothing to me, James. You did nothing wrong.'

'That's right. So why are you sulking?'

'I'm not sulking.' Her gaze steadfastly refused to meet his in the mirror and her lips were tight.

James tried again. 'It's not like you, Emma. You've scarcely spoken a word since I came home. Nor at breakfast time neither, come to that. What's that if not sulking?'

She turned slowly on her stool and surveyed him with eyes full of sadness. 'Tell me, James—how often do you dream of Annie? Was last night the first time, or does it happen often?'

He groaned and sat down on the edge of the big bed. 'Listen, love, I've told you it makes no difference to how I feel about you....'

'How often, James?'

'Now and again. Not often.'

'Three years we've been wed. How often in all that time?'

He felt the irritation rising again. 'Oh, how can I tell? But listen, love, Annie and I were wed for over twenty years—you can't expect me not to think of her once in a while. She were a fine wife and mother too. It'd be unnatural if I didn't think of her and even dream of her. She were a big part of my life.'

'And I'm not, I suppose.'

'Don't talk rubbish. Now please hurry up, love, or we'll be late.'

Emma snapped on the jet earrings and began pinching her cheeks vigorously. Then, picking up a bottle of lavender water, she dabbed a sparing amount behind each ear. 'Very well, James, I'm ready,' she said, and the coldness in her tone troubled him.

He touched her elbow gently. 'You know it doesn't affect how I feel about you, love, don't you? You know how much I wanted you, still want you?'

Avoiding his gaze, she looked down at her hands, toying with her wedding ring. 'You always said so, and I believed you, James. But there were things....'

'What things, love?'

'Well, like not letting me give anything of hers away—those china dogs, for instance. I don't like them, but you still keep them on the mantelpiece. Sometimes I wonder....'

'Now that's silly. I keep them because the boys like them. I told you that.'

'Edward does, you said. But don't you think it's morbid, James? He can't remember much about her now. And anyway, I'm his mother now, not Annie.'

'You're not his mother.' James's tone was unintentionally sharp, and he saw her startled look before anger leapt into her eyes.

'That's the trouble, James, don't you see? If I had had your son....'

'Emma—do you know what time it is?' He took out his watch and flourished it in exasperation. It was not the hour that angered him, but his own guilt. Just how many sleepless nights he had spent thinking about Annie he could never reveal to Emma, for she would not understand. It troubled his conscience now, as it would do until the end of his days, that he had wished his wife dead so that he could have Emma, who seemed to promise all the vitality which Annie, through no fault of her own, bless her, had lacked. He had been filled with desire for Emma and now he was paying for the sin of lust. Emma gained was not half so beautiful as Emma unattained. Who was it who once said that a man's worst punishment was to have his dreams fulfilled?

Emma was pulling on her jacket. 'You pushed me away last night when I went to touch you,' she murmured. James held the door open for her. She stopped in the doorway to look up at him with such vulnerability in her dark eyes that he suddenly saw again in her the helplessness which had first touched him.

'I'm sorry,' he muttered. 'It won't happen again.'

'No, James. It won't,' she agreed, and swept past him. With a heavy heart he followed her downstairs. It was curious, he reflected, how he could only now appreciate just how noble and loyal, uncomplaining and undemanding Annie had been. At the time it had all been taken for granted.

Eddie was squatting on the living room floor tinkering with pieces of a bicycle wheel laid out on sheets of newspaper. Emma gasped in horror.

'Edward! How many times have I told you not to bring those horrid oily things in here? Now just you get them out in the yard this instant!'

James could see dejection in the set of his son's shoulders, but there was no time to question. He was just ushering Emma out of the front door when she suddenly turned.

'That gas mantle on the landing—have you put a new one in yet, James? I asked you when you came home. And while I think on, it's about time we got a new hearthrug—Edward's things have made a right mess of that one, and anyway you must have had it for years. We'll get another on Saturday.'

He sighed as he took her arm. Somehow the anticipation he had been feeling all day for the evening's entertainment had completely dissipated. It was just as they were climbing the flight of steps leading up to the impressive entrance of the town hall that Emma fired her final shot.

'Whatever about Edward,' she said stoutly, 'I know for a fact that Harold regards me as his mother, or why else should he write me a letter every week? Time was when I might have been glad to disown him, when all those letters kept coming saying nasty things about him, but I stuck by him. He's always called me Stepmother, I know, but it's not every lad as writes home regularly to his mother, hardly ever to his father. He thinks a lot about me, does Harold.'

James made no reply. He could have countered by saying that the boy had little alternative since he was too polite to ignore her frequent letters, but instead he moved forward to shake the hand of the alderman standing nearest to the door.

'Good evening, Alderman Lawson. I don't think you've met my wife, have you?'

Having refitted the wheel, Eddie propped his bicycle against the house wall and looked up at the starlit sky. He was in no mood to go back into the house alone, so, turning up his jacket collar, he walked down the yard to the gate and looked along the main street. Under the glimmer of the street lamps there was no one to be seen, only the sheen of damp clinging to the cobbles.

He was acutely aware of the emptiness of his world without Sally Parkinson. All his days and his nights stretched empty and hollow without her, and he thought bitterly once again how shallow was the love of woman. Not like his love, burning and eternal, a passion which would dominate his life until the day he died. Until only the other day his life had been filled with meaning and delight, and now it was desolate, and all because of her fickleness.

'Man cometh forth like a flower...and is cut down.'

She had done this to him, robbing his newly acquired manhood of meaning. What was there left now to utilise all that vigour and energy? He could have used it all up in the war if only he had been old enough, out there in the mud of Flanders like Hal—in fact, that was just what he would do when the time came. But now was the problem—what was he to do now? Every day he saw her in the mill yard, laughing and joking with the other girls, but never once did she speak to him. And though he looked for her every night at the mill gate, she was never there.

The clock tower struck nine. He looked down the street and could just discern the silhouette of the church spire against the night sky. Thin and graceful it rose, like a prayer to heaven, as he had once said to Sally. He grunted. Heaven had not listened to his prayers.

The sound of distant footsteps came pattering towards him. As the figure came nearer, it passed through the arc of light from a gaslamp—and he recognised the shape of a shawled woman. As she reached the lamp nearest to him, he saw with a start that it was Sally.

'Hallo,' he said jerkily. 'Where are you off to?'

Her quick smile showed a trace of embarrassment. 'Just off to see someone, that's all. Taking some buns I've just baked.'

'Oh aye? Bit late to be out on your own, isn't it? I'll walk with you, if you like.'

She was walking on by. 'No need. I'm only going to East Street. I'm nearly there.'

'East Street?' Suspicion dawned. 'At this time of night?'

'Like I said, I've only just finished baking.'

He hurried after her. 'East Street? You know nobody there, 'less it's the Dentons. You're not going to the Dentons', are you?'

'And what if I am?' she said airily. 'It's nowt to do with thee.'

He seized her arm, forcing her to stop. 'You're not having owt to do with that Denton lad, are you? You couldn't do that, Sally—tell me you're not!'

She glared up at him. 'What I do is my business, Eddie Pearson, and nowt to do with thee. I don't have to answer to thee for anything. If my mother and dad are satisfied, then that's all I have to care about.'

The fury in her eyes gave him pain, and he looked away, staring instead at the darn in her shawl. 'You wouldn't, Sally, you couldn't....'

'Couldn't what?' she demanded.

'Give me up—for him.' The words came out in a disbelieving whisper, and he hated himself for the weak sound.

'Couldn't I?' The sneer in her voice drove like a stake into his heart. 'Tha must be daft, Eddie Pearson, if tha thinks a lass wouldn't rather have a man than a boy. He's a hero, is Denton, tha knows. All the lasses in Lindley are after him now—but they're too late, they are. They'll soon learn as he's spoken for.'

'Spoken for? Do you mean—you—'

She sighed. 'Aye, I mean me, lad. Tha mun find a lass of thy own, for I'm promised to Billy Denton. Now leave me be and let me get on afore he starts worrying where I am. Goodnight to thee, Eddie Pearson.'

She was about to go on, but suddenly touched his elbow. 'Don't fret over me, lad. Tha's a good-looking enough fellow and tha'll break a heart or two I reckon, in time. But the fact is, tha's nobbut a lad yet, not like Billy. He's a man, and he's a hero and all. Thy turn'll come one day. Goodnight, lad.'

He watched her slim figure as she hurried away into the darkness until all that was left was the fading scent of freshly baked buns. He could visualise Denton's thick fingers ramming her buns into his greedy mouth, and he felt sick with disgust and jealousy. The nausea and misery still lay heavy upon him when Father and the Iredale woman came home.

'Such a pity you couldn't have come with us, Edward,' she enthused as she made the bedtime cups of cocoa. 'It was a lovely do, fair grand it was, and you'd have been proud to see how all those grand folks treated your father. Quite the respected gentleman he is to them, seemingly.'

Behind her back, as she bent over the range Eddie caught sight of his father's glance. It was a thoughtful, brooding look, and Eddie wondered whether it was imagination that he felt he could see his own desolation reflected in that look.

Vincent Gregg was exhausted when he finally drove the lorry back into the compound of base camp. Behind him the night sky was glowing as bright as day with shellfire, and the air reverberated with the insistent pounding of heavy mortar fire.

The duty sergeant looked up from his lists as Gregg shambled in. 'Bad night tonight,' he murmured.

Gregg muttered something under his breath; there was no point in remarking that it was the worst night ever, since every night was the same. God knew how much longer men could go on slaughtering each other like this.

'Lieutenant Colville left a message for you—he's been moved up front. Note's in the pigeon-hole,' the sergeant added. 'I'd get meself a hot mug of cocoa if I were you—you look all in.'

His frozen fingers, curled around the hot tin mug, began to thaw out, causing them to throb with pain. At last Gregg unfolded the note.

Orders came too suddenly for me to bid farewell, Gregg. I hope that we may be able to renew our common interests one day. If war prevents our paths crossing again for some time, bear in mind that I shall always be glad to see you again in London.

I promised to help advance your interests, along with my own. I keep my word. My flat in St John's Wood is always at your disposal—look me up there when the bloody shooting match is over.

Gregg sighed and tucked the note away inside the pocket of his uniform jacket. It was a pity the partnership had to end, just when it was proving so profitable too, but right at this moment he could not find it in him to feel regret; he was so bloody tired and his eyes burned from all that smoke and sheer fatigue. In an hour or so, when he had rested, the disappointment would begin.

He flung himself on his bunk and closed his eyes, longing for sleep. Distant gunfire still boomed, and he could see in his mind's eye those mud-filled foxholes where the front-line men had to endure hunger and pain alone. He stretched his body to ease the ache in his back. His was not a bad war compared to some poor devils.

It was nearing dawn when Sister Lilian, her starched apron now blood-streaked and her eyes hollow with sleeplessness, pushed the hair out of her eyes with the back of her hand and looked up at the orderly.

'Is that it for the night? We've done, have we?'

He nodded. 'All that you can do anything for, Sister. There's just one out there on a stretcher, but I reckon he's a goner.'

Her brisk manner returned and she straightened. 'Let's have a look at him—the doctor's still operating, so we'd best see if he's a chance.'

But as she bent over the crumpled figure she could see at a glance that he had no chance at all. Not only were there gaping holes in his body where shreds of khaki still clung to the flesh, but his face was almost obliterated. Eyes still moved as if crying out silently for pity, but his head was so mangled that serious brain damage was inevitable. The most she could do for him was to alleviate the torture he must be enduring.

Her hand brushed against his, and the fingers seized hers. She let it lie, feeling the grip tighten.

'Poor lad,' she murmured, and looked up at the orderly. 'He's one of yours, isn't he? He's wearing the medical insignia.'

'Aye, seemingly.'

She was puzzled. 'What happened? Where did you find him?'

He turned his grimy face away. 'It weren't very nice, Sister. One of those things that happens now and again, but we don't talk about it as a rule. The officers don't like having to report things like that.'

The fingers relaxed. The man was dead. Lilian faced the orderly.

'Now come on, Corporal, tell me. What happened?'

'Well, so long as you don't tell. He was a conshie. Our lads can't abide 'em. Sometimes they show how they feel, like with him. War does funny things to a man, doing things they'd never dream of doing at home.'

Lilian felt a shiver of apprehension. 'What are you saying, Corporal? That our men shot one of their own?'

He shook his head. 'Nay, they'd not do that. But they tied him to the barbed wire out in no man's land and left him there. That's where I found him. I reckon he must have tore hisself to ribbons trying to get free long before a shell got him. Poor bugger. Still, his suffering's over now. I'd best get back to my unit.'

Lilian watched him go towards the abbey entrance, her mind unable to register the horror of his story. War had thrown up all manner of obscenities, but this was unbelievable. A man killed by his own comrades—or at least exposed to certain death?

'Did you know him, Corporal?'

His weary voice drifted back over his shoulder. 'Nay, I didn't. He's not the sort you want to know. It were a rotten way to go, poor devil, but then he were a conshie.'

SEVENTEEN

Lieutenant James Colville had grown heartily sick of the war. At the Front, actively engaged in the daily battle, he could find no escape from the horrifying reality of it all, and he had yearned for the end of war and a return to civilian life.

Lice, dysentery and colic had been constant dangers, though he himself was mercifully spared all but the lice. Mud, horses, motor bicycles, gunfire and the cries of wounded and dying men filled the senses unremittingly. If it wasn't the sweet, nauseous smell of blood everywhere it was the acrid gas attacks the Jerries had begun to fling at them, blinding men or seriously burning their lungs and stomachs. Cries for stretcher-bearers never ceased.

Brutality on such a scale seemed to blunt the mind, he realised. War produced heroes, but it had revealed the lesser men too—like the day when two men, terrified out of their minds, had tried to run away rather than go over the top again. Pursued, caught and dragged back, weeping piteously, they had been forced to submit to the recognised punishment for their crime. Cowardice merited death, and one of the runaway lads, an apprentice from Sheffield, had stared disbelievingly at the firing squad before the bullets ripped into him. His own best friend was one of the detail.

Shit-scared he was, thought Colville, just like so many who had to be forced to go over the top. Others, less lucky than himself, perhaps, had gone out of their minds and had to be shipped home. And who wouldn't become demented, he reflected, after collecting the corpses and severed limbs of their comrades, pushing the heap of human remains into foxholes and shovelling mud over them for hasty burial. The blast of shell-explosions would complete the task if the corpse-rats didn't get them first.

Morning birdsong over a silent, deserted battlefield had seemed the height of irony, and even now, with the Armistice and the celebrations of victory well behind them, Colville could still not find it in his heart to find any glory in war. Experience had shattered youthful illusion, as it had for so many other young men. Those of them who had survived, that was, for countless thousands lay dead out there in Flanders. London seemed curiously full of young women and old men, but young men seemed hard to find.

One should make the most of life while it lasted, for one was lucky to be granted another opportunity. There were pickings to be had for the young and ambitious, and if Colville had been ambitious before the war, experience had strengthened it. But civvy life was not turning out to be a bed of roses—far from it.

'I'll find a way to make money,' he promised himself. 'A land fit for heroes, they promised us, but if a man's going to get anywhere, it has to be by his own effort. I'll find a way; by God I will.'

Robert Hardcastle could hardly believe what was happening. After all these years, Vincent Gregg had come back; but he was no longer the gentle, considerate man he once had been.

'I wonder you found me, here in London,' he said icily. 'You must have been very determined.'

'I was. I needed money, Robert.'

'Then you've come to the wrong man. I'm not the impressionable youth you remember, Vincent. War has changed all that. God, I wish you wouldn't smoke those foul cigarettes in here. It makes the furnishings smell awful.'

'I didn't expect a welcome with open arms from you....'

'Good. Because you won't get one.'

'But I did expect you'd react suitably when you knew what I proposed to do. These letters, Robert—remember them? I don't think you'd really care for your father to see them. That could mean the end of your handsome remittance, don't you think?'

Robert paled. 'You couldn't— you wouldn't...'

'Couldn't I? It was not only you who changed in the war, Robert.'

'You rotten blackguard, Gregg! I would never have dreamed you could stoop to this! Get out of here this instant, or I'll have you thrown out!'

Gregg smiled. 'My, my, we have changed, haven't we? But believe me, I am in earnest, Robert. Come on now, be reasonable. I would help you if the situations were reversed. Let me have a hundred or two, or I swear these letters will reach Sir Marcus tomorrow.'

Robert reached for the bell. 'I'll call your bluff, Gregg. Even you wouldn't do that to a sick old man. Be gone by the time the janitor gets here, or else....'

Gregg tossed his cigarette into the fire and rose lazily. 'Very well, Robert. But don't say I didn't give you fair warning.'

Robert stared angrily at the door as it closed behind Gregg, then crossing to the window, he opened it wide and fanned the air with a newspaper, trying to rid the room of the foul scent of French cigarettes.

'Are you sure you don't want to come to the spiritualist meeting with me, James? You might get a message from Harold, you know.'

James lowered his newspaper. 'I've told you, no, Emma. I don't believe in such stuff, and neither should you.'

Her black eyes opened wide with an innocence which would once have charmed away his disbelief. 'Why, James, it's not like you to scoff! You can't disprove it, you know.'

'And you can't prove it neither.' He picked up his paper again, but Emma had not finished.

'How can you say that, dear, after what happened. It was a sign, I know it was. I'd never have found out that Harold wanted to get in touch with me but for that day down East Street.'

James sighed. It was useless to argue with her. She swore that just as she was about to go into a cottage to deliver some outgrown shoes of Edward's to a poor family, she had had a sudden vision of a small boy in a tin bath and an old man seated at a table. And when she entered, the scene was exactly as she had foreseen. If Emma wanted to believe in something, nothing on earth was going to dissuade her.

'It's no coincidence, James. It can't be. The little boy was in the bath in front of the fire, just as I'd seen it, all covered in soapsuds, and the old man knocked his jug of beer off the table. Even the shape of the stain on the linoleum was just as I'd seen it.'

'But why, Emma?' James had protested. 'What's the purpose of Harold trying to get in touch?'

'How am I supposed to know? Happen he wanted to get in touch with me because we were close, me and him. It was me he wrote to every week, think on. Or happen it's you—he might have a message for you, James.'

'He's dead and gone, love. You saw the telegram—killed in action. A credit to us, he was. Let it be, Emma. Leave it at that.'

'Very well, dear. You don't want to come. Never mind, I'll go on me own. Time I got ready.'

Rising from her chair, she hummed a hymn tune as she put on her coat. Funny, thought James, either she was slow-witted and did not recognise that he would prefer her to leave this spiritualist game alone, or she was a very wilful woman who would always have her own way with a pretty smile on her face as she did it. You could never quite tell with a woman.

After she had gone, James busied himself reading over the notes for the forthcoming union meeting due to take place in London very shortly. He was still engrossed when Edward came home from the Band of Hope. The boy looked around curiously as he took off his jacket.

'Is she out?'

'Your stepmother? Aye, she's at the spiritualist meeting.'

'Oh, that.'

'She wants to know what you're going to do about that bike of yours,' James murmured absently. 'Cluttering the place up, she says, and you not using it much these days.'

'No. Reckon I'll get rid of it.'

He had scarcely touched the machine since his brother's death. Perhaps because it was Harold's and he hadn't the heart to ride it. James felt touched.

'I've outgrown it now, Father. I'd rather have a motor bike so I can get farther afield.'

'You're not having a motor bike, and that's that.'

The boy sighed. 'Reckon I'll be off to bed then. Goodnight, Father.'

James put away the union notes and

picked up his newspaper again. He wanted to re-read the account of Sir Marcus Hardcastle's death. A sudden heart attack, the report said, shortly after dinner in a London hotel with the ex-MP Vincent Gregg. What a shame, thought James—not so much about the old man, skinflint that he was, but a shame about Gregg. Such an eloquent man, and he had been so full of conviction about the cause. And such a charmer too. He could have gone a long way, if only he had been able to practice a little moderation....

Vincent Gregg hummed a dance-hall tune as he stroked shaving lather on to his face and then stropped his razor on the leather. He was looking forward to the evening ahead—dinner with Gilda by candlelight and the prospect of an hour or two alone with her after the cab ride back to her villa. She was a woman with everything that appealed to a man of taste—beauty, wit, charm and that tinge of mystery that set a man's heart thudding. And there was the added excitement of danger, with her husband's movements being so unpredictable.

Right now, life was being good to Gregg. A week or two ago there had been disappointment, when old Hardcastle died so suddenly that Robert's letters had proved useless as a source of income, but since then things had definitely looked up. Maundy Gregory, despite all his undoubted acumen, had proved far easier to blackmail than he had anticipated; and what with that and his official income for speech-making for Lloyd George, it was proving possible once again to live the life-style he so desired.

And the possible sources of income were not yet exhausted. There was still Robert, in an indirect way. Word was, over the society grapevine, that he was having trouble paying the huge death duties on his father's estate, that he was thinking of selling off his Hawksmoor land if a wealthy enough buyer could be found. Now if Gregg could, through a third party, get a deal set up and take a cut in the proceeds... Life was full of possibilities if one had the wits to use them to one's own advantage.

If he continued to prosper like this, building up a nice little nest-egg, the day would surely come when he could afford to buy himself a villa in Antibes. When the moment was ripe, he could just vanish to his sunny hideaway and no one would be any the wiser. No one, that was, but whichever companion he would choose to share his good fortune.

'Play your cards right and it could be

you, Gilda,' he murmured to his reflection in the mirror as he began to stoke the razor across his cheek. Then he swore aloud. It was a foolish thing to do, to talk to oneself while shaving. He reached for the styptic pencil in the bathroom cabinet and applied it to the scarlet line just above his jaw.

Eddie awoke bathed in sweat and shaking. It took a full minute before he realised it had all been a terrible dream. He lay shivering under the bedcovers, his blood feeling ice-cold in his veins.

It had all seemed so real, so agonisingly real. He could still feel the tearing of his flesh and hear the sound of it cracking, see the blood gushing from his body and streaming down his limbs. It was Hal again, he realised, not he who lay dying, as if Hal wanted him to know the full horror of war. He cowered under the bedclothes and prayed.

'Oh, Hal! Forgive me for hating you so! I didn't mean to—I was just upset over Sally. I didn't know how terrible it was to die! I didn't know bullets felt like that, or shell, or whatever it was. Oh, Hal, forgive me! I did love you, honest I did.'

Some weeks later, it was a chance meeting with Vincent Gregg which opened Colville's eyes to the possibility of quick gains on a scale hitherto unparalleled in his life. His one-time batman was just coming out of the Ritz as Colville was passing.

'Gregg, my dear fellow!' Colville greeted him, appraising in one quick glance the well-tailored suit and silver-topped cane. 'You look splendid! Life is treating you well, it seems.'

Gregg gave that slow, easy smile he remembered so well. 'Not too badly at all, I'm glad to say. Come and have a drink with me and we'll talk over what's been happening to us both.'

He gave little away over that drink, or the next three, but it was clear to Colville that the fellow must be on to something very good indeed. He was living, he said, in a service flat near Piccadilly. Over the fifth whisky he became a little more forthcoming.

'I'm working for the Government, you might say, touring the country to make speeches.'

'Speeches? What about?'

'Calming the people, you know—explaining why the houses and jobs they were promised can't be provided overnight. There's a rather restless air, and my job is to soothe them—tell them a start has been made on new housing, be patient and so on.'

Colville nodded. 'You're right about the

restlessness, that's for sure. The working people are on the verge of revolution. So you're in the pay of Lloyd George now, are you, using your popularity to good effect?'

Gregg smiled depracatingly. 'I haven't changed sides, if that's what you think, and it earns a crust. Havelock Wilson often goes with me on these tours.'

'The Liberal MP? He's in undercover work for the Intelligence Service, I'm told.'

Gregg's gaze slid away. 'Ah, he has his finger in many pies. I see a lot of Horatio Bottomley these days too.'

'A right-wing friend too? Bread buttered on all sides, eh?' Colville gave him a knowing smile.

'He's not as helpful as Wilson,' replied Gregg. 'Now *he*'s put me in touch with really influential people.'

'Oh yes? Who, for example?'

Gregg looked over his shoulder before replying, then lowered his voice. 'Ever heard of a man called Maundy Gregory?'

'The man who sells titles for Lloyd George?'

'That's the one. He gets his cut for every title sold. Not a bad income, when you consider it costs ten thousand for a knighthood and as much as a hundred thousand for a peerage.'

Colville's lips rounded into a silent

whistle. 'What's his percentage, then? And how does that benefit you?'

Gregg's eyes narrowed as he stared into the bottom of his empty glass. 'Don't ask too many questions, Colville. Just let me say that I have no problem paying my dues these days. You taught me a great deal in Flanders, and I'm grateful to you.'

Colville laughed and clapped him on the back. 'Then show your gratitude by cutting me in on whatever the deal is, Gregg. You owe me that much. Another bottle of whisky, barman.'

By midnight he had managed to loosen Gregg's tongue, but only partially. Gregg soaked in drink was even more verbose and complex than Gregg sober, but it seemed that Maundy Gregory was the source of Gregg's affluence, and the name of the head of the Intelligence Service cropped up frequently. Both he and Gregory were homosexual, according to Gregg's ramblings, so their sexual preferences could be the link which had brought Gregg into their circle. Strange, thought Colville, but until tonight, when Gregg kept muttering obscenities about an encounter with a youth named Robert, he had never known of his batman's inclinations.

He looked at Gregg's handsome face through a cloud of tobacco smoke. He seemed miles away, maudlin almost, in his brooding reverie.

'Well, are you going to cut me in with you, old boy?' he teased. Gregg turned a sober look on him, then shook his head.

'Can't do that, old boy. But tell you what....'

'Yes?'

'I could put you on to something that might be of interest to you. If you know of a millionaire who's looking for a good investment, that is.'

Colville's hopes retreated. He knew of no millionaires—still, he might as well hear the plan.

'Friend of mine wants to sell a large estate in Yorkshire—Hawksmoor actually, my old stamping ground. Really large—cost a million or more, I reckon. Desperate for cash. Could be a nice rake-off for the intermediary who sets up the deal.'

'How much?'

Gregg shrugged. 'Like I said, he's pretty desperate. Name your own commission, and I'll take ten per cent.' He ground out his cigarette in the ashtray. 'I'm for bed. Call me a taxi, there's a good fellow. Georgian Mansions, Piccadilly—that's where you can find me if you find your man.'

Colville lay awake far into the night. At only one per cent commission, he could get ten thousand for setting up this deal. Ten thousand—less one thousand for Gregg, of course, but that still left nine thousand. Not a figure to be sniffed at. It was well worth making a determined search to find a millionaire. At the Duchess's ball next week, perhaps? He would keep his eyes and ears open.

But a few days later Fate seemed to play directly into his hands. It was a most unpromising meeting, but then life could be like that. He was hailing a cab when he discovered that another man was about to climb into it.

'The cabbie saw me waving,' the man remarked, opening the door. 'Which way are you going?'

'King's Cross, actually,' said Colville.

'Aye? Well, hop in. I'll split the cost with you.'

Colville smiled. The fellow was clearly a Northerner from his voice, and they were renowned for thrift, if not downright meanness. For a time they sat side by side in silence as the cab wended its way through the busy traffic.

'Up in town on business?' Colville asked equably.

'Aye. Union business. Catching the two o'clock train home.'

'Yorkshire?'

'That's right. Hawksmoor.'

Colvile's jaw sagged as the word seared into his brain. Hawksmoor. Ye gods, of

315

all the coincidences! He gave the fellow a sidelong glance. Decent coat and hat, but clearly not the sort of fellow who would know millionaires. Still....

'Hawksmoor, eh? I've heard there's a large estate there coming up for sale shortly. It'll take time to find the right buyer, I guess, it being such a huge one.'

The man looked him full in the face. 'I've heard nowt about it, and I'm a town councillor. Whose estate is it?'

Colville spread his hands. 'I'll say no more—perhaps I've said too much already.'

'Nay, I want to hear. Tell me what you know.'

Colville glanced at him sideways. 'We're talking of a great deal of money here. The buyer would need to have a million or more at his disposal.'

The man nodded. 'I reckon I know which estate we're talking about now.'

'And are you interested?'

The man's blue eyes were direct and uncompromising. 'I reckon I might know of someone who is. Give me your name and where I can get in touch with you.'

Heart leaping, Colville took out a pencil and a piece of paper and wrote. 'There. Ah, here's where I get out. Here's my share of the fare—and incidentally, what's your name?'

'Pearson. Councillor James Pearson. You'll be hearing from me in the next week or so, Mr Colville. One way or the other, I'll be in touch.'

The council meeting was at an end and most of the councillors had left the chamber. James Pearson was gathering his papers together when Alderman Lawson passed by his chair. James nodded, and the alderman bowed his head in acknowledgement.

'Excellent recommendation of yours, about utilising that money to build the nurses' home,' said James. 'You have my full backing.'

'Aye, I noticed you voted for it. Thanks.'

'Nay, I vote regardless of party when it comes to the town's welfare. I note you usually do likewise.'

Lawson permitted himself a thin smile. 'That's one area where we have like minds, Mr Pearson, I'll grant you that.'

'Same as we'd both like to see Hawksmoor own itself outright, I'll be bound,' murmured James.

'Indeed we would. 'It's long been my wish to see the town released from the Hardcastle's ownership. If only I thought I could live to see the day....'

'Aye, well, stranger things have happened.'

Lawson glanced up at him from under

317

bushy eyebrows. 'Are you hinting summat, Mr Pearson? If so, I reckon I don't rightly follow....'

James straightened and stood up. 'No need right this minute, but if you chance to be in town on Monday, I'll be having my lunch at the Pack Horse. I'd like a private word with you. Come on your own, Mr Lawson, and don't tell folks what's been said. One o'clock. Corner table by the window.'

Lawson was already seated and sipping a glass of port when James arrived the following Monday. He waved an invitation to take the chair opposite him.

'Care for a glass of this excellent wine, Pearson?'

'Thank you, no,' said James, drawing out the chair.

'Pity about Sir Marcus, wasn't it? Lady Hardcastle has taken it badly, I hear. Had to go into a sanatorium in Switzerland. Fancy the roast beef?'

The first course was cleared and they were about to start in on the steamed pudding when James brought the conversation round to the purpose of their meeting. 'Now, about this business of Hawksmoor owning its own land.'

'Aye,' said Lawson, 'that'd be great. It'd be the first town in the country that did own itself. But it's not very likely to happen. I don't even know that it can be done, legally. Not without a Bill of Parliament, that is, making it legal for councils to buy land.'

'True, there'd be problems.'

'And you don't think young Hardcastle—what's his name, Robert, isn't it?—will be any more likely to want to sell out to us than his father was, do you?'

James shrugged. 'There was certainly no love lost between them and the town council. But the position could be altered.'

Lawson paused, spoon half-way to mouth. 'How?'

James's eyes glistened. 'Ways and means. If I were sure of your discretion.'

'You'd tell me. Well, I'll do nothing against the law.'

'No need. What I wanted to know was simply whether I could count on your support if and when the money could be found—and your discretion. I simply ask for silence.'

'I'll tell no one, if that's what you want.'

James pushed his plate aside and leaned across the table. 'The Hardcastle estate is up for sale, seemingly. Young Hardcastle never lives here nowadays, in any event, but on top of that he needs the money for death duties. That estate is near enough three and a half thousand acres—it would cost a fortune. Where are we to raise the kind of money that would call for? And, as you said, the transaction cannot legally take place.'

'Not without a Bill—but we could put that forward, of course. It'd take a little time. But that still doesn't take into account whether or not Hardcastle would sell to us—I'm damn sure he wouldn't.'

'Happen not, but to a stranger, that's a different matter.'

Lawson's eyes gleamed as he rubbed his chin. 'Ah, I catch your drift. A man acting as middleman, who'd be willing to re-sell the land to us. Very astute, Pearson. A stranger with a great deal of money.'

'Aye, that's the question. Who's got that kind of brass? No one as I know of, but happen with all your contacts, you being a stockbroker and all....'

Lawson grew thoughtful. 'There's plenty of well-off millowners and the like in Hawksmoor, but none as I can think of in the millionaire class. Now, wait a minute!'

He flung a hand in the air so abruptly that he almost knocked a tray from a passing waitress's hand. 'There is one—boyhood friend of mine—met him purely by chance in the Wool Exchange in Bradford last Thursday.'

James looked up. 'Rich, is he? Very rich?'

'As Croesus. Just come back from Australia after making his pile there from sheep farming and property deals. Now this might just be up Sam Topping's street.'

'It'd have to be a man we can trust,' James remarked.

'Not to want too much profit out of us, aye. Sell it to us at what he paid for it.'

'There's always the risk, of course, that we don't get the Bill through, and whoever buys that land could be left with it,' James pointed out. 'Reckon he might be willing to take that risk?'

'There's only one way to find out. We mun ask him.'

'Right,' said James, waving to the waitress to bring his bill, 'then you arrange a meeting and we'll see him just as soon as ever we can. There's no time to be lost.'

EIGHTEEN

The old year had given place to the new, and Eddie Pearson wished with all his heart that it would treat him more kindly than its predecessor. Nineteen-twenty. It had a ring about it, twenty, the same as his age would very shortly be, and then there'd be only one year of his apprenticeship left to serve.

'Come on now, eat up your porridge,' Emma said as she spooned yet more of the thick stuff on to his plate at breakfast time one morning. 'Stick to your ribs, it will. Keep you warm.'

'I'll be warm enough,' he grunted. 'I can wear that scarf me dad gave me for Christmas.'

'Nay, that's for Sundays, not for work,' she said firmly. 'It's showing off, wearing summat new to work. Can't have that. Showing off is vulgar.'

She was always full of sayings like that, thought Eddie, one for every occasion, and always one that suited her argument. He resolved to wear the scarf whether or not.

She glanced at the mantel clock. 'Come on, shift yourself or you'll be late. Snap tin's ready on the side. And don't forget to let that Clayton fellow know as I need some more kindling for the fire.'

She came out on the step after him. 'Think on, now, don't forget. I've never known a lad like you for having his head always in the clouds. Your dad'll have summat to say if you forget.'

She didn't notice the scarf. Neither did Father when he walked stolidly alongside Eddie on their way home from work that night. Father seemed to notice little these days, least of all anything that concerned Eddie. That was one of the reasons why the boy felt so restless. Maybe, he thought, he failed his father, not being able to match up to Hal in his eyes. No one could match up to Hal—or Father's fond memories of him.

'He was a grand lad, was Harold,' Father would sometimes murmur, and his total lack of comment about Eddie's efforts convinced his son that he was not, and never could be, in the running by comparison. Never mind that Eddie had scored ninety marks out of a hundred in the mathematics examination just before Christmas; Father's only remark had been that it could have been higher if he had worked harder.

'Too much time mooning around in that room of yours, or wandering about the woods. Time you learnt how to apply your time properly, son.'

Eddie knew he didn't mean to be critical, only to help, but somehow the result was always the same. Father had no time for him, it seemed, fully occupied as he was with Co-op and Temperance and union and party and bench and things that really mattered.

They were nearing home, just passing the clock tower, when Father cleared his throat.

'We've had little chance to talk of late, Edward. How about us going for a walk on Sunday, eh, just thee and me? We could take a stroll up by the old house.'

Eddie smiled as he nodded. 'Aye, I'd like that.' The old house Father mentioned, Cragg Heights, had been his grandfather's house, where he'd been brought up as a boy. It meant a lot to Father still, though he'd never revisited it since his grandfather died. It had passed to the second wife, he'd said, and she and her feckless son had soon dissipated the old man's wealth, but Father always maintained that the spot on the moor edge was Stott land from centuries back.

'Makes no difference who lives there now, it's still home to me,' he used to say, and Eddie too shared a kind of affinity with the place whenever he walked nearby.

They turned in the gate. 'No need to mention to your stepmother where we're off to,' Father murmured, and Eddie felt his heart lighten. It was a conspiracy between the two of them, shutting the Iredale woman out, and he rejoiced. There was still a corner of Father's heart that only he could share.

On Sunday afternoon a keen wind was blowing a crisp edging of snow against the drystone walls as father and son tramped up to the moor. Eddie was glad of the warm woollen muffler snug around his throat.

'I saw that lass of Parkinson's talking to you in the mill yard the other dinnerbreak,' Father remarked. 'Not walking out with her, are you?'

Eddie did not meet his keen gaze. 'Nay, she's nobbut a friend, Father. She's walking out with Denton—has been for some time.'

Father grunted. 'I see. Pity. She's a bonny lass, and a good 'un too. No one else, is there?'

Eddie's reply was as casual as he could make it. 'Nay, I'm not interested in lasses. Too much work to do.'

'Right enough. I don't mean to pry, lad. It's just that I don't rightly know what's going on in the family these days, being so wrapped up in work myself.'

'Aye, I know you're busy.'

His father slowed his steps. 'It's important work, you know, lad. I wouldn't give it so much time, else. It's all important work—the Band of Hope, the bench, all of it—but right now there's work on hand that might change our whole way of life here in in Hawksmoor. I can't say more, but I promise you its summat worth my time.'

'I'm sure it is, Father.' Eddie could hear the ring of sincerity in his father's tone, but there was more than that, a kind of eagerness he had never heard before. He studied his profile as he leaned against the wall and gazed down into the valley below.

The older man pointed. 'See that mill down there?'

'The paper mill? That were your grand-father's once, you told me.'

'It was, and long years before that it were a farm. Stotts farmed there since Methuselah.'

'You told me. Many a time.'

'And did I tell you that the Hardcastles had land nearby? They were farmers too, same as us.'

Eddie frowned. 'Hardcastles? Rich Hard-castles? They were once only the same as us, do you mean?'

'Aye. Hard to believe, isn't it?'

'I've never even clapped eyes on any of them, but I though they were always rich, like kings.

'Nay, lad, just ambitious. Greedy, some might say.'

'Seemingly the Stotts weren't, then, or we'd not be poor today.'

His father turned and smiled. 'Money's not everything, Edward. We've not done so badly, any of us. Stotts are still here, and thriving, and that's summat.'

But not Harold, that's what he was thinking, Eddie thought. Father was gazing into the smoky distance, deep in thought for a moment, and then he took a deep breath.

'You know, Edward, you've an important part to play,' he said soberly. 'Now Harold's gone, you'll be the last remaining Stott after me. It'll be up to you to keep the family name going.'

Eddie stared. 'Me? But I'm a Pearson—it was your mother who was a Stott.'

'Aye, you're right—she was the last of that name, but she gave it me as middle name. And I gave it you.'

Eddie bowed his head. He knew the pride Father took in the ancient family name, and was proud that its continuance was being handed on to him. It was a matter that struck too deeply for either of them to squander it in inadequate words.

'I understand. I'll see it's right,' he murmured.

His father touched his elbow. 'I knew you would.'

Together they turned and walked along the heather-spattered ridge, past the blackening stone of Crag Heights and back towards the road. Icy sleet was beginning to sting Eddie's ears. Father quickened his step.

'Hey up, it's starting to snow in earnest. Let's get back, and happen your stepmother'll have the kettle boiling on the hob. I could do with a nice hot cup of tea.'

Vincent Gregg poured a glass of whisky for his guest and one for himself. Before handing the first to James Colville, he tossed off the second and re-filled the glass.

'So you managed to come up with a customer?' he said. 'That didn't take long.'

'It was the most incredible stroke of luck, as I told you, but this councillor fellow came up trumps. I've just exchanged the names of the solicitors for the two sides, and the whole deal will be completed before you can say Jack Robinson.'

'No haggling over the price, then? The buyer must be filthy rich in that case.'

'Hardcastle asked a million and a half.

This Topping offered a million. They settled at one and a third.'

'Well, I'll be damned.'

'So there'll be a nice little rake-off for both of us. I've got to hand it to you, Gregg; you've learnt how to prosper, that's for sure.'

'Yes.'

Colville swung his legs over the arm of the chair. 'What's up, Gregg? You look as if you'd lost a thousand, not just earned it.'

Gregg scowled. 'Life just never runs smoothly, does it? Just as I thought I'd got everything taped....'

'What's wrong?'

Gregg flung an irritable arm upwards. 'Oh, this woman's damned husband is after me, threatening me if I see her again....'

Colville laughed. 'I see you haven't changed. Can't leave your *affaires* alone, can you?'

Gregg glared at him. 'Don't be flippant, Colville. Can't you see I'm worried?'

'About a jealous husband? Oh, come on, Gregg.'

'He's savage, I can tell you, even threatening my life. And that's not all. This fellow I've been relying on for income has come over strange—he's threatening me now too.'

Colville's puzzled expression gave way to a smile. 'Oh, I see. You've been blackmailing him and now he's had enough.' His smile took on a cunning look. 'It wouldn't be Maunday Gregory, by any chance, would it? Have you been blackmailing him over the honours sales? If so, that was very silly of you, Gregg. You must have known he had contacts in the Intelligence Service—they could very quickly make short work of you.'

Gregg banged his glass down sharply on the table. 'Stop talking rubbish, Colville, trying to put the wind up me. Just get that cheque paid into my account as quickly as you can, there's a good fellow, and let's talk no more about it. I'm going away for a bit and I want things settled.'

'Scarpering, eh, until the heat dies down? Well, I can't say I blame you. I'll probably do the same myself once all that lovely money is in my hands. Don't worry, I won't cheat on you. Never do that, not to a friend, anyway. As for the rest, they can take care of themselves, eh, and the devil take the hindmost.'

Still laughing, he left, and Gregg poured himself another whisky while he fumbled in a drawer to find the railway timetable.

Alderman Lawson looked around the group of councillors seated in his private office:

the mayor, Pearson, the two millowners, and the newspaper editor who was also chairman of the finance committee. For the past few months these men had formed the unofficial committee backing him in the secret negotiations with Hardcastle.

Lawson's eyes were shining. 'Gentlemen, at last the moment has arrived when we can come out into the open and tell our colleagues what we have achieved,' he said with pride. 'This very afternoon I shall present the whole story to the council and exhort them to take up the deal we are offered.'

'One and a third million,' murmured one. 'And the commission to that fellow Colville—'

'Twenty thousand, that's been paid,' said Lawson.

'And what does Topping expect in the way of interest?'

Lawson smiled. 'He's decided to renounce any interest on the loan—he's willing to settle for all the council's insurance business for the next twenty years. He's a director of the Western Australia Assurance Company, you know. Council will be sure to see the wisdom in accepting that.'

Pearson nodded. 'I'm glad it's ready to put to council at last,' he murmured. 'I'm not sorry to see an end to all this cloak-and-dagger stuff, and that's a fact.'

331

The mayor rose to this. 'Sentiments I'm sure we all share, Pearson, but it was necessary. Now all that remains is for us to put the case in such a way that the council will vote for a Lands Bill to be put before Parliament immediately. Time'll come when the town will thank us for this day.'

One of the mill owners was frowning. 'I'm still not clear how we're going to repay this Topping fellow....'

Lawson glanced down at his papers. 'That's all been calculated. In the first instance, after the Bill is passed, we borrow a million from Cardiff and the remainder from banks at a rate of six and a half per cent. Short-term loan only, because I'm sure the rate will fall to four per cent very soon.'

'But how shall we repay those loans?'

'Out of the rates. The estate raises sixty-five thousand a year in rates—do you realise that what we're paying for the whole estate represents only twenty years' revenue? We've got ourselves a bargain, gentlemen, and as the mayor rightly says, the town will acknowledge its gratitude to us one day. Time we made a move to get to the meeting now—let's be on our way.'

Late that night, James Pearson lay awake, listening to Emma's gentle snoring and thinking over Lawson's impassioned speech in the town hall that afternoon.

'If we buy the estate it will forever stamp Hawksmoor as a pioneer in municipal enterprise.... It is likely to meet strong opposition in government departments....'

A good line, that, thought James, calculated to stir their determination.

'It will do away with the necessity of going cap in hand to a landlord....'

Ah yes. Grandfather had talked bitterly of the one-year leases he had fought so long to get extended to ninety-nine. The battle was nearly over.

'It is a particularly good financial bargain.... The undeveloped land stands at five-sixteenths of a penny per yard—can calico be bought at the price?'

A telling phrase, that, aimed at industrialists who understood only too well the force of such arguments.

'It will facilitate modern layout of the town and the housing of its people....'

Lawson had captured them all, men of commerce and of altruism alike. There had been no hesitation on the council's part in resolving to introduce a Lands Bill to Parliament. Sam Topping now owned Hawksmoor, and it was only a matter of time before the town owned itself.

Strange how things worked out, thought James. If Sir Marcus hadn't died suddenly, leaving his son with massive death duties to pay—eight hundred thousand, Lawson had said—then the estate would probably never have come up for sale. And if that mysterious young Colville fellow hadn't chanced to share his cab that day in London....

Lawson's speech had stirred him like no other speech had done since the days when Vincent Gregg enraptured all with his eloquence. Where was Gregg now? He wondered idly. Dismissing the thought from his mind, James uttered a deep sigh of contentment and reached out a hand to touch Emma's flannelled hip. In her sleep she groaned and pushed his hand away.

Mrs Gregg peered out from behind lace curtains to survey the cobbled street.

'No, son, there's no one out there, honest. I can't see what you get so worked up about, really I don't.'

Vincent Gregg lit another cigarette moodily and tossed the match into the fire. 'There was a man out there an hour ago—I saw him. Man in a fawn raincoat, down by the gaslamp.'

'Well he's not there now, that's for sure. See for yourself. Really, Vincent, it's not as if you're famous like you used to be—I could understand you being worried then, when they used to crowd round you, but it's not like that any more.'

There was a tinge of regret in her voice but he chose to ignore it. There was too much on his mind to worry unduly about Mother's disappointment in him. If only he hadn't been so stupid, so greedy....

Mrs Gregg came to sit opposite him, reaching for the poker to liven up the fire. 'Really, love, I don't know what's come over you,' she murmured. 'I know we've not seen much of you since the war ended, but you're not at all like you used to be, so full of life, teasing me and all. There's something up, I know there is. Can't you tell your mother?'

He shook his dark head glumly. 'There's nothing to tell.'

'I know better. Is it that you don't want me to know you're ill again, is that it? Because if so....'

'I'm not ill,' he answered irritably. 'There's nothing wrong at all, really there isn't.'

She sighed deeply. 'You were just like this that time they said you had a nervous breakdown. I hope you're not going to have to go through that again.'

He flung the cigarette into the fire and reached into the packet for another. It was empty. Swearing, he crushed the empty packet and threw it in the hearth.

'Will you go to the corner shop for me

for some more cigarettes, Mother? I can't bear not having a smoke.'

She looked at him in surprise. 'Me? You always tell me I ought to send someone else to the shops, not go myself. Lizzie's fetching my shopping later.'

'How long will she be? I need a smoke, Mother.'

'Can't you go? It's only at the corner.'

He rose and crossed to stand by the window, lifting the curtain warily. 'He is still there,' he pronounced bitterly. 'You couldn't see him behind that lamp post. He's waiting for me.'

She watched his tall, brooding figure with dismay. Either Vincent was ill again, seriously ill, or he'd got himself involved in something he couldn't handle. Which still meant he was ill, for there was a time when Vincent Gregg could take on the world without fear. Not now, that was clear. Vincent was in trouble, and he was not going to let her help him.

'How long are you going to go on like this, love?' she asked gently. 'It can't go on for ever, never going out, never letting anyone know you're here.'

He let the curtain fall. 'Not long, Mother. Once I get away you may not see me for a long time, a very long time, but you're not to worry. Understand that, Mother. If you hear nothing from me, don't fret. I'll be gone soon enough.'

She nodded and sighed. 'Aye, I know. It's happened before. Not hearing for a long time, I mean.'

'So you won't fret?'

She didn't answer. How could she expect him to understand that a mother never ceases to worry.

'Christ!' he muttered. 'If I don't get a cigarette soon I'll go crazy!'

A factory hooter sounded. Mrs Gregg smiled at her son. 'There, six o'clock— Lizzie'll be here any minute,' she said soothingly. 'Not long to wait now.'

Eddie Pearson was among the last to leave the Mechanics' Institute when the evening classes ended. Shoving the exercise book deep into his pocket, he gathered up his books and began the short walk home. Few people were about at this time of night.

As he turned the corner he was aware of two people ahead of him, under the gaslamp on the far side of the street, and of their voices raised in argument. Nothing unusual in that; squabbles often broke out between roisterers emerging from the pubs. But this was different, for the couple were a man and a woman.

'I didn't mean it! Honest I didn't!'

the girl protested, her voice shrill on the night air.

'Then it's time you learnt to keep your daft mouth shut!' the man retorted, and Eddie recognised him then. It was Denton. The girl must be Sally. Eddie kept on walking.

'You shouldn't talk to me like that. You wouldn't if me dad heard you.' The voice held tears, and clearly it was Sally's. Eddie looked back.

'Shut up!'

Denton swung back his arm and slapped her hard on the face. As he heard her cry out, the blood rushed to Eddie's head. Thinking of nothing but saving her from that bully Denton, he dropped his books and ran across the road. Before he could think, he was pummelling Denton's chest and jaw. Denton stared for a moment, startled by his sudden appearance, and then he too began swinging his arms.

Their bodies locked together in a fierce hug, rocking and swaying, and then suddenly they were rolling on the ground, over and over. Eddie caught a fleeting glimpse of Sally, her hands to her mouth and her eyes wide. He was vaguely aware of the blows that landed on his head, but he kept it lowered and kept on punching. Denton might be bigger and stronger than he was, but he was burly

338

and awkward and blind with rage. The loathsome bully, hitting a woman!

Denton's grip loosened for a second and Eddie seized his chance, leaping to his feet and kicking out at the prostrate body. Denton howled.

'You bastard! You hit me on my wound!' he roared. Eddie stood back, aghast. Then he saw that Denton, staggering to his feet, was clutching his backside. Sally started to giggle.

From deep in his stomach Eddie too felt a laugh beginning to rise. Within moments he was leaning against the lamp post, helpless with laugher. Sally was shrieking hysterically. For a moment Denton stared, then gave them both a surly look and lumbered away down the street, still clutching his bottom.

'I don't believe it,' Sally gasped. 'I always thought as it were a hip wound he had.'

'Nay, shot in the arse, seemingly—oh, love, I'm sorry, I didn't mean—'

She giggled again and went to pick up his books. 'Think nowt of it. I'm grateful to you, Eddie, truly I am. Thanks.'

He looked down at her with concern. There was still a red weal on her cheek. 'Does he often do that—thump you, I mean?' he asked gently.

She shook her head. 'Not often. And he

won't do it again, because he'll not have chance—I won't see him again. Oh, Eddie, you're hurt!'

She reached up to touch his cheek. Eddie shivered and put a finger over hers, feeling the wet smear of blood. 'It's nowt,' he muttered, and took the books from her hand.

'You're not going, are you?' she asked, and there was a tremble in her voice, and then her tone changed. 'Come on,' she said brightly, 'you can't let a girl walk home alone, can you?'

At her gate she paused and looked up at him shyly. 'I know I treated you rotten, Eddie Pearson, but I want you to know as I'm sorry. Denton were no good. You're a gentleman, a real gentleman.'

He could feel his cheeks reddening. 'Don't be daft,' he said roughly, but inside he felt aglow with pride. 'I'd best be off home now. Sure you're all right?'

She smiled, 'I'm fine, thanks to you. See you at dinner break tomorrow?'

Eddie walked home on air, completely oblivious to the trickle of blood running down his cheek and on to his collar. Denton the war hero had fled before him, and the lady had smiled upon him. What more could a man ask for?

The news Alderman Lawson had been

eagerly awaiting came at last—the Lands Bill had been passed by both Houses. He could scarcely contain his excitement as he broke the news to his fellow conspirators.

'Just think, all that opposition from the Bishops because of the advowsons of those churches on the land, but still we've got it through! The deed between Hardcastle and Topping and the council is to be signed today, and Hawksmoor owns itself!'

After the congratulations and delight, his tone had become more serious.

'We have a solemn duty and a great responsibility now, gentleman, for we are landlords and estate managers, trustees of the estate on behalf of its new owners—the ratepayers. It is a great responsibility, but a burden I know we are honoured to share.'

James Pearson was filled with a sense of quiet pride and triumph as he made his way home to Lindley. The job was done, and successfully done. From now on he would have more time, not just for the bench and the union, but for family too. Now at last he could reveal just what had kept him from them for so long.

Eddie was cutting his toenails by the hearth, the tin bath up-ended against the wall. Emma was reading one of those novelettes Mrs Charnock kept bringing in for her.

'Hello, love, I wasn't expecting you back just yet,' she remarked, without laying the book aside. 'Have you had your tea?'

'Yes thanks.' He took off his coat and hung it behind the door, glad to be back in the peace and warmth of his home. Eddie picked up the nail clippings carefully and threw them on the fire, then pulled the chair forward for his father. James sat down.

'Had a good day?' he asked. He would keep his own news for a little longer.

Eddie opened his mouth but Emma was quicker. 'Oh, yes—did you see the paper? That Gregg chap has disappeared, seemingly. Vanished from his London flat weeks ago and hasn't been seen since.'

James sighed. 'That's happened before, love. Drank too much, poor fellow. He'll no doubt wake up in some club or other and turn up sooner or later.'

'No,' said Emma. 'The landlady says two men called for him one night and he went with them. Weeks ago. Paper reckons he might have been kidnapped.'

'Hasn't there been a ransom note then? Kidnappers would have got in touch by now.'

'The paper says he might have got amnesia again, like he did once before. Does that mean forgetting who he is, James?'

'Near enough. He always was highly strung. He might simply have gone away by choice, you know, for it's been said he was getting mixed up in some funny business. But in any event I wouldn't fret over him, Emma. No one's likely to do him any harm.'

She shrugged, and placed her book down on the table. 'I wasn't fretting over him, James. I hardly knew him. I'll go and put hot bricks in the bed.'

Taking the bricks out of the oven and wrapping them in pieces of old blanket, she left the room. James looked down at his son, who was still kneeling on the hearth.

'I heard about you today, Edward.'

The boy looked up at him, and for a moment James's heart caught in his throat. Just sometimes there was in his young face an uncanny resemblance to Annie.

'Heard what?' the boy asked.

'Fellow at work coming out of the Fleece last night. Said he saw you in a scrap with young Denton.'

'Oh—that.' The boy's face fell.

'Did you think I'd heard summat else then?'

'Aye, happen.'

'Like what, then?'

Edward uncurled his length from the floor and sat down in the chair opposite him. He was growing tall, the lad, and his shoulders filling out too. 'Well, I thought someone might have said as I'd won the award for top apprentice,' he murmured. 'It were announced today.'

James leaned forward eagerly. 'Top apprentice? That's wonderful, Edward! Well done—I'm right proud of you.'

He could see the lad's face glow at the unaccustomed praise and felt a pang of remorse. He could have done more over the years to encourage and advise, but the heart had gone out of him after Harold's death. Now things were different. Now there was so much to look forward to....

'And congratulations on dealing with that Denton lad too,' he murmured. 'He were getting far too big for his boots, that lad. What was it? Sneering at your brother again, was he?'

Edward shook his head. 'No, but I'd have hit him the same if he had.'

James listened. He could hear Emma's footsteps on the stairs. He leaned closer to his son. 'I'm glad. I'm that proud of you, Edward. I should have told you that before. I'm proud to call you son.'

Emma entered the room and stood by the door, listening. 'What's this? Have I missed summat?' she asked. 'You always keep the best bits till I'm out of earshot. What's the news then?'

Eddie stood up so that she could take his seat. James rose too and put his arm across his son's shoulders. 'Two of the best pieces of news a man could hear, Emma. My son is the top apprentice of the year, and after months of work Hawksmoor is the first town in the country to own itself.'

Edward was staring at him in disbelief. Emma just blinked at him. 'Is that what you've been keeping so quiet about all these months? You mean Hardcastles don't own the town any more?' she said.

'No, and they never will again. Hardcastle's stranglehold on the town is broken,' James said with pride. 'Hawksmoor is a free borough at last. It's been a battle, lass, but it were well worth while.'

'I knew it,' she said with sudden conviction. 'You didn't believe me, but I told you Harold had a message for you. He said there was great work for you to do, and you shouldn't shirk it. He meant it to be. Perhaps you'll believe me another time.'

'But didn't you hear the best bit of news, Emma?' James said quietly. 'My son has won the award—top apprentice of the year. The world's his oyster now. He's going to go a long way, is my son.'

He turned to face Edward, putting his hands on the boy's shoulders and smiling. His son smiled back, and there was such happiness in his eyes that James felt the tears prick at his eyelids.

'Things'll never be the same again, Edward, just you mark my words. Things'll never be quite the same.'

The publishers hope that this book has given you enjoyable reading. Large Print Books are especially designed to be as easy to see and hold as possible. If you wish a complete list of our books, please ask at your local library or write directly to: Magna Large Print Books, Long Preston, North Yorkshire, BD23 4ND, England.

This Large Print Book for the Partially sighted, who cannot read normal print, is published under the auspices of

THE ULVERSCROFT FOUNDATION

THE ULVERSCROFT FOUNDATION

. . . we hope that you have enjoyed this Large Print Book. Please think for a moment about those people who have worse eyesight problems than you . . . and are unable to even read or enjoy Large Print, without great difficulty.

You can help them by sending a donation, large or small to:

**The Ulverscroft Foundation,
1, The Green, Bradgate Road,
Anstey, Leicestershire, LE7 7FU,
England.**
or request a copy of our brochure for more details.

The Foundation will use all your help to assist those people who are handicapped by various sight problems and need special attention.

Thank you very much for your help.

Other MAGNA Romance Titles In Large Print

ROSE BOUCHERON
The Massinghams

VIRGINIA COFFMAN
The Royles

RUTH HAMILTON
Nest Of Sorrows

SHEILA JANSEN
Mary Maddison

NANCY LIVINGSTON
Never Were Such Times

GENEVIEVE LYONS
The Palucci Vendetta

MARY MINTON
Every Street